Flowers for no Occasion

A COVENTRY FALLS NOVEL

ANDRE'A DELANEY

First edition November 2025

Typography by Katie Jaspersen @ K. Jaspersen Designs

Artwork by Hannah Latham

ISBN: 979-8-999-12040-3 (ebook)

ISBN: 979-8-999-12041-0 (paperback)

Independently published

www.authorandreadelaney.com

To those who bury their head in books,
who try to fill the void from the fear
that true love may never come,
look up. You're not alone.

OFFICIAL PLAYLIST

Higher Power - Coldplay

Summer - Calvin Harris

Motive - Ariana Grande & Doja Cat

Kiss Me - Sixpence None the Richer

Fireflies - Owl City

Winners Circle - Anderson .Paak

I2I - A Goofy Movie

The Only Reason - JP Cooper

Yebba's Heartbreak - Drake

The Night We Met - Lord Huron

A Sky Full of Stars - Coldplay

XO - Beyoncé

Chapter 1

My nerves buzz with excitement the closer we get to town, until I finally break out in a wide grin when I see it:

Welcome to Coventry Falls

Stay a while!

Mayor Josie Payne

Est. 1837

The wooden sign swings from the rusted pole it's chained to, threatening to fall off if you even dare to look at it wrong.

"We're here," I sing as I pull out my phone and open the camera app. "Let's take a picture."

Kennedy shakes her head shamefully. "Aubree, I'm driving."

"Come on. Just one." I angle the phone sideways to get us both in the frame and fix the fresh mini twists I'd done late last night to prepare for the summer heat, admiring my handiwork.

Kennedy glances at her reflection in the camera lens. The annoyance in her glare is clear as day. "You said 'just one' the last 20 times."

She's not wrong, but I've practically been away from Coventry Falls for a year, working and studying myself half to death. While running The Quest at Lakeshore University and networking my ass off to find a good job after graduation, I missed being home. I've never been away this long before, so coming back feels different this time—more exciting. Coventry Falls is small, and things never really change there except for the fact that Kennedy found the sudden urge to move back with me. So, I had to capture every moment, no matter how big or small. I took pictures of us loading the car, our empty apartment, us leaving the apartment, and when we stopped to get our favorite wings from this sketchy restaurant attached to a gas station we ate at every Saturday night called Wings-N-Things because, oddly enough, they also served Chinese and Jamaican food. Over the past few hours, plus all the pictures I took at graduation last month, I've probably taken over 200 photos.

"Okay, but really. One more and I'll make it my last." She glares at me briefly before nodding in agreement. "Yay, okay." I raise the phone, turning it sideways to ensure we're both in frame. Kennedy leans over with a sparkling grin on her face. She's always been the photogenic type. Even the pictures I took of her heaving and sweating look damn good. I had to learn to perfect what she can do naturally over the years. The light hits perfectly over the soft angles of her face, her thick hair flowing down her shoulders in large curls. Kennedy's beauty was breathtaking; it was almost hard to believe she never dated throughout college.

Snapping the photo, I sit back in my seat to see how it came out—perfect as it can be in a moving vehicle. Kennedy's smooth brown skin and dimples alone make her look good in any lighting. My smile's a bit crooked, but I look gorgeous nevertheless.

"Am I gonna see that online later?" Kennedy asks, glancing over at the photo.

I roll my eyes. "I don't post everything, Kenny."

"Could've fooled me," she mumbles.

"I don't. Just the things I like."

The corners of her mouth come up into a slight curl as she glances at me. "So, everything."

"Shut up." I giggle. "I won't be shamed for romanticizing my life."

"Who said anything about shame? I'm simply making an observation."

"Right. I forgot how great of an observationist you are. You should think about it as a profession," I remark sarcastically.

"You already know I'm all over it."

I shake my head as I look out of the window and see the town slowly crawl into view. My stomach leaps as I roll down the window and let the cool summer air blow across my face.

Coventry Falls comes into full view as we make our way onto Main Street, and the smell of daisies from Little Miss Flores fills the air. Ms. Flores stands outside the shop, setting up her chalkboard sign of the deals for the week. Several bouquets and potted plants line the outside of the building, and the door rests wide open to reveal even more inside. She spots our car when she turns to go inside, and an enthusiastic grin spreads across her face.

"Aubree!" She waves, and I wave back before she's out of view.

"Who was that?" Kennedy asks.

"Ms. Flores. You never met her before? I feel I would have mentioned her at some point." It's almost hard to forget that Kennedy has only been to Coventry a few times, and each time she was gone quicker than she came. She's hardly met anyone, but Ms. Flores is like a best friend to me, as much as any adult my mother's age can be.

"I don't think so. Maybe I've seen her in passing the other times I was here."

I shrug. "Either way, I'm sure you'll meet her eventually. She used to watch me after school sometimes when I was younger, and my parents needed to go out of town for work. But even when she wasn't watching me, my dad and I were at her shop every Sunday to pick up a bouquet for my mom and whatever flower I wanted for myself." I pause as I recall those moments. Her son, Rafael, and I would run around the shop while my dad picked out the arrangement he wanted for next week. Sometimes, he'd even let me help to make it extra special.

Kennedy coos with admiration. "Your family always reminds me of one of those picture frame families."

"What?" I question, cocking my head to the side.

"You know, those black and white pictures of families that already come in the frame when you buy it? The nuclear family..."

"Oh, right. Well, I wouldn't go that far. I think my parents got lucky finding each other." Luck that has yet to rub off on me, and the heaviness of that reality weighs heavier by the day. A heaviness that becomes more apparent the closer we get to Colleen Drive.

"Turn here." I point to our right down Baker Street.

"But don't we turn down Colleen—"

"Here!" I exclaim forcibly, almost taking the wheel myself.

"Okay, damn." Kennedy slows into the turn, and the release of tension in my limbs that I didn't realize was there slows my breathing. She glances over in concern. "Do we need to make a stop or something?"

"No. I just—there's a koi fish pond this way that I wanted you to see. Have I ever shown it to you before?"

"No?"

"Oh, really? Well, you have to see it this time of day. It's so beautiful, especially during sunset. And the fish, they're... fish-like. It's great, I swear."

Kennedy huffs in annoyance. "Bree, I don't care about the fish."

"That's okay, we can just drive by," I say hurriedly. "This way is *way* quicker to my house anyway, so."

"Do I have the word 'stupid' written across my forehead, Aubree?"

"Well..."

"Aubree!"

"What?" I laugh. "You asked."

Kennedy rolls her eyes. "You know what you're doing."

"So, do you."

"And what's that?" she challenges.

A drift of silence moves in the cramped space, and I shift closer to the door. Why does she have to be like that? I don't want to talk about it, and I don't need to. Had I wanted to, I would have. Better yet, I'd see a therapist. There is nothing to discuss.

The houses pass by one after the other as I try my best to disconnect from it. "Can you not, please?"

"I feel like you need to talk about it. Let it out; it'll make you feel better." Kennedy gives me a pleading smile.

The leather seat makes a squishing sound as I slide down into it. "Take the next right."

A silent pressure falls over us, but I don't do anything to elevate it because if I talk about AJ, I might just fall apart, and I don't have time for that. I can't handle driving down his street because I know I won't be able to resist the urge to see if his car is in the driveway. If he is there, I'd be angry that he didn't bother mentioning his presence so that I could prepare myself. If he's not there, I'd be angry that he didn't have the courage to face me. Irrational? Maybe, but when did getting dumped ever make anyone think rationally?

We round a corner and pull into the driveway of my home, and I'm finally able to get out of my head as my dad steps out onto the porch, a look of triumph on his face and his arms wide as I get out of the car. His long, slender frame and scratchy beard reminds me of all that I've missed out on as he scoops me up into the brightest hug.

"There's my baby girl." My dad fake cries, and he rocks me from side to side.

"Hi, Daddy." I pat his back, letting him know it's time to let go.

He holds me back at arm's length, examining the only child he has. "I missed you so much. Beautiful as always."

"You just saw me a week ago," I remind him.

"And somehow you've gotten even more beautiful in that time. I can't believe it." He wipes away a fake tear like he always does when he gets dramatic.

"Neither can I," I chuckle.

Kennedy steps out from around the car, giving a small wave. "Hey, Mr. Harper."

"Kennedy, don't leave me hanging." He opens his arms to her, and she swoops in with ease. My dad has always been the affectionate and welcoming type; the embodiment of what it feels like to find home. Whenever anyone needs him, he's there ready to play his part, whatever that may be. That included today to help me move my things back into my old room and Kennedy into her apartment right across the hall from Sasha. They hit it off right away when they first met, so it was the perfect scenario when the man in the apartment previously had to move out, and Kennedy suddenly needed a place to stay.

"Where's Ma?" I ask. She's always punctual, especially when it comes to me. It never matters how, what, or when—if her daughter is involved, she's there.

At that moment, she appears in the door frame sporting cream wide legged pants and a sleeveless black top paired with her favorite sling-back kitten heels. Whether she was relaxing at home or hosting an open house, she always dresses as if she could have a "run in with Michelle Obama," as she put it. When I get dressed in the morning, I can still hear her voice, "You never know who you might run into. First impressions are everything." So, being put together on the outside was never not an option for me, except that I prefer pastels over the whole neutral look she sports.

As she makes her way onto the porch, she shifts between Kennedy and I, her face lighting up. "My college graduates," she says as she scoops us into a hug that goes on a little too long, and I swear she's squeezing us tighter by the second. But I know better than to pull back from her unless I want a lecture on how rude it is to deny your mother love, and how she'll be old one day and wants to show us love while she's still in her right mind. Luckily, Kennedy doesn't seem to mind. After coming to stay a weekend with me in Coventry with my parents, she went on and on about how nice it was to be acknowledged and loved on, especially by adults she didn't know. So, for her sake and my sanity, I tolerate it.

"I guess I can't treat you like a little girl anymore," my mom says, kissing my cheek.

"Who said that?" My dad questions, an exaggerated look on his face.

My mom shakes her head, laughing at my annoyed stance. "Ignore your dad. Y'all are right on time. I picked up some Sal's a few minutes ago, and it's still warm."

"Thanks, Ma, but I think we're just gonna drop off my stuff and head to Sasha's complex to help Kennedy unpack."

"Are you sure? It's pulled pork?" my dad says with a tempting ring to his tone, and suddenly, my stomach decides it can't go another second without food. I can't resist a Sal's pulled pork sandwich, especially with a side of mac and cheese? There is never enough to satisfy.

I look towards Kennedy, who answers gleefully. "I'll never say no to Sal's."

"That's what I'm talking about. You all go in, and I'll get Aubree's stuff out of the car. I'm guessing she labeled the boxes?" He asks Kennedy.

"Oh, you know she did."

I try not to groan as my dad bounces down the stairs while my mother ushers us inside toward the kitchen. There's nothing wrong with organization when everything has its place. If anything, it makes life easier to put things in boxes as a reminder of what goes where and why. It hasn't served me wrong yet.

Warm light shines through the windows, livening the room. The green backsplash adds a sense of calm paired with the white cabinets and wooden shelves. The food sits on top of the island in styrofoam to-go boxes, but at the center is a vase of fresh flowers. The smell of lilies sways in the air the closer I get, and a feeling of belonging and peace washes over me with the realization that I'm finally home. I was so focused on my last year of college, I forgot how much I actually missed being here. My comfort place.

I open up the cabinet to grab four plates and grab some forks from the drawer. The smell of the food, still steaming, fills my nostrils as my mother begins to plate it. My stomach rumbles with joy, but this meal isn't complete without grape jelly. I don't know when or why I started putting it on my pulled pork sandwiches, but it's the perfect mix of sweet and savory. As I go to the fridge to retrieve the jar, my dad comes in with way too many boxes that he knows are too heavy for him.

"Dennis, really? Don't hurt yourself," Ma exclaims with heated concern.

"I got it, honey. Don't worry. I got this." Did he just try to flex his muscles when he said that?

"If you throw your back out, I'm not driving you to the ER... again."

"I was just having a bad back day."

I raise an eyebrow and make the mistake of looking over at Kennedy as she tries to hold back a laugh, which only makes me laugh even harder.

"Don't laugh. One day, you'll be this old and know what I mean."

My mother mumbles something about him and his Macho Man act that I can't make out over our giggles.

"I'll go help him," Kennedy says, pushing away from the table.

"You don't have to do that, sweetie. You're a guest," my mom replies as she motions for her to sit back at the table.

"It's cool, I don't mind. It'll help me work up a bigger appetite anyway." She heads down the hall to my room, her steps quickening when she hears a loud grunt.

"That girl is really something. Teaching will look good on her. She's definitely getting that job at Coventry High from what I've heard through the grapevine."

Spreading jelly onto one of my hamburger buns, I nod in agreement. "Oh, she's definitely getting that job, but I still can't believe she's skipping out on medical school."

"And what about you?" My mom pokes my side.

"I'll be a great editor, but I still have a long way to go."

I spent the last year cramming my schedule with meetings and events with every major and minor publication that I see myself gaining the best experience with for my career. I even secured my position as editor with The Quest hoping it'll make me a better candidate. Job opportunities in journalism are competitive. If I'm going to become an editor and run my own publication one day, I not only need to prove that I'm talented, but that I'm the best at what I do. Somehow, I didn't realize that on top of a shitty breakup, the one company I'd crawl over broken glass for didn't see it that way. The Franklin Gazette pretty much ghosted me after my interview two months ago, and I haven't had the balls to say anything or ask why after all the work I put in getting to know the company and all the people there.

It pretty much forced me to rely on the two other jobs I interviewed for about a week ago that were deemed most appropriate for my career goals. I nailed interviews with them, obviously. Now, it's just a matter of hearing back, which could take weeks. I've networked, built relationships, and created my portfolio. I know I'm prepared, more prepared than most, but that didn't stop my anxiety from bubbling up at the thought of receiving the offers. Until then, that meant working as a counselor at the grand reopening for Camp Whisper Lake for a steady income and the chance to regroup since it seems nothing has been going according to plan lately. It's one of the last things I want to do, but it's either camp or working at Stanton's General Store, and I honestly don't want to be here when news gets out about me and AJ if it hasn't already.

"I know you'll be. You've always been so bright." Ma looks up from her plate to make sure I hear her this time. "But what about *you*?" And this time, I understand her.

Why does she have to do that?

A ball of knots starts to form in my throat, and a static like tingling starts behind my eyes. I grip the fork in my hand, the metal biting into my skin as I attempt to make my nervous system focus on a different type of pain.

"I'm good." I turn away from her and grab of glass from the cabinet.

"You know it's okay if you're not."

"I know, but really, I'm good. Things happen, we learn, and life goes on." I turn the ice machine on to fill the void in hopes that it will cause an energy shift in the room. Like this is just a casual conversation and nothing more.

Ma waits patiently for me to retrieve my ice, except that she remains silent and reaches for my hand to still me, giving it a reassuring squeeze. But I can't look at her because I know the tears will start, and I won't be able to stop them. I haven't cried, and I won't cry. I don't have the time to cry right now. I have to stay focused on securing a job and having my last adolescent summer before I officially have to become an adult with real responsibilities. This summer is going to be nothing but drama free, spent with my three best girlfriends—and Beck—at camp. I won't let a breakup or a job ghosting ruin that for me.

CHAPTER 2

T he phone rings one last time, and it's straight to voicemail again.
"Are you kidding me?" I let out a frustrated sigh and kick the door to the apartment.

"Hey, no door violence. This is my apartment now." Kennedy leans up against the wall, scrolling through her phone without a care, like we haven't been waiting out here with all of her stuff for 20 minutes. Thankfully, my dad offered to help us carry everything up because, as much as they like to tease me about how much stuff I have, Kennedy brought almost double what I have, and not a single thing is organized.

Sasha was supposed to be here. I told her the exact time, and she knows I'm never late. But knowing her, I should have told her two thirty instead of three. I love that girl to death, but she's never been one to be punctual. Now it's 4:23 and I have to use the bathroom.

The ding of the elevator draws my attention, and out comes a flustered Sasha whose arms are littered with shopping bags. Her locs are piled high on her head, and paint is smeared on her bell-bottom jeans, letting me know that she was in the middle of painting when she decided to up and leave without so much as a text or sliding the key under the door mat.

Sasha rushes over, pleading several sorrys as she flails her hands in the air, which are also stained with paint. "I know, I know, I should've called. But I left my phone here when I realized I forgot to pick up the key. So, I ran out to get it and then I figured I had a little time to get some more art supplies for the piece I was working on, and... sorry." She winces.

I try my hardest to fake reluctance, but I can't stop the smile that gathers along my lips at her presence. "You're lucky we missed you."

"Lucky? Girl, what would you do without me?" she jokes.

I hold my hand out for the spare key, and she points to her front pocket where I find the shiny gold key attached to a purple wrist band—Kennedy's favorite color. The apartment is spacious with an open kitchen and a large living room waiting to be decorated with everything Kennedy has to offer, and she has more than enough. In all of the randomness she has, it all works so well together. Doing and buying whatever she wants with an "I don't need an excuse until I do" attitude makes it hard not to notice her blasé demeanor. In another life, I want to grow up to be just like her.

Moving things inside is quicker and easier than we thought without my dad's help to do the heavy lifting. However, it was the unpacking that took a toll on our limbs and my spirit. After putting together, taking apart, and putting back together the bed frame, Sasha declared we needed a palate cleanser and turned on *10 Things I Hate About You*. I voted for *A Goofy Movie*, but was outnumbered mostly because they were tired of hearing me sing "I2I".

As much as I love Julia Stiles, I have way too much on my mind to watch a movie. After my breakup and losing out on my dream job, I have so much to fix with my life map—a neatly tabbed and in depth five year plan with everything I needed to stay on track to achieve my goals. Including my planned move to Columbus at the end of the summer. I already have apartments listed, ranking them from best to least best option depending on location, price, and availability. Others prefer spontaneity, but I always know what I want and where I'm going. Time waits for no one, and I won't be left behind.

Reaching into my bag for my journal and pencil pouch, I begin erasing parts of the map with regret as I rethink how losing the job I never had will change things moving forward.

"Put. The journal. Down." Sasha glares at me with annoyance.

"I haven't even started anything yet. I was just—" A Cheez-It hits me square in the forehead, bouncing into my lap. "Did you really—" *Flick.* Another Cheez-It bounces into my lap.

Kennedy chuckles to herself. "Oh, so you're in on her shenanigans now too?" I ask before tossing one of my pens in her direction.

"Hey, she started it first." Kennedy points to Sasha.

"Yeah, and I didn't throw a hard plastic object." Sasha clutches her hand to her chest. "You could have taken her eye out."

"Oh, whatever. Y'all were ganging up on me."

"It's for your own good." Sasha gives a conniving look to Kennedy, who gives a nod in return. I catch on quickly, but not quick enough, because before I can grab the journal, Kennedy takes hold of my wrists while Sasha snatches it from my lap. I try to get up in protest, but Kennedy is stronger than she looks. Sasha runs to go hide the book somewhere in the apartment, the air filled with her mischievous giggles, and Kennedy doesn't let me go until Sasha's returned with a look of triumph on her face.

When did they have the time to get so good at nonverbal communication while I'm in the room?

"Seriously, Sash, give it back," I demand, pushing Kennedy away from me.

"Nope." Sasha slips back onto the floor, resting her head in her hands.

She can't be serious. They can't be serious. "And why am I not allowed clearance to my personal property?"

"We were doing a palate cleanser, and you broke the golden rule," Kennedy says.

"What golden rule?"

"No phones, and no personal shit."

"That's two rules," I retort.

"Either way, rules were broken. *Golden* rules." Sasha crosses her arms.

They're actually serious.

A part of me wants to be upset, but another part of me knows they're right. I know the rules; they've been the same rules since Sasha and I were kids. We established palate cleaners whenever we needed to get out of our heads and take a second to exist. It didn't matter what happened at school, with our parents, or even if we were tired and had a bad day. Those moments are just moments; they don't last forever. I still remember her mom telling us that. How it was okay to live in those moments and feel it, but we can't live in them for too long, or they attach to us, leeching off of us and stealing our joy. It didn't make as much sense to me then, but now I appreciate that advice despite how difficult it is to live by. That's where the idea to become camp counselors for the grand reopening of our childhood summer camp came from. After the longest four years of my life, Kennedy and Sasha convinced me it would be a much needed paid getaway—an extended palate cleanser.

I fall back onto the cushions of the couch with a sigh and close my eyes. I can't deal with this right now.

"Get up." I hear Sasha move closer and sit on the couch next to me. "Get up, I'm not letting you do this."

When I remain silent, she softly tugs on a twist in my hair. "We care about you, Bree. You know that. We know that this whole life map thing is important to you, and I've accepted that that's just your way of investing in your future. There's nothing wrong with that because it's definitely worked for you this far, but lately it's been, for lack of better words, obsessive."

"And we get it. You don't want to talk about it, and you need a distraction. We're gonna have a summer full of them," Kennedy chimes in. "Let's just relax and take it easy for the next few days, yeah?"

Keeping my eyes closed, I break the silence. "It's not that I don't want to talk about it, I can't."

"Okay, so don't," Kennedy says.

"Right. We would never force you to do anything you didn't want to do... except for today." Sasha starts pulling me up by my arms despite my self loathing weighing me down. "Come on, we're going out."

I groan. "Let's just finish the movie."

"Too late. We're going to the Belfry. We leave for camp tomorrow morning. This will be our last chance for adult only fun."

Kennedy claps her hands together. "Oh, I've been wanting to go since Aubree told me about it. Let me do your makeup, and I have the perfect outfit."

Begrudgingly, I sit up and watch as Kennedy sifts through one of her boxes. "It's just the Belfry. Nobody who's anyone to impress is there. Also, I don't want to go."

"You know what? Fuck AJ for making you into this... girl I don't even recognize," Sasha says as she waves her hand over me. "The Aubree I know would never say no to a Saturday night at the Belfry with her best friend, especially when she has the opportunity to kick some guys' ass at pool again. Plus, you've been weird and flaky all year, so you owe me."

"She's not wrong," Kennedy agrees, and Sasha echoes the sentiment.

They stare at me in anticipation as I shake my head. There's so much to do and figure out in the next few days. I have to make sure my mom is set up with my email and my phone before we leave, in case I hear anything back about my interviews. I still haven't been able to make out how to revamp my plan. And what if AJ is there and I run into him? Looking back at my friends and their encouraging expressions, I know hiding here won't help, and I could use a good drink right now. Maybe a little liquid courage will help me get out of my head for the night and stop stressing.

"Fuck AJ."

"That's my girl. Now, let's go." Sasha leads me to the back room, and the makeover begins.

CHAPTER 3

An hour and a half later, and we're sitting at a tall table near the front of the bar. I would have preferred a booth so that I could hide a little longer, but Kennedy insists we sit up front, and I don't want to spoil her first time here. Especially because she spent so much time on my makeup and outfit. She wanted to put me in things way too short and tight for my liking. After some back and forth, I agreed on a skirt that was still a bit too short and a simple top with a slight plunge that shows off the matching sternum tattoo I got with Sasha. It was minimal, but extremely painful.

The Belfry is a smallish bar at the far end of town off Main Street. It's the closest and the most up to date bar in a 10 mile radius, so it's frequented by locals and neighboring towns alike. It wasn't a sports bar, so it was never too rowdy, and it wasn't a stereotypical dive bar, so it drew in a much younger crowd. Despite its dark, musk exterior, the Belfry was almost always lively, especially when a live band was coming to play.

Tonight, music played from the bar's speakers. It's hardly audible over the laughter and conversation that filled the air, the buzz somewhat comforting, which allowed me to relax. A few familiar faces stuck out to me, but no one that I'd want to interact with for more than a few minutes. And most of all, AJ is nowhere in sight.

Sasha comes back with a round of shots for us, and I'm already feeling the headache I'll have from tonight. Not necessarily from the shots, but from her talking my ear off all night. If you think she's talkative now, wait until shot five and she's like a propeller.

The shot goes down smooth enough, but I still chase it with a soda to get rid of the taste.

"What should we do? Pool? Cards? Oh, I know, let's dance!" Kennedy is far more hyper than usual, and you'd think she was sheltered. She's definitely a homebody, so seeing her this excited is always interesting.

"Cards sound fun," I say, happy to do anything stationary.

"No way," Sasha interjects. "There's a few dozen people here, and the night is young. We could have played cards at home. Let's mingle."

"With who? There's literally no one here."

"There are plenty of people here. Kennedy's only been to Coventry a few times, and there's still people to meet and introductions to be made." The door to the bar opens, sending in a gust of wind as a large, muscular man strides in. His curly hair grazes his shoulders, and a tattoo extends the length of his left arm. Sasha's eyes narrow on him with a bewitching glare. "I wouldn't mind introducing myself to him."

My gaze follows him as he slides into a stool at the bar, a small grin on his face as he greets the bartender, who slips him a glass of dark liquid. My eyes don't leave his lips as he brings the glass to them, his tongue flicking out over his bottom lip to catch the liquid threatening to spill down his chin. Just when I think I'm subtle, his eyes find mine—dark and curious. Quickly, I turn away, ducking my head in hopes that I didn't look like a total creep.

"And who is he?" Kennedy asks, her interest piqued.

"I don't know. I've never seen him before," I say, still trying to catch a glimpse of him out of the corner of my eye because who knew Coventry could attack such a fine man.

"Perfect. Go talk to him, Aubree," Sasha says.

I straighten, my eyes wide. "What? No way."

"Why not? He's a total stranger, so it's not like you'll see him again if you embarrass yourself or if you want a little extra fun. Wink." Sasha literally says wink as she winks.

I shake my head. "Now you know as well as I do that I don't do one night stands. Besides, I've never hit on a stranger before."

AJ was my first real relationship. He moved to Coventry Falls in eighth grade, and we always remained in close proximity. Doing debate club together, running the school newspaper, STEM club. So, when we started to naturally get closer after finding out he was enrolled in one of my communications classes junior year at Lakeshore, I didn't think twice. It just made sense. I didn't need to think about it until things changed—he changed.

"Allow me to demonstrate." Sasha walks a few feet away from our table and slides into the chair next to Kennedy, waiting a few seconds before directing her attention to her. "You been here before?"

When Kennedy realizes she's the example, she sits up to get into character. "No, actually, I haven't. Are you local?"

"Depends on the night." A smirk on her face, she makes intense eye contact before breaking it to bring her attention down to Kennedy's jacket. Sasha's hand comes up to gingerly finger the collar before brushing them down Kennedy's arm, making sure her finger tips graze and linger on Kennedy's wrist. "Gosh, I love this jacket. It suits you."

"I got it recently. I thought the color was a little too bold, but I wanted to try something new."

"New is always good. I've been wanting to try some new things myself." Sasha says, her voice low.

"Oh, really? Like what?" Sasha sucks in her bottom lip before leaning over slightly to whisper something into Kennedy's ear. Kennedy's eyes go wide, her jaw slightly slack as Sasha pulls away. "Uh, that's... really?"

"See? Flustered, shocked, but still engaged. Easy." Sasha downs another shot, gleaming over at me.

"I'm not whispering dirty things into a strange man's ear," I decline.

"And you don't have to. Just the act of leaning in and feeling the whisper on your skin is enough."

"Truth," Kennedy adds.

"Just pretend like you can't hear him or something and get close. It's all about proximity. Didn't you notice how Kennedy leaned in closer to me just from barely touching her? It's a simple science, really. Dang, maybe I should start selling an e-book or something."

I roll my eyes. "I can't."

Kennedy places her hands on my shoulders. "Can you try, Aubree? We can't force you, but you're here and newly single with so much to offer. You got this."

Shifting on the stool, I contemplate if doing this is really worth it. I could make a complete fool of myself, and I have plenty of time for flirting and flouncing after I'm settled in my career.

My eyes shoot back up to the guy at the bar, admiring how serene he looks despite the rowdy group beside him. Something flutters low in my stomach. I can't believe I'm doing this.

"Give me another shot." Sasha gladly slides one over with ease. If I'm going to do this and possibly look foolish while doing so, I need some liquid courage. I'm 23 now, this shouldn't be so hard, but every time it's like I'm walking into a lion's den blindfolded on a jumbo screen, so all of my mistakes are magnified. I talk to people I don't know all the time, it's how I get what I want out of life. Networking is like breathing to me. Flirting is a completely different game I've yet to master.

The room feels more silent as I make my way over to the bar. I roll back my shoulders, taking a deep breath before sitting on the stool next to him. He doesn't even look up from whatever he's doing on his phone as I shift a little closer to him. Great, he's either distracted or uninterested. Looking over my shoulder, Kennedy and Sasha give me a thumbs up, which doesn't make me feel any better about this.

Calm down, play it cool. Let's just order a drink.

I grab Jill's attention from the other side of the bar. Her family has run the Belfry for decades, but it wasn't until about 10 years ago that the place started to garner a larger crowd once Jill took it over. The internet can do magical things for small businesses.

Jill lights up as she approaches me, a wide grin on her face. "Hey, when did you get back? I heard from your parents you graduated, but they didn't say you were in town."

"Today, actually. It's just temporary until I hear back from my interviews."

"Well, look at you, city girl." She beams at me. "Don't forget us when you get out there."

"Like I'd ever." I look over my shoulder to see Sasha and Kennedy still watching me. Why does it feel like my stomach is tying itself into knots? "Can I get a rum and Coke, please?"

Jill nods and makes quick work of making my drink. When she finishes, I take my time as I take a few sips of the cool liquid and face the guy once again, who's still on his phone and hasn't looked up once since I've been sitting here.

Alright, let's get this over with.

"Hi," I say, trying to sound as casual as possible.

He doesn't look up from his phone as he gives me a mundane "hey" before continuing with whatever is so interesting on his screen. Rude. Still, I push on because I'm not going to back down now. I like a challenge.

"Have you been here before? I don't think I've seen you around."

"I'm around." No eye contact.

I'm around? Who the hell is this guy? I think I liked him better from where I was sitting, minding my own business.

A ping of irritation stirs in me. "Do you usually not look at the people talking to you when you're *around,* or is it just a me thing?" I ask through a smile.

A slow grin spills on his face as he turns off his phone and faces me. I've seen plenty of attractive men before, but this guy has a quiet power to him that's both sexy and alluring. His tan skin glows in the dim light of the bar, and his features are a mixture of soft and strong edges and curves, creating the perfect balance. His lips are full and plump, and I could only imagine how soft. Wait. Am I staring at his lips? Did he see that?

"I'm sorry, I was just looking over something for work. It's a little urgent."

Well, now I feel bad. "Oh, I'm sorry. I thought you might have been ignoring me on purpose."

"I noticed you as soon as I walked through those doors." When he parts those lips into a smile again, I feel myself start to relax all over. His smile is so inviting and familiar, I almost wanted to jump right in.

Out of the corner of my eye, I can see Sasha, who was now moved to a closer table, gesturing for me to make a move. This girl.

"Your tattoo," I say, bringing the tip of my finger to his forearm. I lightly run them over the lines and patterns, and to my surprise, he doesn't pull away. "It's beautiful. It really suits you. How long did it take?"

Up close, I can see all the detail and intention put into the design. I want to explore every part of it, but I stop myself and instead pull away but leave our hands close.

"About two days." His knee brushes against mine, and a chill crawls up my spine. I cannot be that desperate. "It was actually my dad's idea."

"He's a smart man. Makes me wonder what his son is like." I flash my eyes up at him, and it's as if his gaze darkens as it trails over me.

He leans in closer, and the scent of dark cherry wafts from him. "Hopefully you won't have to wonder much longer."

His fingers begin to intertwine with mine, and his thumb slowly circles my palm. How can something so innocent feel so sensual? This was the single most exciting interaction I've had with a man in months, and all he's doing is caressing my palm. My mind wanders to what other things his hands can do. I feel his other hand cup my leg just over my knee, and instinctively, my thighs part slightly. Holy hell, am I touch deprived. His eyes wander down between my breasts in a way that makes me regret not wearing something more revealing. He leans in closer, and I think he might kiss me until he moves in close to my ear, my pulse leaping.

"How about a quick game of pool before I have to go?" His voice is low, needy. "Unless you want to come with me?"

"Uh." My head spins with everything that could go wrong, but my body continues to pull itself into his magnitude. "I could go for a round."

He sticks his hand out, and I slide my hand into his as he helps me down from the stool. His grasp remains firm as he leads me to the pool table. Swiftly, I help to set up the game, readying two pool cues with chalk before handing him one. He rests against the table, gesturing for me to step forward.

"Ladies first," he says as I step up to the table, trying to shut my brain off long enough to concentrate on what I'm doing.

"So, I guess I should warn you..." I lower myself over the table, aligning with the cue ball before breaking, sending the balls flying. "I always win at pool."

Leaning over the table again to pocket the solid I have eyes on, he moves in closer to my side just as I'm taking my shot. "Do you enjoy being on top?"

The ball spins into the wall as the cue slips from my bridge, and my pulse quickens. So much for getting out of my head. My eyes dart to him, and the heat of his gaze is irritatingly commanding as I face him.

"Are distractions usually the way you go about winning?" I challenge, watching him walk around the table as he perfectly pockets two balls before answering me.

"I wouldn't call it a distraction. More like a special interest." He moves back to my side as I take my turn. "You're going to miss that shot."

"How would you know?"

"I can show you. May I?" He moves to stand behind me, and I feel my heart jump into my throat as I give him a nod against my better judgment. I just know Sasha is eating this up.

His body comes over mine slightly, still careful to keep his distance as he stands off to the side, but his arms fully encircle me.

"Here." His breath blows cold down my neck as his large hands come over mine, then he angles my cue a few centimeters to the right. "Lower yourself a little more for me so you can get a better view."

Doing as he says, I position myself lower, and to my surprise, I can see exactly what he's referring to. Had I hit the ball previously, I would have absolutely missed by a hair. As he straightens, his hand still lingers at my waist, almost comforting as I take the shot and pocket the ball with ease.

"Well, shit," I mumble as I spin around to face him, only a short distance us. "So, you're not all talk."

He steps closer, a renewed look flashing across his expression. "No, but do you think it's just enough to satisfy your friends, Aubree?"

I still as that familiar sly grin appears again. "What did you just say?"

"You're friends seem nice, but they're not so quiet, and I have impeccable hearing." He places his cue against the wall before grabbing his jacket and heading toward the front of the bar.

I don't know if I should be impressed or scared, but in a way, I feel relieved. "You're telling me you heard everything in a bar full of people? I can hardly hear myself." I trail behind him as we reach the bar.

"Well, not everything. The most important part I already knew."

"And what's that?"

"Your name."

I cock my head to the side and furrow my eyebrows. How could he have known my name? "Have we met before?"

"You really don't recognize me?" He laughs.

Confusion turns into realization as I look at him again; I mean *really* look at him. Fuck. How did I not put it together? The tattoo, the flirting, the satisfied smirk on his face when I'm left clueless.

"Mateo?"

He looks so different. His family moved to Samoa at the end of our junior year of high school, and I haven't seen him since. He used to be so small and scrawny, never letting his hair grow past his ears. I never imagined he'd look this good, but then again, I never really thought of him. In fact, the only memories I have are of him being a slacker and a class clown. I wouldn't go as far as saying we hated each other, but that we were on two opposite sides of a spectrum. Regardless, he still did everything to be a nuisance to me, specifically when he was bored with his usual antics. People like him truly never change.

"You still have that naive nature I see," Mateo says as he pulls out his wallet to pay for his drink.

"Excuse me, I am not naive," I declare as my heart rate triples and heat rushes to my cheeks.

"Uh huh."

"Uh huh? That's all you have to say after you just sat here for the last 20 minutes and lied to my face?"

"I didn't lie. I just withheld the truth."

"That's the same thing, and you know it." He knows what he's doing. He knew who I was. Of course he would come back to haunt me now when I'm unarmed and vulnerable.

He only chuckles to himself and leaves the money on the bar before walking around me and out the door.

Sasha and Kennedy rush over to me, but I'm dazed as I watch the door shut behind him.

"What happened?" Kennedy asks, but I direct my attention to Sasha.

"Did you know?"

She shrugs. "Did I know what?"

"About Mateo Opetaia. Did you know that was him?"

Her expression turns sour as she shakes her head. "Of course not. I wouldn't have sent you over there if I had known it was him. I did hear he moved back a while ago, but why does it matter anyway? You looked so into it."

"It was just one of his stupid tricks. That's what he does, Sash." I pick up my bag and head for the door.

The cool night air nips at my exposed legs and arms. I need to get out of here.

"Aubree, are you okay?" I hear Sasha approach me from behind, and Kennedy comes out after saying something along the lines of us remembering to pay before running out of an establishment.

"Yeah. I'm not mad at you, I'm just so embarrassed." I start to tear up. She leads us over to a bench large enough for all of us to sit on. "I think I knew."

"You knew what, Bree? About Mateo?" Kennedy puts her arm around me and squeezes my shoulder.

A pool of tears falls, running hot on my cheeks. "No, AJ. I knew he'd break up with me."

"How could you have known? It's not your fault," Sasha remarks.

"No. We hadn't had sex in months. He would constantly leave me out of the loop and ignore me, and I tried to convince myself that it was the last semester and he was busy, but... I felt like trash." I am full on ugly crying, and as much as I hate it, I can't stop it, and I don't want to.

What fool would date a guy named Arnold Junior anyway? I let him into my space—my sacred space that I cultivated—and he pulled it from under me without warning. I saw the signs. I saw the way his ego grew into greed the more time passed, but I never thought he could be cruel. And I never thought I was stupid enough to stay when I knew better.

I practically begged him to spend time with me, but it was always met with an excuse. I didn't want to push because he said it made him uncomfortable to be around me, so I didn't. I gave him everything, and I got nothing. Tonight was the first time I felt something other than anxiety. And the worst part is that it was Mateo Opetaia who made me realize it, and how little regard I had for myself.

Kennedy pulls me into a hug and pulls out a pack of tissues from her purse, handing them to me. Sasha rubs small circles into my back. I don't want to be questioned or pitied. I don't want to hear the coos of how I shouldn't blame myself and that there are bigger fish in the sea. I'm not an idiot. I just need a moment to feel free.

CHAPTER 4

P acking the suitcases in the car takes longer than expected for just five people. But with enough determination from Beck—and me having to unpack twice, having to get rid of several things, including three different types of mosquito repellent because apparently it's overkill—we're a 25 minute drive away from Camp Whisper Lake.

After last night, I'm feeling more optimistic about summer camp. My insides still itch with embarrassment and shame, but getting out of the town and into the wilderness might help me forget that last night—and the last few months—ever happened. A bit of fresh air and daily exercise never killed anyone. It's like a not so silent retreat. Camp was closed for nine years before now, but the memories I made there never left. I can't wait to see what Josh did with the place. He promised the showers would have hot water this time around, and I was all in.

My muscles relax with the sip of the coffee that slides down my throat, sparking every nerve with its warmth. "How many kids signed up this year again?"

"About 350 kids. For someone who prides themselves in always being prepared, I'm surprised you don't remember," Kennedy answers.

"Well, if someone hadn't taken my journal," I snap my gaze toward Sasha. "And had someone else not been an accomplice, I would know. I'm trying to gauge how much coffee I'll drink before camp ends."

"I love you," Sasha sings as she bumps my shoulder as if we aren't already cramped in the backseat. I give a short "mmm" in response.

"Gosh, I can't wait to get there," Maeve says with a grin as she turns around to face us from the front seat. "I heard there might be horseback riding this year."

"Josh said he made some major improvements to maximize time spent at camp," Sasha says, readjusting her hair wrap.

"I hope that includes canoes we can actually take out on the water." Beck chuckles to himself.

"I think our lake adventures on dry land were pretty fun," I add.

Maeve shrugs. "Yeah, but it would've been nice to actually row a canoe. That would be so romantic at sunset. Right, Beck?"

"Hmm, I don't know. Seems kinda corny, don't you think?"

I watch as Maeve's face falls and she captures her red hair in her fingers, twirling the strands.

"Wrong," I say, making a buzzer noise. "I'm with Maeve in the Hopeless Romantic Club. Any girl would love that."

Beck is such a cute guy, but absolutely clueless. Everyone knows Maeve has had the biggest crush on Beck since middle school—everyone except for Beck, that is. Since then, I've watched this poor girl drop breadcrumb after breadcrumb only for him to choose sticks instead. They've dated other people over the years, but no one makes them light up a room the way they do each other. Hopefully this summer, they'll finally see it for themselves.

"Don't you think it sounds too Hallmark?" Kennedy questions.

"But what's wrong with that? I love Hallmark," I cheer, and Maeve agrees with a nod. "And why can't we expect love like in the movies? I'm tired of hearing how unrealistic it is when men could just step up to the plate. Romance and yearning is a dying art."

"Here, here!" Maeve exclaims, and I thank her for her support.

"I see what you mean. Men should take notes." Sasha says through a mouth full of chips.

Beck shifts uncomfortably in his seat. "Well, I'm a man, and I think I'm pretty freaking romantic."

"Oh, yeah? What's the last romantic thing you've done?" Sasha challenges.

"Uh... there was... Look, I don't know. I've been out of the game for a while."

I pat his shoulder and laugh to myself. "It's okay. We all have to start somewhere."

"I bet you and AJ have tons of moments like that. He's always bragging about it online. Ugh, I'm so jealous," Maeve says with a sigh.

Sasha and Kennedy go silent, waiting to see what I'll say.

I honestly forgot about him for a second, only to be pulled back to reality. I thought that he would have a least told some of our mutual friends by now, or maybe I was just that easy to disregard. I want to lie, but that's always been a slippery slope for me, and I can never keep up with the lies I tell.

"We actually broke up," I mumble into my coffee cup.

I hear Beck coo, and Maeve reaches out to rub my knee. "Why didn't you tell us? I would have totally been there for you."

That was partially my fault. I was so wrapped up in everything, the first person who knew was Kennedy when she realized he stopped coming around to our apartment. I also didn't want to share that detail with them just yet. Maeve just got into the veterinarian school she wanted. I didn't want to bring down the mood with my bad news. Beck is cool, but he was often MIA because of his internship. Sometimes, I didn't hear from him for weeks at a time. Mostly, I was embarrassed. Going from thinking you're the center of someone's world only to realize you were never really in their orbit was hard enough. Talking about it wasn't at the top of my list.

I shrug. "You were so happy about veterinarian school, and Beck was busy with his internship. It wasn't the right time. I didn't want to bring you guys down."

"We're you're friends. None of that stuff would've stopped us from being by your side. You going through something and needing your friends isn't a burden. Don't ever say you're bringing us down because of that." The seriousness in Beck's voice makes my lip quiver, and I hide it through pretend sips of my coffee.

"That might be the single most sweetest thing you've said to me, Beck."

"I try." He smiles at me through the rear view mirror.

The rest of the drive is a blur of random topics and catching up. Maeve went on about her job at the animal shelter and how she just adores all the animals there, going through the names and personalities of her favorites.

Beck and Sasha seem to be the only ones really into it, while Kennedy sleeps on my shoulder.

We turn onto the road that leads up to the front entrance of Camp Whisper Lake, noting the other cars in the lot. We make quick work of unloading the car and head straight to where Josh told us to meet him in the Grub Station that also doubles as the front office. It's the only place on the premises that has wi-fi and air conditioning. To an unsurprising shock, he isn't there and instead left a note on the bulletin board that included a list of all of the cabins and where each counselor would be staying, along with new maps for us to take. The cabins for counselors and campers are all situated on the left of the Grub Station, while more staff cabins are located to the right. I'm assigned to cabin 11—the same cabin Sasha and I stayed in the summer that Camp Whisper Lake closed. It's a bit closer to the lake, so we would sometimes sneak off to take a late night swim when we were sure everyone else was asleep. It wasn't the smartest thing to do, but it felt like such a rush when we were kids.

Surveying the outside, the wind kicks up off the lake as I notice the repaired roof and its fresh coat of green and white paint. The screen is replaced on the door, but the squeak remains the same as I open it. Five bunk beds are positioned along the walls with dressers in between for the campers, and a single twin sized bed is reserved for me. A stack of camp counselor shirts and an information packet sits on the dresser, containing everything I need to know about the camp rules, safety, and our designated camp schedules. While I would love to take a quick nap before our first staff meeting, my eagerness gets away from me as I crouch down, running my fingers along the floorboard.

"Oh my god, it's still here!" I exclaim as I move closer to see the faint writing.

"What is?" Kennedy asks as the door shuts behind her.

"Our initials." I point out the *S*, *M*, and *A* surrounded by a heart at the base of the board. My heart flutters at the memories it brings back, and I almost feel like crying. In fact, I think I was crying the day we did this.

Counselor Kristy was the absolute worst. That day, she took away my recreation block for the next two days because I'd forgotten to help clean up after lunch for the fourth day in a row, even though it was *her job*. Making up an excuse that it would teach us responsibility. The thought of missing out with my friends sounded like a nightmare at 14. I remember sitting in this corner crying my eyes out with Maeve and Sasha trying to soothe me. Sasha decided we should carve our initials into the wood of the floorboard to show that no matter what, nothing could keep us apart. It ended up not really mattering anyway after I told Josh and he reseeded her decision. Still, it's a stark reminder of our friendship.

"Aw, it's still there." Sasha comes up behind me, squatting down to see. "I'm so glad we get to be here together again. Now all we need to do is add a *K*."

"That's sweet, but it's your thing. I'm sure we'll find something to commemorate the best summer ever," Kennedy says as she admires our handiwork.

I stand up and lay my suitcase out on the floor. "Speaking of commemorating..." I pull out a plastic bag with disposable cameras in it, holding it out for them.

Kennedy gasps. "Aw, cute." She immediately grabs one, followed by Sasha.

"You really do think of everything," Sasha says, winding the film.

"I had to. I know I said that this was a stupid idea when you brought it up..." Kennedy eyes me, earning her a laugh. "But once I move to the city, we might see less of each other. I want to remember this summer as it was and nothing less. I even got one for Maeve and Beck, and extra film and cameras too, just in case."

"Please don't make me cry on our first day." Sasha wraps me in a hug, with Kennedy joining shortly after.

The last year was hard enough not being able to be home as much as I wanted to. I learned so much, but I missed home—my friends. I needed this summer to be a reminder—an escape from everything that's plagued me for months on end.

"Okay, we better start unpacking before the meeting," I say, muffled against Sasha's chest.

Agreeing to meet back at Grub Station, I start unpacking what I can. And once I start, I have to admit they were right about me overpacking. I don't need four different pairs of tennis shoes or three colors of the same shirt, but it's better to have it than to need it when I can't get it. Sasha and Kennedy did offer to help me unpack, but I already had everything organized in my suitcase the way I wanted it to be placed inside the drawers. And my sheets needed to be placed on and tucked a certain way, or I wouldn't be able to sleep knowing that the tags aren't on the left side near the foot of the bed, or that the opening of my pillow case isn't facing the right.

After I finish stuffing the dresser, I take my time making my way to the Grub Station. The smell of the pine trees and dark earth sends rays of joy through my system. The stillness of it all is surprisingly comforting. They say spending time with nature is grounding, and that's just what I needed, even if 350 screaming teens and preteens are running around and giving me hell. But I can do this. I'm letting go and welcoming the present. I have my mom to monitor my phone and emails for any updates, and she'll get back to me on the camp's main line if anything major happens.

Everything will work out fine.

The Grub Station is alive with a couple dozen counselors and instructors holding conversations and catching up with others they haven't seen in years. All seems pleasant until I make my way to the front of the hall and notice a dark haired woman sitting on a table nearby. I don't need to see her face to know the terror she is based on her slim frame and lack of regard for everyone around her as she flips her hair into the face of the person beside her.

Picking up my pace, I rush to where my friends sit off to one side of the room. "Did you guys know Penelope was gonna be here?" I plop down at the table, breathy and annoyed.

"No," Sasha groans. "We just found out when we saw her walk in right before you. I thought she was too pretty for nature?"

"Who's Penelope?" Kennedy interrupts.

Rolling her eyes, Sasha waits for others to pass by before continuing. "A nobody who peaked in high school and has been riding that high ever since."

"Do you remember when she poured milk into your rain boots?" I ask.

"Oh my god, yes! And when she tried to 'expose us' for being secret lesbian lovers?" We both explode into laughter while Kennedy looks more confused than amused. "Now that I think about it, maybe she had a crush on you."

"Ugh, don't. Mean girl isn't my type."

"Who knows, maybe she's changed?" I say with a shrug. Sasha eyes me like she knows I should know better, and while I agree it's highly unlikely for her, people can really surprise you.

Footsteps echo from the staircase to our right, and Josh's lean frame comes into view, carrying a box I'm sure is meant for our phones. In all of the years I've known him, I don't think I've ever not seen him in a good mood as he sports an ear to ear smile. The room grows quiet as he approaches us and sets down the box on a nearby table with a thud.

"Good afternoon, staff!" Josh's voice booms, and I wonder if he was ever a PE teacher in his past life. "Thanks for being here. It truly means a lot, and it's great to be back." We clap and whistle before he raises his hands in a calming motion.

"I'm sure you've all gotten a chance to catch up, and I know you're eager to know what's in store for Camp Whisper Lake moving forward. But first, did everyone sign the sign-in sheet on the bulletin board?" When no one gets up to do so, Josh takes that as is sign to continue. "Alright, assuming you all did so because you're responsible adults, we'll talk about some new additions to the camp. First, we have a few new buildings on the grounds: an amphitheater where we'll host movie nights and the return of our amazing camp plays, a greenhouse, and the

Education Center, where certain classes will be held, which I'll get into a little later. The prayer rooms will still be held in the Grub Station on the second floor across from my office."

He goes on to list other new additions, including electricity in the bathrooms as well as new activities, including horseback riding, canoeing, and gardening. He went on about stressing the importance of creating a camp experience that will leave campers inspired and open minded. Each week, campers will have a new schedule of activities to ensure everyone gets a chance to do everything at least once, with the exception being theater.

"Now for the real fun part." Josh claps his hands together, bringing people back to attention who've drifted off. "First day of camp, there'll be a surprise challenge for both you and the campers. First place gets to use the showers first for week one."

Everyone, especially me, sits up with intrigue. A hot shower is the second best thing next to freshly pressed pants. And I do love a bit of competition; I could practically salivate.

"The challenge is about team bonding, so you'll be competing in teams of two paired with a fellow counselor. And get used to it because you'll be paired for most other things around camp too." We all look at each other, a sense of anticipation and excitement suddenly filling the air. Josh goes on to read off the names and cabin numbers for each paired team. When he gets to my name, I'm just crossing my fingers that it's not Penelope.

"Harper, you're partner had to drop out last minute, so you're with uh... Ah, there he is now." Josh gestures to the back of the room at the sound of the large wooden door opening.

I turn around to see who he's referring to and my gut flares with a nauseous loathing.

This can't be real.

CHAPTER 5

D id I do something to upset the universe? Tip the scales and rip a hole through space in time, causing some alternate timeline where I'm punished for not fulfilling some cosmic cycle? First AJ, then my dream job, and now *him*. My perfect getaway—ruined.

Mateo strolls into the hall with that dumb cocky smirk on his face. I turn around, choosing to ignore him rather than get myself worked up. Sasha mouths a "what the fuck" out of the corner of my eye, and Kennedy tries to grab my attention, but I instead focus on the rest of Josh's speech, taking notes here and there in the information packet he provided us.

As the meeting ends, and as my head stops spinning, Maeve turns to face us. "I can't believe I got paired with Devin. This is going to be one long summer if I have to work with him."

"You're telling me," I exhale.

"You got Mateo, though. That should be fun." Giving her a strong side eye, she shakes her head. "Do we not like Mateo?"

"They have their differences," Sasha chimes.

"You don't remember how he used to taunt me in school?" I ask. "I almost got suspended because of him."

"Oh, gosh, I do remember that. Sorry, Bree. I can see why you hate him."

Groaning, I move to make my way toward the doors. "I'm going for a walk."

Concentrating my energy on kicking the rock in my path in rhythm with my steps, I take a few deep breaths, soaking my lungs with as much positive affirmation as I can. But my mind keeps wandering back to that stupid cigarette Mateo insisted on smoking when we were supposed to be working on a class assignment. Of course I got caught up in it when I went to put it out and the assistant principal found us. Technically, we were skipping class, but it was because of Mateo's negligence that I had to, or we both would have failed. The cigarette was the cherry on top.

Unfortunately, my concentration on the rock left me without my hearing, as I didn't notice the patter of footsteps behind me before the low vibrato that comes with it.

"Hey, teammate." Mateo falls into step with me.

"Leave me alone," I dismiss, keeping my focus on the ground.

As he stuffs his hands into his pockets, I can't help but notice the flex of his muscles. My line of vision extends up his forearm, recalling how they felt over my body. Gentle, firm—nope. I'm so not going there.

"So, you really won't talk to me? You do know we'll have to talk eventually, right?" The rock bounces into Mateo's path, and he starts kicking it along.

I don't have the energy to do this right now. "I'm aware. How are you even here?"

"A car would have been ideal, but I've really been into the pogo stick lately."

"Just answer the question."

"Alright," he chuckles, but I've yet to find any of this funny. "I've been up here the past few days helping Josh fix up a few more things before tomorrow. When a counselor dropped out last minute, he asked me, and I said yes."

"Oh my gosh, was that the 'work' you were busy with at the bar?" I question as another shock sweeps over me. "Did you know I was going to be here?" And when he hesitates, I have my answer.

"I didn't say yes because of that, if that's what you're worried about. Things have been slow at the auto shop, and I need the work," he claims.

"Do you honestly think I'd stop you from working? I'm not worried either. Unfortunately, you're here now, and there's nothing I can do about it."

"Is this about last night?"

I chuckle in disbelief. "Please. You took advantage of that situation to get under my skin."

He shrugs. "What can I say? Although I'm flattered you approached me. Way to come out of your shell."

"So, you admit it then. You do it on purpose." I stop to face him.

He smiles down at me. "Do what?"

Unbelievable. I walk faster toward the lake, leaving him to jog to catch up to me.

"Okay, okay—Aubree." He reaches out for me, his fingertips brushing my arm as I turn to meet his gaze. "I apologize. That was a dumb thing to do, and I shouldn't have done it. I got caught up, and I swear it won't happen again."

I look into his eyes for any ounce of amusement. "Nice try, but I've heard that before, remember?" Clearing my throat, I put on my best Mateo Opetaia impression. "'Aubree, I swear I didn't mean to throw that paper ball at you during our test.' 'Aubree, I swear I wasn't trying to make you late for class.' 'Aubree, I didn't think Principal Wilson would catch us outside the school while I was smoking instead of helping you with the school project, even though you told me a million times to put it out, *and* you had to skip class for me just to get it done.' You're a broken record. It's not just about last night—it's everything about you."

His face falls, but before he can give me those timeless puppy dog eyes, I turn away back on my trail.

"Look, you're right, and I can see why you hate me. I quit smoking by the way, so you don't need to worry about that anymore," he pleads as if that makes up for it.

Shaking my head, I almost laugh. "Mateo, spare me. And I don't hate you. It's been five years. I now strongly dislike you."

Mateo nods. "So, there's a chance I can still win you over?"

"Highly unlikely since the first thing you did when you saw me after years was to pretend that you didn't know me and allowed me to embarrass myself." I stop walking to face him once more. "Listen, we're both adults and we're different people now—hopefully. Let's agree to disagree." I put my hand out for him to shake it.

His palm slides into mine. "I'll do whatever you need."

After a late lunch and a mid-afternoon shower, I make my way over to Kennedy's cabin, where she's strategizing all of the possible challenges for tomorrow, all of which make absolutely no sense. Sasha, on the other hand, can't seem to sit still long enough to paint her own toenails as she goes on and on about everything she wants to do this summer. I'm just hoping that tomorrow doesn't totally suck. I have ideas of my own of what the challenge is, but the prize is too sweet to share with my girls.

"Oh, guys!" Sasha exclaims, interrupting herself yet again to go on another spiel. "Do you know what would have been perfect? Is if Maeve would have been paired up with Beck. They could really use some bonding time, and Devin's just dead weight anyway. He'd rather sulk around and act nonchalant."

"True. I wonder what's keeping them apart? They obviously like each other," I affirm as Sasha passes me the nail polish to screw closed.

"Maybe Beck doesn't like her in that way, though," Kennedy adds.

"He does, he's hinted at it before, but there's only one way to find out." Sasha grins, a sparkle not so hidden behind it.

"We are not meddling in their love lives, Sash. What happened to 'this summer is all about us'?" I remind her.

She hugs her pillow close to her. "It still is. That doesn't mean there isn't room for romance for any of us. Plus, we'd be doing them a favor. Think about how happy they'll be if it works out."

"But think about how sad it will be if it doesn't. You can't force people together, it's not right." Kennedy throws her hands up, a hint of agitation in her tone.

"Fine," Sasha groans. "If I can sus out how Beck is feeling, will you guys help me?"

"No," I say firmly. "They're both grown ups. If there's really more than a spark between them, they'll talk through it like adults."

"But, don't you think they need a little push?" Sasha challenges.

"A big one, but that's not our job; we're not in high school."

Sasha frowns, hugging her pillow tighter.

"And leave me out of your match making shenanigans before you get any ideas. I have enough to deal with," Kennedy confesses.

I want to see Maeve and Beck together more than anyone, but it's not my concern to make it happen for them. I've been the victim and witness of more than enough of Sasha's schemes to know that something almost always goes wrong. As great as it sounds in theory, it's destined to be a disaster in practice. Besides, this summer is about having fun and spending time with each other. Not kindling old flames or guys who want nothing more than to be a pain in my ass.

CHAPTER 6

As early as seven in the morning, cars fill the lot as parents, guardians, and siblings drop off campers and their duffel bags full of essentials for the next six weeks. The check-in line continuously grows, but moves along quickly as each camper is signed in and handed a drawstring backpack with a shirt, a folder of information, and hand sanitizer. Impatient parents are packed inside the Grub Station waiting for their turn to speak to Josh about whatever problem they're having that may affect the full summer camp experience their child was promised. Issues ranged from allergies to the lack of service in the middle of the woods in case their child needed to reach them. Other staff members were going around to troubleshoot and answer as many questions as they could to ease the pressure off of Josh; some parents are more reluctant to speak to them than others. Myself and the other counselors stand outside our cabins to greet each of our campers and ensure that they make their way to the cabin to choose their bed and unpack before initiation.

The buzz of excitement in the air brings the camp to life, and my heart races thinking of all the things that could happen in the coming weeks. Somehow, being on the other end of the camp experience as a counselor is just as thrilling as being a camper. It could be first day jitters or the three cups of coffee I've had since five thirty this morning. Either way, I'm ready for the summer to officially begin.

I sway back and forth on my feet as I wait for my first camper, checking and rechecking my list of campers as if I didn't already have it memorized. The universe must be restoring its balance as I see Valarie rush over to greet me with a hug. She's grown to be much taller than me at 16 years old, but then again, I am on the short side.

Valarie and her mom used to live next door to us before moving to a neighboring town when her mom got remarried. I'd drive her to our house some afternoons from the elementary school as a favor, as her mom was working toward her nursing degree at the time and had evening classes. She'd stay over and have dinner with us a few days a week, which my parents were always thrilled to do, and so was I. Most people would find a talkative nine year old exhausting, but I found it fascinating. The way they're experiencing life for the first time and making connections I never did at their age, or even now at 23, was nothing short of entertaining.

"I was so happy when they told me you were my counselor." Valarie sets her bag down to readjust her backpack. Her long braids cascade over her shoulder.

"I was so happy when I saw you on the list. How's your mom? Everything okay in Oakbridge?"

Oakbridge was nothing compared to Coventry Falls, its lack of town cheer or community evidence of it. It was okay for an occasional visit for their large corporation franchises, but Paul, Valarie's mom's husband, insisted they enroll Valarie in the private school system there for a "brighter future" for his stepchild. Valarie only stopped protesting the idea after I convinced her to make some new friends, after which our hour long chats became two minute calls the stronger her friendships grew. I was proud of her, but a little hurt too.

"Yeah, but it's not like being in Coventry." She frowns. "Mom's good too, she dropped me off in the lot because she had to get to work."

"Well, hopefully I can catch her next time." I smile. "Go on in and get unpacked. We have initiation in the Quad in about an hour."

The Quad is where I've made some of my best camp memories. We meet there every Saturday to roast marshmallows, sing songs, tell stories, and reflect on our camp motto: Grow, Change, Become Together. It's what makes Camp Whisper Lake live up to its name; if you close your eyes and listen hard enough, you can hear the echoes of memories made here, according to Josh. Personally, I try not to think about creepy whispers in the woods, especially at night.

The nine other girls assigned to my cabin trickled in one after the other—filling the space with giggles and chatter.

"Alright, guys." I raise my voice loud enough over them to get their attention. "Let's finish unpacking, so we can head up camp."

"Do you think we can go swimming in the lake today?" A girl with two pig tales raises her arm, pinning where the question came from. Dena, I remember from the photos that parents were required to submit before camp so that we can keep track of each camper.

"It all depends on how fast you guys unpack and get to the Quad, and please don't forget to put on your camp shirt."

The girls start to pick up their pace, and I move to look over the roster one last time, noting that none of my campers or Mateo's have any medical conditions or dietary restrictions. We exchanged copies of camper information last night after dinner, but I didn't really have much time to look over any notes from guardians for Mateo's campers. Sleep washed over me after the pot pie we had, and I woke up with the papers crushed and scattered over the bed. I'll have to remember to bring it with me today. Besides, after today, they're mostly his responsibility anyway.

Just as I'm rechecking my notes and my bag for the hundredth time, Valarie pops her head out from beside me, nearly giving me a heart attack.

"You're still as sly as a cat, you know that?" I tell her as I toss my things onto the dresser.

"Yep." She smiles sweetly. "I consider it my special skill among many things. Speaking of skills..."

She hands me a red journal with scrap paper stuffed between some of the pages. I immediately recognize it as the one I gave her last Christmas. A small wave of gratitude echoes within me as I see how useful it's been to her. When Valarie told me she wanted to start writing, I knew it would be the perfect gift. Simple, yet impactful. Thumbing through some of the pages, I'm impressed by how much she's been able to write since then. Lines and stanzas of poetry litter each page front to back. Some with exes and scribbles of the ones she wanted to erase.

"This is awesome, Val. You'll be needing a new one soon." I hold it out for her to take, but she pushes it back toward me.

"No, I want you to read it. I was hoping to get some feedback since we have some time now."

"Oh." It came out more surprising than I wanted it to be. "I mean, of course! It's good to know someone still trusts my opinion."

"Well, duh," she replies smartly, falling onto my bed, and I try not to cringe at the fact that my neat folds come loose. "You won the state poetry contest twice. I want to win next year for sure this time."

I pull her up and into a bear hug, which she's initially reluctant to. "You're gonna win it, and I'm making sure of it."

I feel her relax under the pressure of my arms, as if it was just the thing she needed to hear. Before she can say anything more, the squawk of the loudspeakers turning on brings us to attention.

"Good morning, campers and staff!" Josh says, drawing out the "good" for dramatics. "Please make your way on down to the Quad for initiation. Camp Whisper Lake is officially in session." Cheers break out across the other cabins as kids burst through their cabin doors in their blue and white camp shirts. I hustle the girls out of the cabin and have them wait for me out front, contrary to what Mateo's done with his own campers. He walks out of his cabin at the same time as me, catching each other's gaze. He gives me a wink as he catches up to the rest of his campers, and I loathe the inevitable headache I'll have to deal with later.

As we near the Quad, I find Mateo standing nearby, Penelope attached to his side as he smiles down at her. I'd almost forgotten about the pathetic crush she had on him in school, and by the smug look she gives me when I approach them, I know she's still trying to mark her territory. It's bad enough she's here, but now I'm more of a target because I'm teamed with Mateo for the summer. Ignoring them, I direct my campers to sit beside his, avoiding him as I move to sit behind them.

"I can't get a good morning at least? We're a team after all." Mateo asks as he sits beside me, looking over my frame.

"Good morning, Mateo," I say through a smile, staying on my best behavior for the campers.

"I can get used to hearing that." The words snake up my spine, tightening around me.

"If you're supposed to be proving you're not the annoying a-hole you were in high school, you're doing a really terrible job." Turning to face him, I lower my voice, keeping my smile pleasant. "Just make sure I don't have to pick up your slack today."

The pinch between his brows tells me there's more to say, but when Josh finally appears at the bottom of the pit near the bonfire, a round of cheers break out as he pumps up the crowd with his arms and cheers alongside them. When everyone starts to settle down, Josh begins his first day speech, similar to the one we got, but with specific rules for campers. He always stresses the importance of safety and relying on the buddy system when going around the grounds. He emphasizes how there is a strict no phones policy and that phone calls would be allowed daily by cabin per camp rules to ease the minds of worried parents and homesick campers. In between, he tells corny dad jokes and punchlines that either send laughter or groans throughout the audience. After the last one, I watch as Mateo leans over to Penelope, saying something in a low enough voice that I can't hear, but funny enough that it makes her laugh. It probably isn't even that funny knowing her, and why am I paying attention to him? I turn my attention back on Josh, who's finally moving onto the challenge.

"And lastly—because I know you all are antsy—this year we're doing things a little differently for initiation. You'll all be participating in a little challenge that'll determine who gets first bids on showers for the week." The prize isn't that amazing, but it still sends whispers of anticipation skittering through the campers, many of them perking up after his spiel. "There are 15 teams, meaning each cabin is combined with another for the game. The first team to make it back here will be dubbed the winner. Our initiation challenge this year is.... a scavenger hunt."

Josh lowers his hands to shush the crowd before giving up further instructions. "Your first clue has been concealed in these envelopes." He holds them up for us to see, each of them with cabin numbers that correspond with our teams. He instructs each counselor to come and retrieve their envelopes and stand in front of their group. I take the liberty of going up to grab it since Mateo's too busy flirting—not that I should be complaining.

"Each clue will lead you to a different location on the grounds. The clues not only hint at the location, but to an item you'll need to collect and bring back here in 45 minutes to complete the hunt," Josh says. "Now, if you're all ready, on the blow of the whistle you may begin." The sound of the whistle causes a ripple of excitement as each counselor tears open their envelope and campers gather close for the first clue. Once I get the envelope open, I pull out the note card inside, my eyes scanning the print while Mateo not so subtly leans over my shoulder.

"'Where curiosity and wonder bubble over, and questions and failures leave answers closer. Safety is key for eager eyes; protection is necessary if you're wise.'" I look up at the campers. "Anyone have any ideas."

They mumble among each other before one kid raises his hand, shouting out the answer. "Is it science?"

"Perfect!" I exclaim. "So, that would be the Education Center, but what about the second part of the riddle?"

"We'll figure that out on the way." Mateo steps in front of me, blocking my view. "Let's get moving."

He charges up the stone steps as the group gets up to follow him toward the large brick building at the far side of camp. I remain frozen in place, not knowing whether to confront him now or later. I have no time to decide when I look back and notice Josh watching us, a satisfied grin on his face, and I can't afford to embarrass myself in front of him. My foot up Mateo's ass would have to wait until later.

Other groups part off in different directions based on their clues. When we finally make it to the Education Center, the building is much larger than the rest of the small wooden buildings. The inside looks more like an actual classroom laboratory than something you'd expect at summer camp, its cool tile floors and long black tables adding to the effect. Mateo leads us into the spacious room, and I spot our next envelope against the whiteboard next to some others.

Before I can even draw my next breath, Mateo's repeating the second part of the riddle. "Safety is key for eager eyes; protection is necessary if you're wise." Bitterly, I let him have it as not to cause a scene as I slide my way toward the front where he stands.

The campers look around, some whispering to each other and others seeming as lost as the person next to them. I step forward, moving toward the answer slowly as to give them a clue. "Come on, guys, think about it."

"Safety goggles?" a young boy with short, black curls guesses in a slight whisper.

"You got it." Mateo reaches over me, snatching a pair out of the box from beside me and tossing it to the boy to carry. Before I can turn back to grab the next envelope, Mateo is already tearing it open. I didn't even see him grab it. Heat rushes to my ears as I step closer to him, lowering my voice so only he can hear.

"Sorry, but I was going to do that." I reach for the card, and he moves it out of my reach.

"I'm capable of reading a piece of paper." He waves the clue in front of my face.

"Could of fooled me since it's not written in Buffoon." I reach for it again, and he holds it over his head, and suddenly I'm back in high school. He's been 6'2 since the eighth grade, and I've been the same height since the fifth. This was one of his very many tactics in his playbook of "How Can I Get On Aubree's Nerves Today?" If he thinks I'm going to climb him for that card like I would have five years ago, he's mistaken. Screw him, I'm not fighting him for a stupid card like we're 12.

"This is childish," I say. "We're wasting time."

He points out of the window at the team approaching us. "I agree. I say we split up."

"What? That's not what I—"

"Come on, Aubree. Take a chance." Before I can disagree further, he's already taking half of the campers with him, some of whom are mine, and leaving me with a few of his.

"And where are we supposed to go?" I shout at him as he heads outside.

He turns around, and a wide grin spreads across his face. "The team out here is holding a life jacket; try the lake. This one is going to Arts and Crafts." He holds up the note card that I didn't get to check over to confirm his suspicion. Before I can get another word in, he's gone, and the other team is entering the building.

My face grows hot as I clench my teeth together. He humiliated me again, and this time in front of a group of kids. He could have just handed me the card like I asked, but no. He insists on making things complicated and making me look like the stuck up asshole.

I don't have time to toil in it now, so I rush the campers outside toward the lake. It's a short walk from the Education Center, with the supply shed a few yards away from the dock. I swing open the door before grabbing a life jacket and the next envelope and have one of the campers read it. This activity's meant to be educational, so they can a least get something out of it before securing our win.

"'When bumps and bruises cause quite a scare, you find this place with hands that care. When you're sick, don't spread your germs; put on one of these for a term.'"

"The infirmary," Valarie mumbles.

"Good. Any guesses for the second part?" I ask, looking over the rest of the group anxiously.

"I need to use the bathroom." One camper says, shifting from leg to leg.

"Oh, but the infirmary is on the other side of camp. Do you think you can hold it for a few minutes?"

"I need to go too," says Dena. Another camper nods in agreement alongside another. A bathroom break should have been the first on my list before coming out here, and it's the one thing I didn't think of. There are at least four other buildings to check—because who knows how long Mateo will take—and only 35 more minutes according to my watch. If we hurry, we can make it with enough time left to complete the challenge.

I lead the group up the path, past the cabins, and to the bathrooms. Two more campers go in along with the initial three that needed to go. Pacing outside the doors, I strategize how we can go about collecting the rest of the items. It's probably best for me to answer the clues and collect as we go. As long as we all make it to the buildings as a group, that's all that matters. We can do an official campground tour later.

One group comes running past us toward the lake, Kennedy towing behind.

"Kennedy!" I yell.

She jogs back toward me, her breathing heavy. "Geez, what are you doing here? What happened with you and Mateo? I saw him leaving the Rec when we got there."

"He thought it was a good idea to split up." I contain the eye roll that I've reserved specifically for Mateo.

Kennedy cocks her head to the side with a shrug. "I mean, its not a bad idea. It's definitely faster than ushering around 20 kids."

"But the whole point is to get the kids familiar with where everything is. How does splitting up help?"

"I don't know. Go with it for now, and we can talk later. I gotta go." She runs off, leaving me even more frustrated. Why is she on his side?

Deep breaths, Aubree.

When the kids are done in the bathroom, I check my watch. Less than 25 minutes.

"Okay, everyone ready? No one else needs anything immediate, right?"

They all shake their heads, but as I'm looking over them, I only find nine shaking heads instead of 10. I look inside the girls' bathroom and then the boys. Nothing.

"Who's missing?" I ask. They look at me just as confused as I am as panic slowly seeps into my veins. I throw off my backpack in search of the list of campers I had in the cabin earlier, but as I sift through it a third time, I clench my stomach as my heart drops into a bottomless pit of my worst nightmares.

"Shit," I whisper. Shutting my eyes, I see the paper sitting on the dresser where I left it in the cabin. "Dammit!"

"What's wrong?" Valarie steps forward.

"I left the list of names in the cabin. All I know is that it was a boy; one of Mateo's campers."

Fuck. I lost a kid. How the hell did I lose a whole kid in less than 10 minutes? And on the first day? Now I know how my mom felt whenever I ran off in the store to go look at the toy aisle. A looming terror spins around me, coiling me into its grasp. I need to throw up.

"It's okay. We'll help you," Valarie says. "I'll go get the papers."

"No," I say sharply. "I'm the adult; it was my responsibility. I'm not letting anyone else out of my sight." But I also don't have time to haul them all back to the cabins and run around the camp to find a kid who isn't even one of my campers to begin with. "We need to find Mateo."

Mateo's the last person I want to ask for help, but I don't have very many options, and he's the only one who knows the kid. Regrettably, I should have read those notes sooner—stayed up longer—but I didn't think it would lead to this. I've never lost anything living before, and the grounds are larger than I remember; they could be anywhere.

With the kids in front of me to ensure no one leaves my sight this time, we run toward the Rec Center. He may still be on this side of camp, but it doesn't stop the sinking feeling in my stomach with the realization that I might not find him in time. Anything could happen to the kid by the time we find Mateo, and that alone is scary enough. Josh is a lesser beast.

My heart pounds with each thump of my feet hitting the ground. If he's still here, he's either in the greenhouse or headed back from the stables. I turn right for the greenhouse, allowing my intuition to guide me. Racing forward to reach for the door, it swings open. Mateo steps out, a faint grin on his lips that quickly falls as he scans me over.

His eyes grow wide as he steps closer to me. "Are you okay? What's going on?"

"One of the kids is missing," I manage to reply between breaths, holding a hand to my ribs.

"What the—" He runs his hands through his hair, biting down on his last word. "How did you lose a kid?" He exclaims, his brows furrowed in fear.

"He wandered off somewhere, I don't know? He's your camper anyway. I told you that splitting up was a dumb idea, but you don't listen." Blame hangs like a cloud above us alongside the anger that he dared to try and fault me, fueling its heavy tension.

"Don't put this on me. I gave you a list of notes and the names of my campers—"

"Names, not faces," I correct. "I met them, for what? All of 10 minutes before you went off without me? I had information for my campers a week ago. I can't be held responsible for your last minute call to action to be a counselor."

"Whatever, we don't have time to argue." He scans the campers, letting out a sigh. "Of course, it's Axel."

"So, you knew he was a runner and didn't say anything?"

He starts to pace back and forth, his hands on his hips. "His mom said something to me this morning about how he gets easily distracted, especially when—"

"When what?" I ask, wanting to pull the answer from his tongue myself. Other campers look just as worried, and I wonder if we're scaring them. I definitely wouldn't want a counselor who couldn't keep their cool, let alone keep track of the kids left in their care. I can hear the screams of parents now. This is so fucked.

Mateo doesn't give an answer or tell us where we're going before he starts toward the direction of the Grub Station. I notice other teams all making their way back to the Quad, filing in one after the other. Our time is running out, especially if we want to avoid Josh. I can only hope Mateo knows what he's doing, and he knows where Axel is. Maybe we can swing it that we misplaced him. A misplaced kid is better than a missing one, right?

Mateo opens the door to the Grub Station, and I push forward to follow him inside. My blood runs cold, my stomach forming into knots as the sight of Josh and Axel sitting at one of the tables comes into view—a sandwich smashed into Axel's face, and disappointment stains Josh's expression as he looks between Mateo and I.

Time was never on our side.

CHAPTER 7

The silence in the small office is deafening as Mateo and I sit side by side in front of Josh, the typing of his computer being the only thing to distract me from my own thoughts. I want to say something—anything—to explain myself and how this isn't my fault. That I wasn't the one responsible for him, so there's really no need for me to be here in the first place. Mateo, on the other hand, this is a typical afternoon for him. I don't know if this whole sitting in silence thing is a test or if he really is busy with the report, so I bite my tongue and pick at the fabric of the cushioned chair.

The office chair squeaks on its hinges the moment Josh sits back in it, taking his attention away from the bright glow of the screen and onto us. I've never seen him look so upset before, especially not at me.

"Things can get a little hectic on the first day of camp, so it's understandable to be overwhelmed given that neither of you have done this before. And especially given that I asked Mateo last minute to help out." Josh sighs, folding his hands on the desk. "Still, I'm extremely disappointed in you both."

A weight pushes down on me, so much so that I wish it'd pull me through the floor. This wasn't my doing, yet I'm still receiving the blame. I'm glad that nothing happened to Axel and that he was found safe, but I'm not accepting any guilt. He wasn't my camper, and it wasn't my idea to split up when things were fine to begin with. I didn't ask for this; I didn't ask to be paired with the most incompetent and irritating man on the planet. But I do hope that this will make Josh see how unfit Mateo is to be a counselor. One less problem on my list the sooner he's gone.

"It was an accident, Josh, and I had everything under control—"

He puts his hand up, forcing me into silence. "That's fine and all, but a lack of control and teamwork is what got you here in the first place. Fighting in front of your team, splitting off from each other, trying to outdo the other; you guys know better." He shakes his head. "I'd have to relieve you of your duties."

Out of the corner of my eye, Mateo stiffens, but I swear you can hear my pulse beating through the walls. Going home isn't an option. As much as I hated the idea, I need this summer. I need to be here. I can't be forced back into reality too soon—I'm not ready. This was supposed to be a break, the time I needed to figure my shit out, and now it's ruined.

"*But*," he adds sharply. "I've known you both since you were kids, and I know neither one of you is careless enough to let something like this happen again. You had a weak moment in a rough patch, and no one was harmed. However, I will say that this is your one and only warning."

I let out a breath I didn't know I was holding. "Oh my god, thank you so much."

"Don't thank me yet," Josh says with a grin. "You two still need to learn to work together as a team. So, for the next week, you'll be doing dishes after dinner and helping to prep breakfast in the mornings."

"That's it?" Mateo questions, and I almost kick him.

Josh picks off a sticky note from his computer monitor, handing it to Mateo. "Well, the stables could use an extra cleaning in the mornings, but I don't need any negative energy affecting the horses. But since you so kindly asked, I do need you to run an errand to Millard's and pick up some oat milk and almond milk for breakfast tomorrow morning. I underestimated how many kids don't drink real milk these days, and the next delivery won't be for a while."

"Millard's? That's almost an hour from here." Mateo looks over the sticky note like the few things on the list will magically double at any second. On it are the milks and a few extra things I'm assuming are for Josh's personal stash of goodies.

"Yup." He tosses me his keys. "You can take the old pickup at the front during Block Five before dinner. Be back no later than seven; Ron and Penelope have agreed to watch your campers until then. Go on now, I don't want to *milk* this any longer." Josh laughs to himself.

I roll my eyes both at the joke and Penelope because of course she did. Penelope's only an angel when there's something to gain. Unbelievable.

"I'm sorry, but how is any of this fair to me? Axel's not my camper. Mateo split off from me; he's the reason this happened," I explain. It's a reasonable question, and the more respectful way for me to tell Josh that this is bullshit.

Josh takes a beat before clarifying. "You're a team whether you like it or not. You take the losses and the victories together. No, Mateo shouldn't have broken up the group and gone off on his own, but you should've remained level headed despite it and communicated your concerns with him instead of fighting. Both of you let your frustration get the best of you. I expect better moving forward."

A trail of fire is left behind me with how quickly I storm out of that office. I'm entirely fed up with Mateo, and I honestly don't know how I'm going to get through the next six weeks if every time I turn around, I have a man child biting at my ankles. Camp Whisper Lake was the last place I thought I'd have to deal with this. This was supposed to be fun and happy. Now it just feels like a chore.

My friends are congregated at the bottom of the stairs, Beck's fingers drumming on the railing. Maeve notices me first and comes to my side when I hit the last stair. "What happened? Please tell me you're staying."

"I'm staying," I confirm with a mumble.

"That's great," Kennedy says through a sigh of relief. "Why do you look so gloom and doom then?"

"Because," I reply, trying to suppress a pout. "I'm being blamed, and Josh refused to hear it when it's not technically my fault. On top of that, I have to wash dishes after dinner and help prep breakfast in the morning for the next week with Mateo."

"That's not so bad," Beck consoles. "You know, when I used to work at Applebee's, I'd bus out 600 plates easily on the weekends. It can be super stressful and it makes your hands really dry, but it's also super fun with the right people." He nods, satisfied.

"Yeah, Beck, you're not helping," Sasha says.

"Right, sorry. I'm gonna go get some more sausage." He points to the line where kitchen staff are serving up trays and walks backward towards them after offering me an apologetic smile.

"I'm so screwed," I groan.

"No, you're not." Kennedy pulls me into her side, clapping my shoulder. "The summer is just getting started, and you still get to do Rec. You're still doing horseback riding with me, right? I can't bruise this butt on my own."

"Yeah, I guess," I say, my assurance faltering. Recreation is the only time we actually get a break aside from the rest hour. The time could be used for anything, including a select few activities counselors can participate in, but is it really worth it if I have to spend extra time doing more work?

"I can't wait for Dance. I've been practicing." Maeve breaks out into what looks like the robot, which elicits a round of laughter. Simultaneously, Mateo appears at the top of the stairs, his expression hard and unreadable. His gaze quickly catches mine as he finds his footing to continue down toward us, and for a second, he feels like a completely different person. Mateo's normally easygoing spirit evaporates behind his cold demeanor, and I wonder if he's really that upset about the whole thing. Either way, I don't have the time or patience to worry about him, but Penelope sure does as she swoops in to his rescue. She rests are hand on his arm before moving it up over his shoulder and down his chest. Her pouted lip and wide eyes might trick him, but I know desperation when I see it.

A sudden pinching eats at a hole in my chest as I watch them. How the corners of his mouth turn up at her, how easy it is for her, and the reality that I couldn't get the same reaction out of my ex for months.

"She's such a snake," Sasha says, looking at my line of vision.

"Do you think he likes her?" I question.

"Why? Do you like him?" Sasha's grin turns devious, which earns her a rightful side eye. "What? All that friction between you two? I wouldn't be surprised if there's something more under the surface. Perhaps a spark?"

"That spark is just smoke."

CHAPTER 8

B lock Five rolls around faster than I'd like. I thought I'd have more time to prepare and clear my head, but a five minute breathing exercise was all I could manage as I wait in the parking lot for Mateo. The truck is too hot to sit in, so I manually rolled down the windows to let cool air in and sat in the flatbed instead. A few minutes pass before Mateo finally comes rushing towards me in black basketball shorts and a white muscle shirt. My eyes immediately go to his arms, noticing how the sunlight reflects off every beautifully formed muscle.

"Sorry I'm late," he says as he slows to a walk, the heavy breathing in his chest giving me a new focus.

I snap my gaze away from him, pulling myself back to reality. "Being punctual was never your strong suit." I hop out of the flatbed, making sure to close it shut before handing Mateo the keys. His fingers graze my palm as he takes them, and a shiver runs through me. Shaking it off, I don't take any more time as I slide into the passenger seat. Had I known the seats were leather, I'd have worn longer shorts.

The choice to remain silent for the entire ride up to Springdale is very intentional. I pass the hour by counting how many corn fields we pass and then how many Jeeps I saw once we got closer to the suburbs. Most of the drive is back roads, and then 20 minutes on the highway. I would have fallen asleep because, despite what I think about him, Mateo is a smooth driver. But I was too anxious to get to the store and get back to camp in time for dinner. It's meatloaf night, and I do love a good lump of meat covered in ketchup.

Millard's is always busy and crowded, no matter what time of day you come. Luckily, Josh had already called ahead and had the milk set aside for us, and the rest of his personal shopping list is pretty straightforward. The quicker we get things in the cart, the less time I have to spend with Mateo, but that doesn't stop me from looking for a few things myself.

We walk down the chip aisle only to find that they didn't have the ones I wanted, but they did have the huge variety pack of Doritos that Josh wrote on the list.

Mateo grabs two of them off the shelf. "There's no way he'll eat all of these by the time camp is over."

He definitely would. I once watched Josh clear out a tray of 25 wings at Sal's in one sitting, and he still manages to remain fit and healthy at his age despite his eating habits. I look up from the list in my hand to find Mateo eyeing me for a response to his assumption, but I don't give him the pleasure.

"I'm going to go get the sushi tray." I hand him the piece of paper, not waiting or caring for his acceptance of it.

The smell of rotisserie chicken makes my mouth water as I make my way to the cooler section where a group of people gather around as they wait for the next batch of chicken. I spot a tray I think Josh might like since he didn't give specifics. As I grab it, I notice a guy handing out samples of some kind of fancy cheese. I don't waste another second before taking one of the toothpicks and popping it into my mouth. The taste of it is mild, but sweet and nutty at the same time—nothing like anything I've had before. It would go great on one of Sal's pulled pork sandwiches, and I find myself doing a little happy dance at the thought, making a mental note to come back for it later. Just what I needed to boost my mood. Enough of a good mood that I don't automatically shut down in annoyance when Mateo comes up behind me like a stalker.

"Must be good," he says, moving to my side.

I grab another toothpick and hand it to him. "See for yourself."

He raises is brows in what I hope is delight, signaling his approval. "Not bad."

"Not bad? It's *amazing,*" I correct. "I would buy some now if it weren't so expensive and I had somewhere to put it."

"Maybe next time." Mateo tosses both of our toothpicks into the little trash can beside the guy before taking the sushi tray and placing it in the cart.

A lady walks by with a variety pack of Baked Lays in her cart, my nose scrunching up. "That lady has my Lays," I whisper.

"And they clearly have your name written on them," Mateo says teasingly, his arm coming around me to grab the cart. His breath blows over the tip of my ear, causing me to flinch back.

"Yeah, well, you win some, you lose some," I reply hurriedly as I walk in front toward a section I'm not sure we're supposed to be in.

I let him finish things up on the list as we shop in silence. It was hard enough to stand in line for 15 minutes as irritation looms over me like a dark cloud, but then as we approach the front, Mateo excuses himself to the bathroom, leaving me to check out on my own. I make quick work of scanning the items so that I don't hold up the line, and pay the register with the cash Josh gave us, which covered just enough to leave him with a few cents left over. Thankfully, Mateo had enough sense to park near the front. I try my best to pack everything neatly into the crates in the flatbed, but I eventually give up and do what I can, letting Mateo handle the rest. I don't see him when he comes out, but remind him to tie everything down once he's finished.

When we're finally back on the road, I go back to playing my game of Count the Jeeps in quiet, which must be killing Mateo because when we've made our way on the back roads, he has other plans.

"Aubree, can we talk?"

"If we must." I sigh as my arms cross over my chest.

"Please, don't be like that," he says, glancing in my direction. "We got along well enough in the store, so can we not start this back up again?"

"Start what up again?" I challenge as my eyes dart to him. "You haven't even apologized."

"Why apologize when you don't want to hear it?"

I scoff, sitting up to face him. "You embarrassed me, and I'm the one who gets the blame *again*. I'm not like you, okay? I don't need you making shit worse for me here too."

"Is that what you think I'm trying to do?" He shakes his head, and when I think he's about to implode, his voice softens. "I am sorry, Aubree. I should have put the team first; what I did was selfish. But I'm tired of you treating me like a giant, walking disappointment. I get it, I've fucked up a lot, but I'm trying. Can you do the same? For the sake of having an easy summer?"

My chest feels hollow as my heart sinks. Admittedly, I have been harsh on Mateo. It's easier to discard him as an obnoxious clown than it was to admit that he's a person living life too and trying his best, even though it doesn't always feel that way. But he apologized. I know better than to believe it, as history tends to repeat itself with Mateo. Rarely do his apologies act as a form of redemption, but if I'm going to turn the page this summer, that means putting on my big girl panties. I don't have the energy to keep being mad; that's not the kind of person I am, and I don't have to be

"I can try... And I'm sorry too. Regardless of the fact that Axel is your camper, I should have made sure he was with me before leaving the lake." I try to keep my focus on the empty grass fields passing by us, but I can still feel the victory smile on Mateo's face burning through my scalp.

"Thank you." He smiles, sitting up comfortably in his seat. "Now, let's play a game."

"Please," I groan. An apology was one thing, but this is pushing it. Then again, when has Mateo ever not pushed his luck?

"Come on," Mateo begs. "Josh sent us on this trip to bond, so let's bond."

"I'm good," I reply, completely dismissing the idea.

"Fine, then I'll let Josh know."

"Are you serious? You're gonna snitch on me?"

Mateo holds up a finger. "One game. That's all I ask, and I won't bother you for the rest of the drive."

How about the rest of the summer?

I've spent most of my life dealing with Mateo's shenanigans. That being said, the last five years have been glorious without him. Knowing him, I'm sure he has no problem finding ways to provoke me somehow. Ignoring him has never been enough, and I'm not cleaning the stables.

"Fine," I mumble. "What's the game?"

"Glad you asked." His tone is raunchy. "Two Truths and a Lie."

"That's your game? Two Truths and a Lie?"

"It's an icebreaker, but I can always make it Truth or Dare." He grins.

My fingers pick at the stitching of the leather seat. "Just go already."

"Hmm, let me think." Mateo's fingers drum at the steering wheel one after the other. My patience grows thin as he scratches at his stubble, humming to himself. "Got it! Ready?"

"No—"

"Great," he says with a little too much enthusiasm. "I once sang the national anthem at a baseball game, I can eat two large pizzas in one sitting, and I never learned how to ride a bike."

My brows draw together as I rerun his answers in my mind. It seems unlikely that he sang the national anthem at a baseball game, or someone would have brought it up at some point. And not knowing how to ride a bike sounds odd unless he skipped the training wheels and decided skateboarding is where it's at. He could also be telling the truth about everything ,which wouldn't be shocking that he isn't playing by the rules.

"You can't eat two large pizzas in one sitting," I conclude with confidence.

"I can actually. Well, almost if I don't eat the crust," he admits proudly, a new height in his chest.

My head cocks to the side, debating the other two answers. "Then it's the national anthem."

"Nope."

"You can't ride a bike?" The shock in my voice is deemed appropriate with the nod of his head. "But you skateboard."

"My uncle taught me back when my family used to go home to Samoa every summer when I was little," he explains as he shrugs to himself. "Riding a bike isn't as hot."

"That makes sense for you, but that isn't nearly as surprising as knowing that you can sing."

"We all have our secrets." He winks, and there's this soft flare behind it that warms my insides. My eyes fall over every soft curve of his face, noticing the way his lips are parted slightly before his tongue flicks out to wet them. I want him to say anything that will break this moment and stop my heart from racing, but he doesn't have to when the truck starts to sputter and jerk before it comes to a complete stop.

"What the heck just happened?" I ask, trying my best to keep my voice calm.

"Um, I don't know I..." Mateo tries starting the truck again and again, but each time it sputters and then stops.

"Let me try." I move him out of the way and turn the key. Nothing. "Dammit."

I knew we shouldn't have driven this hunk of junk out here.

When I go to try it again, Mateo stops me. "Let me have a look first, okay?"

I nod and sit back against the seat while he pops open the hood. I just can't catch a break. I want to get out and look with him, but what was the point if I don't even know what I'm looking at? I don't even fill my own coolant.

When he's done being Inspector Gadget, he seems calm as he makes his way around to my window, putting me somewhat at ease. "It could use an oil change, but the battery's dead."

"Oh, the battery. For a second, I thought you screwed us and forgot to check if there was any gas in the tank," I joke over the panic that's rushing through my veins.

He smirks. "For a second, I thought you might have a little more faith in me."

"I don't exactly trust you, but you're a mechanic, so I would hope you check first before pulling out of the lot."

"I always check before pulling out." His smirk grows more sinister, and the beating in my chest grows louder.

"Don't be gross," I say, frowning as I attempt to pull myself together. "What are we going to do?"

He looks back from where we came, nodding in that direction. "There was a farm back that way. I saw some lights on. I'll see if they can help us."

"Um, no. That was three miles back, and the sun is starting to set."

"You're not scared, are you?"

"A little, yeah." I'm not afraid to admit it. We're between fields and woods, and people are crazy. Anything could happen, and I don't need his possible death on my conscious unless I'm the one doing the killing. "Someone will drive by soon. Worst case scenario, we have to wait for Josh to notice we're missing."

Turns out, it would be the latter. It's been almost an hour according to Mateo's watch, and not a single car has driven by. Darkness engulfs us as the sun sets, inviting in the coolness of the night. There are no street lights on this road, the moon and the starlight being the only things keeping us from total darkness. I'd forgotten how brightly stars shine being cooped up in my apartment most nights. It's stunning. Under better circumstances, I would sit in the back of the truck and take my time looking at every star as it twinkled, but the fear of possibly being eaten by something or someone was greater than my desire. At least the milk will stay cool.

Staying on high alert, I missed what Mateo had said to me. "Hmm?"

"I asked if you're okay?" Mateo asks again, more clearly this time.

"I'm fine."

"Then why are you hugging yourself and looking out of the window like we're being watched?"

"How do you know we aren't? We're in the middle of nowhere, Mateo. Have you never listened to a true crime podcast before or watched *Cold Case Files*? It can happen anywhere at any time to anybody." I don't take my eyes off the darkness, although I'm positive he can guess just how serious I'm being by the tone of my voice.

"Then, I'll distract you. Hey..." Mateo grabs my hand gently. "Look at me."

I want to, but I can't. "If I tell you a secret, promise you won't laugh?"

"Promise."

"I'm actually kinda scared of the dark." I cringe as the words leave my mouth. I'm too damn old to be afraid of the dark, and it's ironic given that I signed up to be without electricity for the next six weeks, but I can't help it. It's okay when I don't notice it, but when I do, I can't stop thinking something is out there preying on me. I watched way too many scary movies at too young an age with my cousin—who I'm sure was trying to psychologically torture me now—and it scared me for life. Even Goosebumps is too much for me at times, although it's my guilty pleasure.

I finally look to him, but he just smiles knowingly as his thumb glides over my knuckles. "It makes sense. It explains why you never stayed past sunset at the back to school bonfires every year."

"It was in the woods with no adult supervision. You'd be crazy to stay," I object. "I didn't realize you noticed that."

"Sorry." His voice is almost a whisper.

I offer him a weak smile. "No, don't be. It's nice to have a man be honest with me for once. I think it's all those scary movies I watched growing up that did it."

"I couldn't imagine lying to you and seeing the look on your face when it breaks your heart." His fingers press into my palm, and a sense of comfort sweeps over me.

"Okay, well, now you have to tell me what you're afraid of," I challenge.

"Nah, I think your confession makes up for your turn of Two Truths and a Lie."

"Yeah, right. Tell me," I demand with a laugh.

Mateo chuckles. "Fine, but *you* don't laugh, alright?" I cross my heart, and he sighs. "It's ants."

I look at him, nodding my head slowly, pursing my lips to try and suppress the inevitable laughter that bubbles low in my gut and rises with each second that passes. I start off fine until I look at him, and it escapes me without a fight.

"You said you wouldn't laugh!" he giggles.

"I didn't *say* anything," I correct.

He shakes his head as he joins in my humor. "You're too much."

"Okay, but wait. How did that become a fear? They're so small and innocent."

Mateo rubs the back of his neck in anticipation. "When I was a kid, I unknowingly sat on a small ant hill, and next thing I knew, hundreds of tiny ants were crawling up my body like a mini army. I haven't been the same since."

My face scrunches up just imagining it, my skin tingling at the thought. It sounds like something straight out of a black and white horror film. As I look at Mateo and the wide smile on his face, my mind drifts elsewhere, and my skin tingles with a different sensation.

"Can I ask you something?" I question, my curiosity getting the better of me.

"Shoot."

I turn toward him, biting down on my lip in hesitation. "Why didn't you say anything when you recognized me at the bar?"

Mateo nods, and I can tell he's thinking over his answer carefully. "I was going to tell you at first, and I should have, I know, but a part of me was curious."

I raise an eyebrow. "About?"

"Who you are now. If you'd unlocked that last bit of untamable confidence I know you have." The softness in his voice relaxes me. Still, I wait for the joke or mocking tone to come after, but it doesn't. His sincerity plays in sync with his touch as the strokes of his thumb find the pulse in my wrist. "Can I ask you a question?"

I nod. "Double shoot."

"Do you regret what happened at the bar? You know, before you found out who I was and rightfully flipped out on me?"

Gingerly, I look down at his hand over mine. In my rightest of minds, the answer is yes, but if we're being honest, the truth is more complicated than that. It would be more accurate to say that I wish I regretted it. That night made me realize two things—that I'd spent the last few months of my life chasing a guy who hadn't made me feel the way Mateo did for longer than I thought, and how much I craved that kind of attention. It's bittersweet, yet I can't forget the feel of his body pressed against mine, or the way his breath felt on my neck. His touch was just as gentle as it is now.

I bite the inside of my cheek as every memory heats my core. "No."

Mateo moves closer to me, dropping his voice to only fill the space between us that seems to grow smaller. "Tell me, what don't you regret?"

"Umm..." I pause as to not stutter over my words. "It's hard to say exactly."

He brings his hand to my hair, tucking the twists behind my ear, and I find myself leaning into his touch. "I know you're not that shy, *manamea*."

Everything within me melts instantly, and I need him to say that again, but he waits patiently for my response. The words dance on my tongue, threatening to take the leap. I want that feeling again, and he'd give it to me in a heartbeat. Would it hurt me to be honest now when he sees right through me?

"Maybe it was just the way you made me feel," I confess. A subtle confession, but a confession known the less.

"Is that code for how I touched you?" His fingers graze up my arm.

"Maybe."

"Would you stop me now?" Mateo's hand slides over my neck, cupping my cheek. His thumb traces my jaw, and my lips part intentionally. He lingers on them, smiling before grasping my thigh and bringing my leg over his knee. "Don't be afraid to tell me when to stop." But god, I don't want him to. My nerves are on edge, and I can't find it in me to say the word.

He slides his hand up my leg, stopping at the inside of my thigh. I brace my hands on his broad shoulders as I shift my hips forward slightly, daring him to inch his fingers forward. My pulse quickens when his fingers reach under the hem of my shorts, the pads of his fingers cooling my flesh. He hesitates there a moment before his eyes find mine once more. A hungry aroma clouds the air between us, proof of it flashing in his expression. He leans closer, dipping his head down my neck, his lips grazing the skin of my collar, teasing me. My body sings for his touch, but I needed his lips on mine. As I pull away, forcing him to face me again, a sudden panic aches in my bones; the ghost of a stark reminder. If I kiss him now, there's no going back.

"Wait." My hand comes to his chest as I pull away from him. "We can't do this. I can't."

"That's okay. There was no pressure—"

"It's not that," I interrupt. "I can't go there with you. Everything's different—we're different people."

"Oh." Mateo falls back into his seat, a grimness in the way he stares straight ahead, away from my sight. "Of course. That makes sense."

"I don't mean anything bad by that, it's only that I don't think it's the best idea," I explain, the words leaving my mouth like I'm reading from a script.

"You don't have to justify it. I should've expected it."

An anchor drops in the pit of my stomach as I realize what I've done. What I said was out of caution, but it's also the truth. I can't waste my summer getting caught up again, no matter how tempting it is. I debate on trying to explain myself further—let him know it's not to do with him—when headlights round the corner and a blue truck comes into view. Josh. I look to Mateo, but he's already out of the car and opening up the flatbed while the weight of guilt pulls me down.

CHAPTER 9

Sleep is truly a luxury. I'll never drink another cup of coffee again if it means I can get a good night's sleep and wake up looking flawless every morning.

After Josh picked us up, Mateo and I were still made to wash the dishes, which took up two hours of our evening. After an hour, the smell of the ketchup from the meatloaf that was served started to make me gag. That's another food on the list of random foods I won't be eating for the next nine months. Last time it was overnight oats. Two weeks of having it back to back every morning, and suddenly my brain decided that overnight oats is the equivalent of eating vomit.

The two hours might have gone by faster if either one of us thought to speak, but I didn't want to overstep. I kept wanting to say something to ease the tension, make him see that what I said had nothing to do with him, but he hardly looked at me. And every time I looked at him, from the outside it seemed like he didn't care, but a wounded grimace was wired into his body language. I think he's said a total of 10 words to me since the car incident. Maybe he expected me to apologize or explain more, but for what? It was complicated; explaining it wouldn't help, and I have nothing to apologize for. It still doesn't explain why I couldn't sleep between thinking about the look on his face last night and the guilt that was burrowing a hole in my chest. This morning wasn't much better. We worked around each other, only stopping to help me with the powdered eggs after I spilled most of the bag on the floor.

Sitting on one of the tire swings near the lake attached to the large oak tree, I watch as a few of my campers try to row a canoe. In particular, I'm watching one kid spin herself in circles while the instructor yells at her to stop before she hurts someone or herself. The most entertaining thing about water sports at camp is watching kids go rogue over their excitement for water. It could be the heat causing their bodies to have a visceral reaction from being overheated all day, acting on their need to cool down. As fun as it is to watch, I need a break.

The camp store inside the Grub Station is calling my name, and I could go for a chocolate fix right now. Technically, campers don't have to "pay" to get anything from the camp store, but it comes out of their camp tuition and fees. Staff and counselors are a different story. Slowly, I can see a nap fading into existence as I reach the shelf where the chocolate is. Before I can grab one, Josh steps out in front of me.

"Aubree, just the person I was looking for," he says, chomping on a beef stick and cheese.

"Here I am." I smile woodenly.

"Your mother rang earlier." He pauses, drawing out what I know we already agreed on. "You can use the computer in my office to check your email."

My nerves vibrate with excitement, putting me on edge as I thank Josh just before rushing off to his office. Wide eyed and buzzing, there's a kick in my step as I hurry to make my way up the stairs. The chair rolls slightly as I practically jump into it. The clacking of the keyboard fills the space as I type in my login information, and a new email from Helen at Fizz Magazine floats on top of the other emails offering various discount codes and electronic bank statements for the month. There's a pulsing in my ears, and everything feels like someone turned on the slow motion effect.

Granted, Fizz wasn't my first choice, or second, but it was still a big publication, only taking four interns per year with a guaranteed permanent position at one of their smaller publications, given that each intern meets their standards. It's still a huge deal to be considered at all. As I recall, my interview with Helen went smoothly, and we hit it off instantly over our love of Ann Lowe. From there, it was a walk in the park.

My mouse hovers over the email as I take a shaky breath in before clicking it and drawing my hands back as if it would explode. I wonder if I should call my mom first before reading it for the sake of some moral support from a real adult, but I decide against it. My mom is my biggest supporter next to my dad, but I wanted to read this on my own first because, regardless of the outcome, I'll need time to process without their influence.

I scan the email, skimming over the compliments in the beginning while trying to keep my heart rate down. My gaze drifts to the bottom of the paragraph in hope of catching sight of the expected, but there's only one word that knots my spine; *unfortunately.*

My nails dig into the arms of the chair, my hands feeling tingly. I can't bring myself to read any further.

Unfortunately.

I've never gotten an *unfortunately* before.

The pulsing in my ears moves to my temples. My face feels hot as I quickly click out of the email and rest my head on the desk. Immediately, my mind races back to the interview, wondering what went wrong—what I might have done differently. If Fizz, a major fashion magazine, doesn't want me, then what are the chances anyone will? But I did everything right. I catered my resume and portfolio to their interests, I researched every editor and designer they've worked with, studied their last five years' worth of editions... Where did I go wrong?

No, I need to go back to the drawing board, and it's not too late to go home. If I plan it all out now, revamping what I've already done, I might be able to fix this—better my chances with other companies if there's still time. I can always apply somewhere else and talk it out with my parents. As I reach for the office phone to dial my mother's number, footsteps sound in the hall. I perk up, anticipating that Josh is coming to check on me and probably make sure I'm not taking anything out of his snack drawer. I shake my hands out, working myself up to a place of acceptable consciousness when the door swings open. Mateo steps inside, the shock on his face a reflection of my own.

"Hi," he says hesitantly as he holds up a stack of paper. "Just coming to drop these off."

"Right. I mean, it's not my office, so..." The shifting of our attention from the floor to the walls, and back to each other makes this moment more awkward than it should be, especially after our almost kiss last night.

"So," I say, because one of us has to speak, "I'm done here anyway. The office is all yours."

I gesture to the desk as I move for the door, or more like my escape. Mateo looks at me, confused as he continues to stand in the way of the door. I could squeeze past him, imagining the feel of him as we move across each other, but I only stand there waiting for him to notice he's in my way. I know that he's not so quick on his feet when it comes to common sense, but this is ridiculous.

"Excuse me—"

"You okay?" Mateo says over me.

"I'm fine." I blink up at him. "I was just coming to make a personal call."

It seems like Mateo is somehow taller now, looming over me as he squares himself in front of me. "In the office? We have a phone outside for personal calls."

Fed up, I move to push him out of the way, but he's faster. Mateo catches my waist, his finger tips pressing into me and only pulling away to keep me in his sight.

"Why are you really up here?" If Mateo's one thing, it's observant. It was evident in the truck, and even more so now as he softens with concern.

My face falls as I begin to pick at my nails. "It's nothing. I don't really want to talk about it."

"You can trust me, Aubree," he insists, the words caressing me in all the places you can't touch.

I stare at him, wait for some ulterior motive to jump out at me, but all I find is openness in the depths of his deep, brown eyes. "I was rejected from one of the jobs I applied to."

Mateo shifts on his weight, and I can tell he's not sure what to do with his hands as they seem to subtly reach out for me. "I'm so sorry, Aubree. I know you were really looking forward to it."

"And how would you know?" I snap. "You don't know me so well, despite what you think."

Mateo sucks in a breath slowly, his lips pressed for another apology, but he shakes his head. "You're right. I don't know you that well, but what I do know is that you've always talked about being a journalist—how it's your one dream to be an editor and run your own publication. It's what you wrote as an icebreaker every year in school since I've known you, and knowing you, I doubt it's ever changed. I know enough to know that." He shifts uncomfortably, but doesn't waver.

"I applied for other full time positions, so you don't need to be sorry for me," I say, ignoring how his sentiments wash over me like a blanket—gentle, affirming. "My failure isn't anyone's burden."

"But, you didn't fail, Aubree. It was just a no this time." Mateo steps closer to me, his curly hair falling forward as he looks down at me. "I may not have been around for the past five years, but from what I've seen, you're the same determined, ambitious, and stubborn Aubree who gets what she thinks she deserves no matter what. That didn't happen this time, and it's hard, but that's life. You didn't get it this time, but that doesn't make you any less deserving or a failure. The work you put in says otherwise."

Truth hurts. Writing for a fashion magazine wasn't what I saw myself doing for the next 10 years. I wouldn't mind it, but it's not where my heart is. I don't doubt that people find joy and revelation in fashion, but when I really sit with it, I don't feel the same joy or stroke of genius that others do from it. I don't see myself spending hours writing and editing articles about what I mostly see as just stitched up fabric. I want my work to not only reflect what I believe in, but what is relatable and relevant to the everyday, average person. Fizz wouldn't supply me with that ability.

Mateo cracks a smile, a small chuckle escaping him. "And let's not forget how you arm wrestled the school board into giving the high school equal funding for all programs just so the drama club could put on their production of *Mean Girls*."

There's a tug at my lips that I slowly give in to, remembering how I rallied other students and teachers behind me as I stood in front of the board and demanded the arts "required equal respect with equal checks."

I shake my head as I cross my arms over my chest. "I'm going to pretend that you didn't essentially say that I'm spoiled and focus on the part where you admire my hard work. And Maeve had been itching to audition for the role of Karen since middle school, and before they pulled funding for the arts programs only to give it to the athletes. The arts are just as important, if not more important. We do live in the home of the second largest theater district. We need inspired young actors if we want to keep it that way."

Mateo steps closer, and I breathe in his warm cherry scent. "You're friends are lucky."

"It feels the other way around."

For a moment, everything's tender, untouched, simple. The air feels lighter, and it's just us. The way his nose crinkles with his smile, and the way the sunlight highlights the brown of his eyes. I fall into the space between his full lips and the sweet sighs I could whisper into them. My mind goes back to the truck and how his hands felt as they gripped my thigh, pulling me toward him. How easy it would have been to slide on top of him and let him take me right there. I must stare for too long because the fantasy I was building is broken when he clears his throat. The fantasy is completely desecrated when Penelope bursts through the door like she's the FBI.

"There you are, Mateo," she says amiably and ignoring my existence. "I could really use your help with something."

He analyzes my reaction, to which I shake my head, not wanting him to show any sign of pity, especially not in front of Penelope.

"You've done enough, thanks." I offer a weak smile, avoiding making any further contact as I exit the room hurriedly, feeling the heat of his gaze on my back.

Mateo deserves more than a thanks or a pat on the back. What he said stirred up emotions that I haven't felt in so long. But admitting it would mean starting something I can't finish—things I can't hold space for. I need to leave any thoughts of Mateo—negative or otherwise—behind.

CHAPTER 10

Dusk beats at the sky when I'm rewarded with a well deserved break, if I can really call it one. Horseback riding is much harder than it looks, but Kennedy seems to have gotten the hang of it quickly since her lesson yesterday. Meanwhile, my thighs and hips are on fire as it takes everything in me not to fall off of Lola, a chestnut American Quarter horse who is just as lively as she wants to be. She's young and easily distracted, much like Beck. But, all in all, this was relaxing, especially after being rejected from Fizz. I debriefed both Kennedy and Sasha on it at lunch, leaving out the part where Mateo comforted me and all I could think about were his lips. They both gave me their best pep talk before leaving me to recreate my life map and rethink my best plan of action moving forward, which I still don't know how to do from the wilderness.

"How are you staying on so well?" I question as I adjust myself when I feel a cramp coming on.

"Just relax," Kennedy giggles. "Trust your horse."

"That's physically impossible with Lola."

"So, go with it. Don't try to control her so much; loosen your grip some."

"You learned all this in an hour?"

She shrugs, holding her head high. "I guess you can say I'm a horse girl now."

We ride in silence a little longer, admiring the sunset as it falls behind the trees. Being in the open like this is thrilling. Some part of me wants to ride off into the sunset like in those old western films and never look back. Just me, Lola, and the great outdoors. It'd be ideal if I had actually paid attention in Survival Skills Training when I was a camper. I'd likely die from eating a poisonous mushroom the minute I got hungry.

"So," Kennedy says, dragging out the anticipation of her question. "What really happened yesterday with Mateo?"

I shake my head. "Nothing. It was just a weird vibe. So, when do you hear back about that interview for the teaching position?" I ask, quickly changing the subject.

"Don't lie to me, Harper, and stop trying to distract from the conversation. You and Mateo have been avoiding each other all day."

I'm still wrapping my head around it myself. Mateo's not a bad person, but just not good enough for me to open myself—or my legs—up in that way, not even as friends. In a perfect world, sure, but here and now, he's the complete opposite of what I need. He's irresponsible and questionable at best. I prefer certainty and security at my worst, while he'd settle for the thrill of spontaneity. Besides, I'm not even looking to date right now, especially not after everything with AJ. I'm stepping away and moving on to better. Unfortunately, I was still desperate to talk about it, or I might just explode and do something I regret.

"I love her, but don't repeat any of this to Sasha, okay?" Kennedy nods, giving me the space to leave it all out on the table. "When the truck broke down, Mateo and I got to talking and... one thing led to another, and it was looking like we might, you know... have afternoon delight."

"Okay, *Grandma*," Kennedy teases, rolling her eyes at my reluctance. "But also, *okay*, Grandma. Look at you getting back in the saddle, if you catch my drift."

"Ha ha," I say, squinting my eyes in irritation. "No one is getting a ride out of me except for Lola. I stopped him right before we were about to kiss. I told him it was because I couldn't go there with him, but I don't think he took it well."

"Aw, that's sad, but I can't blame him." Her horse trots ahead of mine, forcing me to have to coax Lola into doing the same, trying to steady myself as she does.

"I'm sure you don't, but it's not my fault. I was honest, and if he doesn't like it, it's on him. I don't need to hear a lecture on it; you asked, I answered."

"Oh, you're gonna hear it." There's an edge to Kennedy's tone, causing me to sit up straighter. "First of all, knowing you, you probably could have said it nicer. Second of all, there's nothing wrong with admitting you have feelings for him, or at least your vagina does. Imagine having a steamy night with a guy not once, but twice, just for him to turn around and reject you *twice*. You'd be pissed. And another thing—"

"Okay," I hiss. "I get it. I could have been nicer, I'm a bad person, yada yada. I could have said, 'Sorry, but you're just not up to par with the men I typically go for.' Now that's mean. I can't sugarcoat everything for people."

"It's not about sugarcoating," Kennedy counters. "It's about being clear. Yes, you rejected him the first time, but then you went in for a double dip just to do the same thing. If you really don't like him, you can't do that again."

I hate it when she's right. I should stay far away from Mateo, but since our cabins are practically teamed up this summer, that would be a challenge. Despite that, something keeps knocking at me to keep him closer, to allow him inside me—figuratively, of course. There's something so different about him, but I can't be sure of what it is, and I won't get close enough to find out.

"Maybe you can try to smooth things over and start fresh," Kennedy suggests, snapping me out of my thoughts only to put me down again.

"I'll make you a deal," I wager, coming to a realization. "I'll smooth things over with Mateo if you finally tell me why you suddenly wanted to move to Coventry."

She tenses, her fists clenching at the reins. "How about you do the right thing, start fresh, admit you might like him for your own sanity, and I don't tell you anything because there's nothing to tell."

"I know you're lying, and I don't know why, but fine. I'll try because maybe I feel a *little* bad." Kennedy gives me a vicious side eye, and I hear Lola grunt incredulity. "Okay, I feel awful, but I don't like him."

And I don't. We're opposites, and last time I checked, two wrongs don't make a right.

CHAPTER II

O ur weekly bonfires were always full of laughter, singing, and tears before Camp Whisper Lake closed. Now that the tradition has started again, all of those memories come flooding back. Eating marshmallows while huddled in blankets with Sasha and Maeve, and talking about whatever juicy camp gossip we heard that week. The bonfire is meant to bring us together and help us reflect on our week. The first one always happens in the middle of the week to give campers a sense of comfort as they bond and continue to adjust.

The large fire crackles and sparks as its flames reach up toward the night sky. Looking around the Quad at the campers, I miss when life was simple and easier to navigate. When the littlest things felt like they would cause a cosmic shift, and when adulthood felt more like a dream than a reality. Despite coming in dead last for showers because we didn't finish the scavenger hunt, which earned Mateo and I the evil eye from some of the campers, this was almost a perfect first bonfire.

As I sit close to the fire next to Sasha, toasting a marshmallow for my s'more, Valarie takes the empty space next to me with a smile.

"Is now a good time to ask what you thought about my writing?" She questions, looking down at my pick, the marshmallow practically melting off.

"Sure! I did read a few, but let's go grab your—"

"Harper!"

Groaning internally, I don't need to look to know it's Josh that's approaching us, graham cracker crumbs spilling over the front of his shirt. It seems like every time he's approached me these past few days, it's been bad news, and I can't afford another sleepless night.

"Yup," I say, trying not to seem annoyed.

"Life jackets and canoes need to be put away in the supply shed. I need you to get on that."

I look around at the other counselors in the Quad and shake my head. "Just me? I'm kind of in the middle of something." I nod to Valarie.

"Go ahead, I can wait," Valarie says, throwing me in the deep end.

"Please, it can wait," I whisper through my teeth, my eyes larger as to clue her in.

She looks over at Josh, shrugging. "It's okay. I want to catch up with some of the other girls anyway. Dena's teaching me how to make those little key chain things with the plastic string."

"Don't worry, Maeve is already down there, and she requested your help to keep her *afloat*." He laughs, shaking his head to himself as he walks away to retrieve another s'more.

"Great. Just great," I mumble to myself. First, the dishes, and now more chores. This is exactly how I imagined my first bonfire to be.

Maeve is scrambling around the dock, picking up life jackets and organizing them by size. It takes her a minute to notice me, and relief washes over her features. I almost want to dart in the other direction. I know that look all too well.

"Finally, you're here," she breathes. "Okay, so I've handled the canoes, but the life jackets are everywhere, and I'm pretty sure some are missing." She rushes past me in a flurry.

"Um, where are you going? I can't put this stuff up by myself."

"Sorry, but I have to pee, and I can't hold it any longer. I'll be right back—I promise!" she yells over her shoulder, and she's gone before I can say another word.

Hunching over, I look over the piles of jackets as I scratch my head. I didn't know we had this many to begin with. I thought that I'd get a break tonight, but nothing has gone right for me this summer, so why should I be surprised?

I look back at the Quad, hearing the sounds of lifelong memories in the making. Truthfully, I'm happy to be back here again. Out here, it feels like I can breathe. Like a weight has been lifted, and I don't have to worry about the constant reminders that my childhood is over and it's time to let go. At camp, I can hold on just a little longer and a little tighter. If not for that email the other day, I could stay in this fantasy without the sudden jolts of my reality that strike through me like lightning.

Begrudgingly, I get to work on the life jackets, making sure to avoid the small stick keeping the shed door propped open. These things are heavier than they look, especially when you're carrying more than one. As I slide them onto the rack, I hear shuffling outside, and a sense of ease comes over me.

"That was fast," I yell out of the shed. "Let's get this over with so we can get back to the bonfire. Hopefully, Sasha and Beck saved some cider for us." There's silence, and I wonder if Maeve heard me. "Maeve?"

I stop fumbling with the life jackets and turn toward the door so that I can listen for any noise coming from outside, but I only hear the echoes of everyone at the Quad alongside the chirping of crickets.

I set the rest of the jackets I have looped on my arms down and creep toward the door when I hear more rustling. My instincts kick in, and I grab a nearby paddle before moving into the shadows of the shed as much as I can with the little space provided. I brace myself when I hear footsteps coming closer, my heart beating out of my chest, and my ass clenched. If I die out here, I swear I'll come back to haunt Maeve for the rest of her days.

The closer the footsteps come, the more I raise the paddle over my head and tighten my grip. Jumping out in front of the door, I let out a battle cry and prepare to swing when another voice screams back at me. Mateo drops his pile of life jackets, raising his hands over his head.

"Oh my god, what the fuck are you doing?" I huff.

"I came to help you," he exclaims, panicked. "Maeve was talking with Beck, and I figured that would take a while, so I came to help out. Can you drop the paddle, please?"

Mateo's eyes dart to the paddle still raised above my head. I relax and drop my arms, setting the paddle with the stack on the wall. "Sorry, but you need to learn to announce yourself. I could have taken your head off."

I can't believe Maeve ditched me for Beck, but at the same time, I'm not mad at her. Maybe the magic of the bonfire swept up their spirits and made them realize what they've been missing with each other for years.

Mateo picks up his floored jackets, eyeing me. "When you said you were afraid of the dark, I didn't think you meant *really* afraid."

I wave him off, going to pick up my own jackets as my heartbeat slows. "Well, now you know. It's whatever, just be careful not to knock the stick off of the—" When I look back, the door is swinging closed and the stick is on its side. "The door!"

I rush to catch it from closing, but it's too late as it shuts inches away from my outstretched hand. I hear the latch drop from the outside. Perfect. Mateo mutters an "oh shit," and I cover my eyes with my hands, rubbing them as if to erase what just happened. Mateo tries to open it with no luck. Tugging and pulling the old door as it rattles under his efforts.

"The latch locked itself from the outside. There's no point," I tell him.

Everything Josh fixed up in this camp, and he neglected the supply shed, which people have gotten trapped in more than a dozen times. His solution? A big stick. Now I'm trapped—twice in the same week—with Mateo Opetaia in close proximity, and I'm starting to believe someone may have cursed me.

Besides the moonlight that seeps through the cracks of the wooden structure, we're engulfed in darkness. It's just enough light to see my surroundings. I park myself on a bucket, massaging my temples and trying not to focus on that acidic feeling in my throat. If I keep my eyes closed and Mateo doesn't speak, I might make it out of here with my pride intact as my conversation with Kennedy reverberates in my mind.

"So," Mateo mutters. "I guess we just wait here."

"Guess so." My response is short as I fight off the urge to say more than is necessary. Trapped in a supply shed was not where I wanted to talk about my feelings and have a fresh start with a man who was the bane of my existence for years. That can wait. I just have to make it until Maeve comes back—if she ever does.

I open my eyes to meet Mateo's shadowed frame. He props himself against the wall near the door. His arms are crossed over his hard chest, except for the constant hand that continues to push back his curly hair from his face. That hand that caressed a path of fire over my skin just a few days before. I shake my head, snapping myself out of the memory I was falling into.

"Stay focused. You're a grown woman," I mutter to myself.

"Did you say something?" Mateo questions as he holds his hair back at the base of his neck.

"Nothing," I assure him, biting into my nail. Even through the darkness, I can feel him fixated on me, and I wonder if he can feel me doing the same. We can't spend the rest of the summer just looking at each other with passing glances, especially not this close.

Just rip the bandage off.

I clear my throat. "Do you want my help?" He turns towards me, the moonlight illuminating the gentle confusion on his face. "Your hair. I noticed you broke your hair tie earlier, and I don't have one, but I can do some french braids if you like."

"You don't need to do that, Aubree."

"No, really," I say too quickly, causing me to purse my lips. "We don't know how long it will be before someone notices we're missing, and watching you constantly flip your hair is starting to get distracting." I move the bucket over where there's more space for him to sit as well as moonlight, and gesture for him to come over. Gingerly, he shifts his weight before lowering himself down between my legs. Despite my being more elevated, I still have some trouble seeing over the top of his head.

I decide to do two french braids and work on parting off his hair, splitting it in two down the middle. Taking my claw clip from my own hair, I clip one section off and work on finger detangling.

"Let me know if I'm hurting you," I say, focusing on making sure I get out every knot I can without a comb. Paying extra care to the smaller ones at his nape.

"You're not, and thank you." He goes quiet again, the tension getting thicker with each second.

All I have to do is keep talking so I don't lose my nerve, or at least until this feels less awkward. "I used to braid hair in college as a side hustle, so I think I've gotten pretty good. I know your sister used to do yours sometimes. How is Jami by the way?"

"She's okay. She graduated high school this year."

"Oh, that's right." I smile. "Does she think she's going to college?"

"Yeah, in the fall. Lakeshore."

"Good choice." I use the claw clip to hold the section I finished and move to the other side. "Do you miss being in Samoa with your family? I know you guys are really close."

He shakes his head lightly. "All the time. Sometimes, I think about going back, but I love Coventry and this is where my heart is, you know?"

"Your heart?" I question. "What about your family?"

"I miss them, but they understand. *E lele le toloa ae ma'au i le vai.* Samoa will always be my home, and I'll always carry it with me, but there are things here that I'm not ready to let go of yet. Something I'm missing."

I nod, not knowing if I should keep prying or bite the bullet.

Come on, do it.

"Mateo," I say, my voice barely above a whisper. "About the other night in the truck..."

He shifts uncomfortably. "We really don't have to talk about it."

"I know, but I need to say this." I bite down on my lip, waiting to exhale. "I haven't been the best person when it comes to being honest about how I feel. This past year has been hell, to say the least. I'd been working my ass off just to be ghosted by the job I wanted, and my boyfriend turned out to be a complete asshole after using me to get what he wanted. For the record, I meant it when I said I don't regret what happened at the bar, but I shouldn't have let it happen again in the truck. You're not the same person I thought you were, but I have to hold true to the promise that I'm not interested in a relationship or any... intimate distractions this summer."

I breathe out, working my hands as I wait for a response from Mateo. His silence is suffocating, and I wonder if I might have made it worse. "Mateo?"

After a few seconds, he responds softly. "I know."

"You know what?" My nerves are set on end as I wait for him.

"I understand you, and I respect that."

"You can be honest with me, Mateo. I know it's been confusing, and that's my fault."

Mateo pulls forward to turn around and face me. "It's not all on you, Aubree. I pushed it, and I'm sorry about that."

"Thank you." My gaze softens, admiring his honesty. I pull him to face forward so that I can finish off the braid I'm working on that extends down his shoulders before working on the next one. He lets me work in silence as I concentrate on gripping the thick strands of hair into a neat braid. My hands are a little sore; I probably should have done four braids instead of two, but when I'm done, I admire my handiwork.

"All done," I say as I rest my hands on his shoulders, signaling him to stand up. Mateo instead holds onto them, turning his head slightly, his breath dancing across the skin of my inner thigh. His thumbs caress my wrists. "Aubree, can I ask you a question?"

"You just did," I tease.

He huffs out a laugh. "Seriously. I need to know something."

"Okay, ask away."

"When did you start to hate me?"

"What?" I laugh. "I don't hate you, Mateo."

"Yeah, but you also don't like me."

"Fine. You nearly crushed me with a tree." He backs away slightly from me with a confused look on his face. "Our third grade Christmas recital?"

Realization arches his brows. "Oh, shit. I forgot about that. I got into so much trouble for that."

"As you should have," I chuckle. "That tree came crashing down right in the middle of my solo, almost knocking me over. Not only was my big moment ruined, but Mrs. O'Neil's was too. It was her first year teaching, and she worked so hard to keep us together."

"I felt so bad. I swear I barely touched it."

"If you call tugging on the branches barely touching it, I'd hate to see what else you can do."

"Is it too late to apologize?" he says, holding my hands to his chest, and I try to ignore the way his touch ignites every muscle in my body.

"Better late than never." Mateo's smile grows, and I can't help but match his.

"Can I ask you another question?" he says as I stand up.

"You're just full of them."

He looks to the door. "Seems like we have time."

"Alright," I sigh.

"What's so bad about having a little distraction while you pursue your career?"

The question hits me unexpectedly, lighting up a part of my brain I rarely ever visit. There was no considering it in my mind. I've seen what happens when people get too involved in a situationship, causing them to lose their morals and responsibility. I went through it with AJ. Even though we were an established couple, I was treated as less than, and I lost myself. I won't go there again.

I take a second before clarifying his question. "You mean like a fling?"

"A fling, a one night stand, fuck buddies..."

"Yeah, I'm good." Waving it off and rejecting the notion entirely.

"What about lust and adventure?"

I smirk up at him as he draws closer. "I have a magic wand that does just the trick."

His grin turns mischievous as he looks over me. "Touché. But don't you want the experience?"

I shrug like it should be obvious. "Why waste my time like that?"

"I don't know. It's just a little harmless fun."

"A fling isn't a little fun to me or harmless," I challenge. "It's more like a burden that lingers over you until one of you is smart enough to end it before it gets messy. And from what I've seen, most people aren't that smart." I pause debating on if I want to say the next part, and why I even care to entertain his curiosities. Mateo waits patiently, and I can't believe I'm being vulnerable with this man again.

"I believe in the power of romance, and I won't settle for anything less. I want to be able to dance around the kitchen and run in the rain while holding hands before it ends with a kiss. I want passion and for a guy to stand outside of my window with a stereo playing my favorite song because we had a stupid fight. I want love letters and sunsets, sneaky glances, and flowers for no occasion."

I let out a shaky breath. "My parents have that, so it can't be a crime that I expect the same. Maybe I'll never get it, but I want to one day experience a love so great that I'd say yes to it in this life and the next, even if I have to die trying."

Mateo faces me again, and I look down at the smooth contours of his face. "What if I said you could experience that, even if it's temporary?"

I laugh. "Sounds great in theory, but logically it doesn't make sense. Someone will get hurt, and that someone is likely me."

Mateo slowly steps closer to me, leaving a short distance of space between us. "I couldn't imagine hurting you."

Mateo's always been a thorn in my side. The despicable clown who has no care in the world about what really matters—that's how I've always remembered him. But the man I've experienced lately suddenly looks different. This Mateo has been slowly replacing the one I knew, and I can't tell which I can trust more. I've given my trust too many times to be betrayed again like that.

The latch on the door sounds as it lifts, and the door opens. I jump back to see Maeve and Sasha standing in the doorway.

Sasha sighs with relief. "There you guys are. The bonfires over and—"

"Finally!" I shout before turning my attention to Maeve. "And what happened to you?"

"Uh, it's a long story."

"A long and hard one, I'm sure." Maeve blushes, and we walk past her out of the shed. I turn back to Mateo, who matches my pace beside me as I try to shake off whatever that was in the shed. "What do you say we start fresh, maybe try to be friends this time around? No more assumptions or dishonesty?"

"I can agree to that." His gaze feels like heat as he stares down at me, his eyes darkened.

Easier said than done.

Chapter 12

Breakfast prep was far less awkward than usual this morning. Mateo and I actually managed to keep things friendly, a stark contrast to the usual grunts and accidentally bumping into each other. It was actually nice, and maybe a little too nice after last night. He's supposed to be my fellow camp counselor, not the guy my mind wanders to when I try to think about literally anything else. I like my life to be uncomplicated and simple. Mateo is neither of those things, well, maybe simple in the best ways. I have to practice keeping my distance. We're just coworkers. Coworkers, who are respectful and cordial, and nothing more.

"Aubree."

I look up from my tray to see Liz standing in front of me on the other side of the table. "Sorry, did you say something?"

"I asked if it's okay if I go back to the cabin really quick and grab my sketch pad. I want to show Ellie what I drew yesterday."

"Breakfast is almost over, you can show her after," I reply, my voice monotone.

Her face falls as she heads back to her group of friends who await her sketchpad-less hands.

"Liz is so adorable. That was kind of mean, Bree." Maeve stabs her sausage with her fork, taking a bite off each end.

"Life's harsh like that."

"Ugh, will you stop moping?" Sasha grunts. "You've been doing it all morning, and it's bringing the mood down."

I move pieces of hash brown around on my tray, making hair for the smiley face I made on my toast. Broken up bacon for the smile, blueberries for the eyes, and ketchup for some rouge. "Why focus on me when we can focus on Maeve abandoning me for Beck?"

"Oh my gosh, I forgot about that." Kennedy inhales excitedly. "What did Beck say? You looked so cute together by the fire."

Maeve's cheeks turn pink as a smile spreads across her face. I follow her gaze to where Beck is seated on the other side of the room. He's showing some campers how to make the perfect paper plane with a napkin, and the campers are fascinated. I suspect they'll be paper planes all over the grounds that we'll end up having to pick up, but I have to admit Beck is cute when he's focused.

"Well," Maeve draws out. "We talked about camp, and all of these old memories were brought up. Then he admitted that the bonfire made him think about how much time had passed, how he felt like he missed his chance... Anyway, yeah. So we agreed that we might want to see where things go."

We all shriek in excitement, but a bewildering heaviness still lingers over me as I remember the look on Mateo's face when he told me I could potentially still experience the love I want. I stayed up most of the night trying to figure out what to make of it, going in circles trying to make it make sense. Was he offering? Because that would be, well, ridiculous and impossible—inconsiderable.

I blink hard, escaping the spiral I'm in, when Kennedy shakes my arm.

"Earth to Aubree," Kennedy sings. "Now you have to say what happened last night. You're barely here."

I shake my head. "Nothing really. I helped with his hair, and we talked."

"About?" Kennedy raises her eyebrows.

"Our hopes and dreams," I say sarcastically as I shove a blueberry in my mouth. "We just talked, you know? Passing the time since *someone* ditched me."

"But I really did have to pee!" Maeve defends herself. I ignore her plea as I dig into my eggs.

Sasha frowns. "Well, you guys weren't clawing your eyes out when I got there, so I take that as a good sign."

"It is." I look up to see Mateo heading in our direction, his gaze trained on me. "I have to go."

The entrance is calling my name as I push through its doors, the daylight temporarily blinding me as I make my way to... anywhere, really. The Arts and Crafts building catches my eye, and thankfully, it's unlocked. Inside, three-dimensional paper stars hang from the ceiling like lanterns, all with different designs and patterns. Drawings and paintings line the walls alongside ceramic mugs and bowls on shelves. Everything in this space is either new or left behind by previous campers, and yet, each one whispers a story—a memory held dear. One painting sticks out to me in particular, and I immediately recognize it as Sasha's. It's a pastel drawing of the lake, with the large oak tree stretching out to the right of the frame. I remember her being so proud of this when it was finished that Ms. Divya hung it near the window that faced the lake to admire the similarities, but Sasha's piece was strikingly different. The colors and lines made the lake more eye catching, like you could picture a perfect day there, and feel how warm the sun feels on your skin. Sasha always had an eye for the beauty that others can't see.

I hear the door open and my nerves calm when I notice it's Sasha.

"Can you believe it's still here?" Sasha questions in surprise, her expression bright.

"I can. It's gorgeous." I pull my disposable camera out of my back pocket and direct Sasha to stand in front of it. "Give me your best artist pose." She laughs instead, and I snap the picture anyway, capturing her in her element.

I wind the film before sitting down on a stool behind us. "Why'd you follow me?"

She moves the stool next to me to sit facing me. "Because you ran out of there like you saw your worst nightmare."

I kind of did, but I wasn't sure I could describe it.

"Not for gossip?" I question.

"You know I love gossip, but I love you more. Talk to me." Sasha pats my knee.

I waver, tapping my toes on the muted rainbow colored floorboard. I don't know why this feels bigger than it really should. It's just Mateo—a man of no real significance to me—but I can't stop thinking about the things he says, and how much I'm starting to warm up to him. His freakish charm is starting to rub off on me, and I don't know how to embrace it or if I should. On top of my plans going awry, it's all too strange and too much.

"It's everything," I confess. "The job search, the breakup, and Mateo. He's... I don't know."

"The job thing will work itself out; you know that. You did all the interviews you could, and it's out of your hands. AJ is a piece of shit asshole, that's nothing new," Sasha says, earning her a laugh. "What don't you know about Mateo?"

I bite down on my lip as last night sweeps through me like a bad habit. "I don't know. It's a lot, and I don't really know if it makes sense."

"Try me."

Sasha isn't going to let me leave without me spilling like Kennedy would. Her version of care and kindness is laying it all out face up for all the world to see. It's effective, but difficult for me. Sometimes, I need to keep things to myself or write things down so I can connect the dots and make sense of it later. I want to believe that Mateo and I can really connect, but a part of me is still stuck in the past. And with the way he seems to always find ways to send a swarm of butterflies into my stomach, it's even more confusing.

"Okay." I swallow hard, forcing everything to the front. "That night in the truck, Mateo and I almost had what would have been hot car sex." Sasha starts, and I hold my hand up to stop her. "Then we had a moment in the shed. Not like sexual, but intense. We went from joking and agreeing to a clean slate to talking about love and relationships. It was so strange."

Sasha bobs her head up and down strategically, trying to collect herself. "So, I'm struggling to see the problem here."

"It's just weird," I exclaim, slapping my hands on my thighs. "Mateo's always been the guy to stay clear of, someone I'd never look twice at. Now, he comes in with his tattoo and long hair, talking all sweetly and making sense, and it's confusing."

"I see what you mean, but can't you bend your rules just a little? He's fine, and he clearly wants to start over with you. He's been following you around like some lovesick puppy, and he's obviously not the same person he was in school. Didn't you say people can change? Why does that logic stop at Mateo?"

I groan. "It doesn't, I mean—I want us to get along, but it's hard when he's so him and admittedly good looking. He said he can respect that I don't want to move forward that way, but I still don't want to accidentally fall into something I can't finish or don't want. I can't get caught up again and lose myself like I did with AJ."

Sasha shifts on the stool, her hands reaching out to clasp mine. "Bree, you have to relax. None of what you're stressing about matters here. You're too in your head. We've got five and a half more weeks left, and it's like you're wasting it worrying about the same stuff you said you wanted to let go of this summer." Sasha takes a deep breath, her expression turning serious. "You and Mateo will work things out, but you can't if you keep running away thinking you'll fall onto his dick—not that I don't support that cause because I would love that for you. If you're afraid you will, talk to him about it. Draw a clear line in the sand."

I look out of the window, watching as the water flows and shimmers. Sasha's advice is the exact opposite of what Kennedy told me to do. Avoiding it is hard, but so is not talking about it. Arguably, it's better not to run around camp like a chicken whose head is about to be cut off.

It would let me breathe a little to talk through it. Plus, we go hiking in a few days for our Survival Skills Training workshop, and I'll need a clear head to actually earn the badge this time. On the other hand, it's likely best to keep quiet and handle it on my own.

"Thanks, Sasha, but I think I can handle it. You're right, I'm too in my head and stressed for nothing."

Sasha captures me in a hug, and we stay like that until I'm finally ready to let go. There's still a lot I need to think about, and I'm still not sure about Mateo and if I can trust him, but I need to be more willing to try.

Chapter 13

"How do I look?" Turning to Kennedy, I show off my outfit for today's Survival Skills Training workshop. The hiking boots I bought before camp were expensive enough, so I wanted to make sure I at least looked good, as good as you can while sweaty and out of breath going up hill. I landed on a simple Camp Whisper Lake t-shirt that I tied back just to show a sliver of my stomach and denim shorts that stopped mid-thigh.

"Like a hiker." Kennedy's sarcasm lands with Sasha, but earns her a side eye from me. "A beginner, to be exact."

"I'm no beginner. I used to hike all the time."

"'Used to' being the operative phrase," Kennedy counters, a smirk on her face. "But at least your boots match mine."

"How cute," Sasha chimes, her eyes drifting between us with a shrug. "Wish I had matching boots."

Going through my checklist, I recheck everything in my backpack, triple-checking everything in my first aid kit. "It was last minute, and you and I matched enough in middle school."

"I guess," she tugs at her leggings before giving me a sheepish smile. "Doesn't matter anyway. I'll see you guys when you get back."

Finishing up my checklist, I then check over Kennedy's back before heading back to my own cabin, where I make the girls hold up each item we'll need for the workshop, including their packed lunch. Upon successful completion of the workshop, each camper and counselor will earn their Survival Skills badge. It really means nothing since you'd have to do it again next year, but it's good practice and something I've only managed to earn a few times since I always struggled to make a fire. After getting everyone together and making sure everyone has what they need, I instruct my cabin to meet out in the Quad.

As I make my way outside, Mateo catches my eye, and I immediately notice his rigid expression as Sasha continues a conversation with him. As I make my way over, Mateo's head snaps up, stopping Sasha as he walks over to me. His hair is pulled back into a bun as he sports a sleeveless shirt that has the light emphasizing every taut muscle down to the veins in his forearm.

"What was that about?" I question, nodding toward Sasha. "Everything okay?"

Looking over his shoulder, Mateo lets out a sigh. "Oh, yeah. She was just telling me about you, actually. She's kinda bummed about not being able to do the workshop with you and Kennedy. Maybe you should talk to her."

I shrug. "Yeah, well, that's Sasha. She's always been a little brat-ish about stuff like this. She'll get over it."

He falls silent, and I try to ignore the way his eyes linger over me, scanning the most prominent parts of my figure as we make our way up the path.

"Are you going to speak or keep acting like I can't see you staring at me?" I question him, keeping my voice low.

Mateo grins. "Sorry, I got distracted."

"That's not unusual for you." He shoves me gently, knocking me slightly off balance as I laugh to myself. "Hey, I'm just speaking facts."

"Yeah? Well, let's see what you have to say about distractions after this workshop."

I narrow my gaze at him, tilting my head to one side. "Are you challenging me, Opetaia?"

"Why? Do I make you nervous?"

"If by nervous you mean rabid, then yes."

"Hey! I thought we were starting fresh?"

Shrugging, I threw my hands up. "Yes, and being more honest. I'm still building trust, especially if you're challenging me."

"It's only a challenge if it's a fair fight." He winks down at me before catching up to the other three cabins gathered at the Quad.

Luckily for Mateo, I never back down from a challenge.

The hike up to the campsite was more brutal than I expected. After a half mile, my calves were burning with the threat of a cramp if I didn't take it easy. Kennedy stayed back with me behind the group, even though she really didn't need to, especially because we were going at such a slow pace anyway. She's far more athletic than I am, and the entire hike made me realize just how much I missed my morning walks. Mateo seemed to go with ease as he helped lead us to the vast open space, perfect for a group camping site. He occasionally looped back to check on Kennedy and I, but each time I shooed him away. Talking while doing exercise irritates me, and I didn't want to take that out on him since we're trying this whole "friends" thing.

"He's been giving you some extra attention." Kennedy elbows me, and I follow her line of vision over to Mateo who's saying something to his campers.

"I don't know what you mean," I say as I pull tents out of the wagon in front of the instructor.

"Oh, you know what I mean, Aubree." Kennedy moves around me to take tents of her own. "Checking on you every 10 minutes, offering you his water... It's kinda hot."

"I have water, and he was just being nice," I protest, trying not to sound annoyed. "Since when do you care? I thought you didn't care about stuff like that."

Kennedy rolls her eyes as we head back to our group of campers. "Just because I don't date doesn't mean I don't have eyes."

My attention is drawn back to Mateo, whose gaze finds mine. Except it's not the usual sweet, caring look he's been giving me, but one of determination and confidence. Matching him, I stand taller, trusting that what I've learned over the past few days will come to me easily.

A whistle blows, demanding our attention to the front of the groups where Mr. Foreman, our Survival Skills instructor, stands with a clipboard. His shaggy hair and small frame makes him look younger than he really is, despite his being an instructor at Camp Whisper Lake since I was a kid. I think he's a retired veteran, but I can't exactly remember. Mr. Foreman's a serious man with a hard exterior, but on an individual level, he was actually pretty kind and patient.

He waits until he finds all of our eyes on him before continuing. "You all are the first four cabins who will complete this workshop today, putting the skills you've learned this week into real practice." His voice echoes out toward us, his gaze shifting between us like he's afraid we'll miss a single word.

"Today, we'll be going over four basic skills: forging, tent construction, building a fire, and first aid." Mr. Foreman instructs counselors to pair our campers in groups of five to start the first exercise, setting up our tents. There's no time limit, but to make sure that each tent is facing opposite the wind and staked to the ground properly. But from the way Mateo is moving, I could tell it was a race.

Working quickly, I hand off both tents, working with Valarie's group first. It would be easy to do it all myself, and faster, but this training is more for them than it is for me. Still, I try to help them as much as I can, as quickly as I can, moving between both groups.

"Okay, wait a minute," I say to Valarie and Liz as they start to stake their tents. Angling their stakes down a little more, I remind them of their positioning. "Don't forget that your stakes need to be at a 45 degree angle. We don't need it flying away."

"Does it matter?" Valarie asks as if being inconvenienced. "It's not like we're sleeping in them."

"Yes, it does," I huff. I glare up at Mateo, whose campers already have one tent set up like it was nothing, while we still haven't even opened the rain fly. "Just do it correctly, okay? We're almost done."

They groan in unison, but I don't have time to argue about it. Not only did I not want to redo the tents if we got it wrong, but I wasn't going to lose to the secret competition I was running against Mateo, who conveniently is heading my way.

"Need any help?" He moves in to inspect one of our tents, to which I push him back.

"We're good," I reply, finally opening up the rain fly to stake it down. "Maybe you should go inspect your own tents."

"You can inspect mine if you want." His voice low, dropping into my ear for only me to hear. The feel of his breath has my hair standing on end.

I look back to find his face inches from mine, but I don't give him the satisfaction of indulging him. "Your tags are wrong."

"What?"

"The colored tabs on the trap and the tent aren't a suggestion." I move around him to point out his mistake, clear as day. "Looks like you're starting over."

Mateo mumbles something under his breath as he rushes back to his tents, giving my soul the appeasement it needs.

The rest of the tasks were pretty simple and moved swiftly. I even managed to start a decent fire this time. The only one left is foraging, which I'm not too confident about. Mushrooms are hard for me to identify, so I left my instincts to the berries that littered the wooded area, while some of the girls managed to find chanterelles on our trail.

After collecting a few morels and the wild onion we managed to find, we make our way back to the site, following close behind the girls. As I'm admiring the basket of our foraged goods that I'm sure is more than what Mateo's cabin can manage to find, one of the girls moves off the trail toward a small stream. Yelling for her to get back on the trail, and following her beyond the marked poles that lead back up to the site, a different cry escapes me as I fall to the ground. My ankle stings with fire as I roll to my side to try and push myself up. A note of curses fly from my mouth like jets as I go to touch the already swelling area, pain radiating through my entire calf at the slightest graze. Footsteps crunch over the twigs that surround me as someone shouts my name, but I'm too busy trying to breathe through the pain to notice who it is. More come until I'm surrounded, and I feel a hand come to my back.

"Aubree, are you okay?" Mateo's voice breaks the barrier between the pain and the embarrassment I feel, but only enough for me to shake my head as I try not to move. "It'll be okay, I'm getting you back to camp."

That declaration alone is enough to force me to try to get up. "No, I'm okay. I can get up; I still have one good ankle."

"You're in pain," he says calmly, but it doesn't undermine the hint of panic in his tone.

"They're bringing the stretcher," I explain, hoping that will back him down.

"It's back at camp. It'll be more than an hour."

"Oh, for fuck sake!" I hiss as the pain turns into a hard throb. "I just need an ice pack. I can wait—"

"No, you can't, Aubree. You're hurt now, and I'm not going to sit and watch you in pain. I'm carrying you back to camp." The firmness in his voice tells me there's no objecting, and that he's made up his mind for both of us. He was taking me back, and that was it.

CHAPTER 14

The entire hike back, I was worried he might hurt himself or pass out with the way he was breathing. He only stopped to readjust as I clung to his back, but he never complained or stopped for a break. I'd offered him water, but he shook his head, fixated on getting me back safely.

Once the campgrounds were in sight, Mateo's pace managed to quicken despite how tired I knew he was. Thankfully, the infirmary is close, and the nurse was already waiting after she was radioed that we were on our way. She already has ice and cold water waiting as Mateo set me down on one of the beds to rest before picking up the ice pack to hand to me. The nurse takes her time examining my ankle, careful not to touch it too much, and I notice just how bruised and swollen it is. I can tell that it's just a sprain from the looks of it, and given the way I rolled my ankle when I missed the thick root that was protruding from the ground of the trail.

After carefully wrapping my ankle, the nurse allows me a dose of pain reliever as I sit with it elevated, the ice pack resting on top. Mateo took it upon himself to make sure my cabin got to their next block activity, leaving me alone to rest and curse myself for being so clumsy. Had I followed my own advice and stayed on the trail, I wouldn't be here.

Sulkily, I fall back onto the bed, my head hitting something firm. I reach above me to the realization that it's Mateo's backpack. Grabbing it to toss onto the bed beside me, a small book falls out of the side. Cursing myself, I slide it over with my good foot to retrieve it. Upon closer inspection, the pages are yellowed with dog-eared creases running at the corners of almost every page. The light blue cover is heavily worn, and the title *Hamlet* is written across the cover in bold letters. Mateo is the last person I would think to have a copy of *Hamlet* hidden in his backpack, especially not a copy with so many notes in the margins.

"Why is this kinda hot?" I whisper into the pages as I read over his notes. "'The subconscious mind descends into madness...' interesting."

The sudden sound of the door to the infirmary opening and closing sends a violent jolt through me as I hurriedly attempt to toss the book onto the bed with the backpack. Of course with my luck, it bounces off the edge and falls flat to the floor. Perfect. My eyes dart to the door frame, still empty. With a wince, I pull myself to the edge of the bed, stretching myself as far as I can to move it back, but it's no use.

This is what you get for being sneaky.

"What are you doing?"

"Nothing!" I shout as Mateo strides into the room, his mouth taut. I move back onto the bed, a stiff smile drawn on my face.

Mateo bends down to snatch up the book, holding it up. "Were you looking through this?"

I shake my head. "No, what? It fell out, and I was just trying to pick it up."

"So, you didn't have your grimy little fingers all over it?" he questions playfully.

"That would be an invasion of privacy." Handing him the ice bag, I move to change the subject. "It's not my business what you do in your free time. Why you hide it is a better question."

"I'm not hiding it." He puffs his chest as if that would make the truth any less apparent. "It's just not something I share."

"So, you're hiding it," I challenge as I lower my gaze. "No shame, it's clearly your special interest. It's kinda cute."

"Thanks, I guess." Mateo shoves the book back into his bag. "You can at least ask next time."

"Sorry," I giggle. "But, I'd love to read your notes sometime if you'll let me."

Mateo places a fresh ice bag on my ankle, wrapping it in a towel to make it more comfortable. "Maybe when you're feeling better, *manamea*."

"What is that?"

"What is what?" he asks, adjusting the pillow under my foot.

"*Manamea*," I repeat. "You keep saying it."

"Oh, yeah. It means 'sweetheart' in Samoan... Does that make you uncomfortable?"

His gaze drifts to mine, a gentle sincerity flowing in his eyes. Withdrawing, I focus on folding the blanket in my lap, stretching out time as much as I can until the leap in my chest subsides. It's so beautiful the way it rolls from his tongue with ease, just the same as it did the first time he said it.

"It's okay with me."

CHAPTER 15

I rest in a shaded area across from the lake as I munch on apple slices with crunchy peanut butter. The initial pain I had had mostly subsided in the past few days of rest as Josh demanded I not leave my cabin for any other reason than to eat, shower, or use the restroom. So, the crutches I was given temporarily got little to no use. The one thing I didn't think to pack was compression socks, not thinking I'd find myself in need of them. But today I'm determined to get up and moving. I'm tired of watching all the fun from the window.

Kennedy steals one of my apple slices, neglecting the peanut buttery goodness on the side for dunking.

"Don't eat my apples if you're not going to pair them with the peanut butter," I declare.

"Nobody eats crunchy peanut butter unless they're insane," she says, flipping to the next page of her book.

I roll my eyes. "I portioned it out evenly to get the perfect ratio. Now I'll have leftover peanut butter and nothing to put it on. And how do

I know your hands are clean while you're digging in my apple slices like that?"

She ignores me, too immersed in her book to care. In the lake, campers are splashing around while others squirt water guns from the dock, enjoying their free time before the next block starts. Their laughter fills in between the trees and lifts with the breeze. I pull out my camera to photograph the scene and try to find the right moment when my lens falls on Mateo. His arms flex as he tosses water at campers, joy radiating off of him. Droplets of water shimmer and glide down his toned core, and my gaze lingers on the seam of his shorts. I suck in my bottom lip, bringing the camera down for a full view.

"What are you doing?" Sasha questions mischievously.

"Nothing," I say, sucking in a breath and bringing the camera back up. I snap a picture randomly and toss it to the side.

She looks over to where I averted my gaze. "Hmm, admiring the view I see."

"I don't know what you mean." Crunching down on an apple slice, I sit myself up. "I'm simply admiring the joy nature brings out in others."

"And that man is all nature," she teases. "That muscular dad bod thing he's got going on is doing wonders for him if you don't mind me saying."

"I have no claim on him, Sash, nor will I make one." I finish off my peanut butter, licking some off my thumb.

"He seems to have one on you." She nods in his direction.

Mateo stands tall in the water, his gaze intense and trained on me. Specifically, my mouth as I remove my thumb from it. Something like admiration dances across his face as his eyes wander over me. When he notices me staring back, the corner of his mouth ticks upward until he's blasted by a water gun, immersed back into the fun.

"No one stakes a claim on me; I'm my own woman."

"Okay, but the way he carried you back to camp?" Kennedy coos. "Ugh, it was disgustingly romantic."

"It was just a favor." I toss my things into my bag, using my crutches that I really didn't need anymore to help me up.

"He brought you all of your meals for the past 3 days—dropping whatever he was doing to be at your service—and you're telling me there still isn't a spark?" Sasha cocks her head to the side, giving me an "if you say so" shrug.

Ignoring her, I carry myself to the cabins to change my bandage again before the bell for the next block sounds. The cabins are usually quiet at this time with everyone grabbing a last minute snack and hanging out with friends, or taking a nap if you're Beck. As I near the cabin, frustrated groans and sighs grow louder as I reach the door. Through the screen, Valarie sits on the floor, balling up and tossing pieces of paper that scatter and skip across the room. She doesn't notice me as I climb the steps and swing open the door, startling her.

"What's going on?" I question, kicking a ball of paper toward her as I ease myself down to the floor beside her.

"Nothing," she says dismissively before tossing the ball back on the other side of the room.

"This doesn't look like nothing." I look around at the dozen crumpled paper balls. "Writer's block?"

She shakes her head, frowning at the blank journal page in her lap. "Nothing I write is good enough."

"Valarie, don't say stuff like that. You're making art."

"You haven't even seen any of it, so how could you possibly know?" she spits.

Her words twist in my chest. I did promise her I'd read more of her work, and I really did mean it. This past week has just been a whirlwind of good and bad, taking me for a trip I couldn't have predicted. Rewardingly, Valarie's been the one person to be the most patient with me, and I can admit that I've taken that for granted. Sitting here for the past few days, I had more than enough time to read through her journal, yet I was so caught up in my own problems that I didn't think once about it.

"Valarie, I know you're frustrated and have been trying to show me for a week now, but art is subjective. You don't need my validation to write what you feel is a good poem."

"But I do," she confesses.

"No, you think you do. I'll always encourage you, but my word isn't final."

"You can say that because you're good at everything you do. You've always been good enough, and I can't be like you." Tears roll down the curve of her cheeks, softly hitting the paper below. Shifting toward her, I wipe them with the backs of my hands.

"Why do you need to be like me? I screw up too, and I have my days just like everyone else."

"My whole life feels like that, though. Everyone always talks about how successful you are and how you'll do big things one day, even my mom knows it. I want to be that good. I want people to see me in that way. But if I can't even write a couple of sentences, then why bother trying at all?"

"Oh, Valarie." Her sobs soften as I pull her into my arms, running my hands up and down her arm. She hiccups, and cracks slowly burst in my chest as the hammer of truth drums within me.

Valarie has always been like a little sister to me. I always thought it was cute how she wanted to follow in my footsteps, but I never thought it would lead her to feel like this. I neglected her, believing that she would naturally find her footing because I've been where she is. The pressure to be perfect, to please everyone, and to make those closest to you proud. No, she doesn't need my validation, but she needed my support the same way I did when I was her age. It's so easy to get in your head and forget that you're only human. I think I've forgotten myself.

When Valarie's sobs have quieted, I lean over slightly to allow her room to prop herself up on my shoulder. "I'm so sorry, Valarie. I haven't been the best person lately."

"It's not your fault," she sniffles.

"Don't make excuses for me. I've been so caught up in my own shit that I didn't think to check on you, especially now that I see how it's hurt you. I'm so used to being a type A control freak, I forgot what's important to me. I forgot you." I pick up a ball off the floor, flattening it on my leg. "A breeze rolls off the sea / tangling with the coils of my hair / laughing between the folds of my dress... Valarie, this is beautiful," I coo.

"It's okay. I don't know what else to write."

"How about tonight, I help you finish the rest and take a look at your other poems too. I want to read every last one." She nods her approval, and I give her the tightest squeeze I can manage. She helps me up, and I finish wiping away her remaining tears and fix her braids. Stepping across the path, I spot Mateo walking towards the cabins. His hair drips water down his jaw and over the tip of his nose, a soft cloud-like halo surrounding him, making him all that I see.

His expression turns cocky as he slows to meet me. "Looking for me?"

"Yes, actually. Don't get excited." I wave him off as I balance myself.

"And I was just getting started," Mateo retorts with a grin.

"You're too sure of yourself."

"That's just my charm, and I love the way it's growing on you."

"Keep dreaming," I say as he helps me to the stairs to sit. "We should have a bonfire tonight. I think it'll be good for our campers to bond and whatnot."

His expression turns sour at my suggestion, and I raise an eyebrow. "You don't think it's a good idea?"

"No, it's a great idea. I was just thinking, is all. Maybe we could invite Kennedy's and Sasha's cabins too. I'll be nice."

"Awesome! Yay, I'm so excited." Clasping my hands together, Mateo looks at me with a stillness I can't put my finger on. "What?"

"You're cute when you're excited." The seriousness in his tone causes me to tense, and that fuzzy cloud surrounds him again. Everything comes to a hum, sucking me in until a group of campers rushes toward us, declaring a water gun fight, and we attempt to move away with defenseless joy as we take cover.

CHAPTER 16

Night falls quickly, the temperature dropping just low enough to enjoy the warmth coming from the small bonfire reserved for the cabins. The crackling of the fire provides a sense of comfort, harmonious with the jubilant sounds of the campers. The sparklers I brought to camp prove to be a great addition as they run and draw various shapes in the air with them. My camera snapped photo after photo, making sure to get one with the infamous "I Heart U" sparkler writing.

I nurse a can of pop as I lean onto my knees, looking down into Valarie's notebook. Cocking my head to the side, I point to a line that she wrote.

"What if you change 'my feet kick in the sand' to 'skip in the sand' so it goes with the fluidity of the rest of the poem. That way it's more like a dance—light and airy."

Valarie's pencil taps her thigh in contemplation. "Hmm, I like it. Makes more sense too."

She goes to close the notebook, and I block her. "Hey, I wasn't done."

"We've been at it for an hour. Sometimes, you just have to leave well enough alone and view it with fresh eyes another day."

My finger taps my chin in mock consideration. "Sounds familiar..."

"I learned from the best," she says with a grin. "Please, I want to join in the sparkler action before they're all gone."

I grin and nod in acceptance as she skips over to a group of girls who debate on who can make the best star shape with their sparkler. I sit on a log next to Sasha and Kennedy, who are also debating on the best way to roast a marshmallow.

"No, no, no," Kennedy says, pulling hers from the fire. "It has to be slightly burnt on the outside or you don't get the full effect and taste of a crispy campfire marshmallow."

"Golden brown is the way to go. Aubree, would you tell her?" Sasha gestures to me.

"Sorry, Sasha, but Kennedy's right. Anything cooked over a fire should be slightly burnt. It's a requirement."

"Yeah, for barbecue, not marshmallows," she pouts, resting her chin on her fist. "When did you start liking them that way anyway?"

I giggle watching her in her solace. "Camping trip Kennedy and I went on with some friends. It's elite. Try it."

Kennedy drives the marshmallow to Sasha's lips like an airplane, engine noise and all. Sasha backs away, giving us a hard side eye before taking the stick and taking a hesitant bite. The caution in her chew turns into a heavily satisfied head bob. "Okay, y'all were right. I'm throwing in the towel," she says as she finishes off the rest in one bite.

I grab my own stick, sticking on a marshmallow when Kennedy leans down into my ear. "Looks like someone's got an admirer," she singsongs.

Through the flames and the sparks that fly into the air, I find Mateo, who takes not so subtle glances up at me as he helps some boys figure out how to pile the empty cans of pop to make a tower, smiling all the while. But I somehow know it's reserved for me.

Heat flushes my cheeks as I shake my head, taking a sip of my pop—peach Faygo, the ultimate pop brand.

"Oh my god, are you getting... shy?" Kennedy teases. "It's like I've stepped into an alternate universe where Aubree is embracing being... perceived?"

"Alright, enough," I say. "Nothing is happening between us, and it never will. I've just decided to be friendly until he gives me a reason not to."

"With the way he looks at you, you'll be more than friendly this summer," Sasha says with a hint of lushness.

They quiet their fun as Mateo approaches us. His strides are determined and almost anxious the closer he gets.

"Ladies." He nods to Sasha and Kennedy as they lean in close to my sides. "Can I borrow Aubree for a little while?"

"Be our guest," Sasha says a little too enthusiastically, making me roll my eyes.

"For what?" I question suspiciously.

"You'll see." He holds out his hand to me. I look up at him with reservation, the corner of my mouth ticking up. When logic—my fatal flaw—fights to swim to the surface, I take a breath in and release all that threatens to trouble me.

It's only a few minutes. Don't think too hard.

I place my hand in his. As he pulls me away, I look over my shoulder at Kennedy and Sasha, but they shrug just as confused as I am. He allows me to lean on him for support, and when we're a ways away from everyone—a little too far for my comfort—I stop him.

"Where are we going?"

"Do you always need to ask questions?" he asks, tugging my arm forward.

"I do when I'm venturing into unknown territory with the man who tormented me for half my adolescence," I scrutinize.

"I thought we moved past that?" He grins down at me.

"Yeah, well, the past is a silent killer."

His laughter is deep and sultry, causing a sudden flutter low in my gut. "Stop asking questions and come on. It's only a little further down."

Although the glow of the moon provides some light, I still find myself moving closer to Mateo, checking my surroundings every so often. He leads me to the far side of the lake, and up ahead, I make out something spread over the ground. My first instinct is that it's a tarp and I should be running for my life by now, but when rationality replaces fear, I notice the flicker of lights around it. The lights—that I now see are fake tea light candles—sit on the edge of a blanket with a basket resting on top.

"Uh, what is that?" I question, confusion and shock consuming me at once.

"It's our own private bonding experience," he confirms, his arms stretched out toward the display.

Uncertainty turns in me as I remember our conversation in the shed. "I told you I can't—"

"Stop saying you can't." He slides his hands down my arms, taking my hands in his. My heart pumps double time as his thumb caresses my knuckles. "Don't think of it as anything other than two people enjoying each other's company."

This man is too smooth. With every word that falls off his lips and the gentleness that he has with every touch, I ease into the idea of him even more. It's scary, and wonderful, and inexplicable—and I don't know what to make of it. But for once, I don't want to think anymore. I don't want to cry my eyes out every time things feel too hard, or too impossible, or out of control. I want to feel and experience things the way they are. I want to be liked and seen without the innuendos, and—as much as I hate it and will likely never get used to it—Mateo makes it seem possible. And thanks to Valarie, I'm willing to turn a new leaf and try something outside of myself, even if it's just for a night.

I allow Mateo to lead me to the blanket, and I sit without fuss. My hands fidget in my lap warily as I watch him.

"Don't be so nervous," he says, setting the basket between us.

"I'm not nervous," I reply as I avoid looking at him and instead look around at the woods around us. The hummed swooshing of the lake works against the dark, the only element providing a calming sensation.

He sits beside me, his movement a distraction from the mixture of emotions churning in me. He opens the basket, and I lean over to witness its contents.

"Oh my gosh," I gasp. Wrapped in cling wrap is a wooden cutting board with an array of meats, cheeses, and crackers. What truly catches my eye as he lifts it out of the basket and onto the blanket is the cheese that we sampled at Millard's. "You got the cheese?"

"Yes, and..." He reaches back inside the basket pulling out a small bag of Baked Barbecue Lays, and presents it to me.

"Shut up," I exclaim. "How? There were none left."

"I might have convinced the woman who had it in her cart to give them to me. Had to pay her 25 bucks though."

I raise my eyebrows. "That's more than what the box costs. You really didn't need to do that."

"It was worth it to see the shock on your face." There's mischief in his smile as he unwraps the board.

"Well, I'm paying you back—for all of this."

"I'm not expecting any money from you, Aubree."

"It'd be inconsiderate of me not to repay you after all the trouble you went through to do this."

"It was no trouble," he says softly as he looks into my eyes. "You can repay me by enjoying yourself and indulging in the 45 dollar chips I bought for you."

My chest swells, my heart leaping to my throat, and I lean onto my hands to steady myself. I feel the grass below us to make sure that this is really happening, trying to savor this moment and this feeling. Brick by brick, the wall I was fighting to keep up comes crumbling down, welcoming every heartfelt emotion. And like oil over water, I slowly lose my strength to keep fighting it. No one has ever done anything like this for me. And at first, a part of me still wants to flee out of fear that it's all too good to be true. But Mateo's not the same person I thought he was, and maybe I never knew him, but I want to.

"Mateo," I say, barely above a whisper. "I don't know what this means, and I'm still trying to wrap my head around everything that's happened this past week, but you know I don't do casual, right?"

"I've already started writing my wedding vows," he teases, and I poke him in the side.

"Seriously, Mateo." I laugh. "Is this what you meant back in this shed. A temporary experience?"

He relaxes with a nod. "And you wouldn't be taking advantage of me. I don't care about sex or you returning the favor in any way. I know that's not you, and I admire that about you. But I want to do this for you. Let me." He cups my cheek, the warmth of the gesture steadying me.

My eyes fall to my lap, and he lifts my hand to his chest, placing it over his heart. It's fast, but steady... predictable. I find his eyes looking for any signs of dishonesty, but all I find is promise. I think back to our school days; the teasing, the distractions, and everything that's happened between us since that night at the Belfry. The way his eyes always seem to find mine when I'm searching for his.

"What happens at the end of the summer, or if one of us wants more?"

"We go our separate ways and remember it as the summer of a lifetime. I know I'm irresistible, but that's just how these things work."

I playfully push him away, breaking the intensity lingering in the air. "You're full of it."

"I had an excellent teacher." He winks.

"I don't know, Mateo. I leave at the end of the summer—"

"So, just give me the summer," he says, almost pleading.

Looking around at the candles and the neatly curated snack board, I wonder what it would be like to just give in. To push away the voices that scream at me that this is wrong, that I shouldn't waste my time. I've been here before, but this feels different. Still, caution pokes at me with a hot iron as my gaze drifts over Mateo.

"Don't take this the wrong way, but I can't say yes—not now. This is amazing, but I need time to think about it."

"Take all the time you need. I'm not going anywhere. I'll take a 'not right now' over a 'no' from you any day."

"What makes you think I'll say yes?"

He shrugs, caressing a finger over my cheek. "Time heals all wounds, right? Plus, you know me better than to give up."

A giggle escapes me as I lie down on my back, admiring the stars in all their glory. Mateo follows suit, and in honor of embracing the unknown, I move closer and lace our fingers together. My body is alert, lost, and afraid of what's to come. It's unusual, but freeing. But my mind is waveless as I bury myself in the present.

CHAPTER 17

I avoid going to breakfast as long as possible this morning. Not because I'm not starving, but because I need to prolong the airy feeling I have for a while longer before feeding the beasts of which are my friends. I'd already concluded that I wouldn't be giving them more details than necessary, and I'd been practicing my poker face since last night. Although nothing much happened—we only stargazed and shared what we thought was the best combination with the meats and cheeses he bought, smoked Gouda and pastrami being the clear winner—they'd still bleed me dry looking for answers where there are none. Thankfully, my trio of friends are my only issue since I'm officially no longer on dish and breakfast prep duty, and my ankle feels so much better. Penelope still mostly glares at me whenever I walk by, but has yet to say a word. The only real connection she's made here is her new arm candy, Gale, who might as well walk around with his nose up her ass. But it honestly gives me a sense of peace watching her like that and knowing she's no longer after Mateo—not that I was bothered or anything.

Breakfast is always the more chaotic part of the day. It would be annoying if I were anywhere but camp. I loved the gleeful faces of the campers as they talked about their new activities and what instructors have planned for the day. Valarie could not stop telling me about the jambalaya they're making today in Cooking Around the World. Yesterday, it was gimbap, which didn't turn out to be a complete disaster.

As I make my way up to the Grub Station, a frustrated and hurried voice disrupts the quiet nature of the morning. Edging closer to the side of the building, Kennedy paces back and forth, the cord for the camp phone swinging with her. Her hand flails about as her words grow more urgent, and I try my best to stay back, all the while keeping my ears perked.

"I told you, I'm fine. I don't need you to rescue me, and I'm not confused... It's already been called off. This isn't something you can fix with money, dammit! Will you just listen to me for once?" Kennedy pauses, stopping in her tracks when she notices me standing nearby. Hurriedly, she slams the phone on the hook, untangling the cord that was beginning to wrap around her arm. "You're spying on me too now?"

"No—I mean, I was just worried. You sounded angry, I wanted to make sure you were okay—"

"I'm fine." She cuts through me like a knife, her expression softening when she notices me stiffen. "It was my mom. She thinks I'm making a mistake moving out here and everything, especially after I told her I wasn't going to medical school."

I nod. "Yeah, I get that... Are you okay?"

"Yeah, let's get inside before there's no more breakfast. We saved you a seat."

I want to ask her more, but as we head inside, Sasha and Maeve are already flagging me down. I'm pulled back into the reality that I can't escape their curious minds. I weigh my options of fleeing to where I came, filing into the breakfast line, or entering the lion's den. Biting the bullet and getting the hard part done and over with seems to be the likely option as Sasha looks like she might wet her pants.

Centering myself, I force a smile as I walk over to them. As I move in, Maeve gestures to sit next to her where there's a tray already stacked with buttery pancakes and fresh fruit beside it. While the fluffiness of the pancakes is what immediately draws my attention, it's the heart shaped strawberries that pull me into a pool of warmth. Across the room, Mateo winks in my direction before I throw my head back down at the tray, crinkling my nose.

This is entirely too sweet and thoughtful. A part of me wants to gush, but another part of me feels stuck. I'm so high off the anxious comfort I felt last night that I didn't think about how this would go over with everyone watching. I'm a grand gestures type of girl, but this, I want to keep more private. Speaking of private... As I look at my friends all scarfing down their breakfast, not a single one of them has asked me about last night yet, and this group loves good gossip.

"So..." I clear my throat. "None of you are going to ask me about last night?" None of them even look in my direction. Instead, they all shake their heads, frowning. "Okay, then I won't share."

Maeve peeks up at me, eyeing the other girls. Kennedy shakes her head, and Maeve starts to go back to cutting her pancakes until she peers up at me again and then down at the strawberries on my tray, groaning at how cute they are.

"Of course I want to know!" Maeve bursts. "Kennedy said we should respect your privacy, but I can't help that I'm curious." She mouths a 'sorry' to Kennedy who tosses a grape at her.

"You're so weak," Kennedy complains playfully, suddenly a complete 180 to the person I ran into outside.

Sasha shrugs. "We're not weak. We just like to stay up to date. Besides, you know you want to know too."

"Obviously, but I know how it feels to constantly have to report your relations to close friends and family. It's draining."

"Okay, let's keep it down first of all," I chime in. "Second of all, nothing really happened. We stargazed, he made a little snack board with a cheese I liked at Millard's... it was nice."

"Are you saying you didn't... do the deed?" Maeve whispers.

I giggle. "You expected me to be ass out in the middle of the woods? I don't think so."

"Well, I think that's super cute," Kennedy says.

"Yeah, we just like seeing you happy and not so bunched up." Sasha smiles with sincerity.

"Thanks," I reply. "It's weird, though. I don't really know what to make of it. Mateo's a great guy, but I don't want to ruin the next few weeks being tangled up in some cozy nest of delusion."

"Well, it's not like it has to be complicated. Just go with the flow; feel it out," Maeve suggests.

"But it is complicated" is what I want to say, but I don't want to drag this conversation out any longer.

Two old classmates hanging out in a romantic way, but with platonic intentions is complicated. Romance is supposed to be about getting in your feelings and opening the door for something new in hopes that it will eventually lead to more. What Mateo and I would be doing has an abrupt end with no linear timeline. It seems nice since there's no expectation to take things further and think about the future, but I also hate the fact that I know there's a possibility for things to fall apart. I like Mateo, and I don't want things to move backward when I think we can actually be friends once camp is over.

"Anyway," I sigh, digging my fork into my pancakes. "How are things with you and Beck, Maeve?"

Her shoulders slump. "Okay, I guess, but we haven't really talked since the bonfire. Maybe I jumped the gun a bit."

"Nonsense," Sasha exclaims. "You know, Beck. He's not really the straightforward, romantic type. Give him some time or just tell him how you're feeling."

"No, you're probably right. We express ourselves differently, so that makes sense."

An aluminum ball comes flying over our heads, hitting a camper in the back of the head a few tables down. Cheers break out from the source, Beck standing over the group as he reinforces how the spork catapult he taught them to make isn't to be used for violence.

"Yeah, give him some time," I say in reassurance.

The bell to head back to the cabins to get ready for first block activities rings, and campers skitter off to toss away remaining trash and stack dirty trays on top of the counter near the kitchen. I take my cup of strawberries along with me after picking up what I can to help the cleaning staff. As I brave the hot air, Mateo is already outside waiting near the door with his usual confidence.

"Mind if I walk with you?" He asks, pushing off the wall of the building.

"I don't mind." I pop a strawberry into my mouth. "Thank you for getting me breakfast, by the way. That was really sweet of you."

"Anything for you." The smile in his voice is infectious, drawing me in.

"Actually, I'm glad you found me," I say. "I wanted to talk to you."

We stop outside of my cabin, away from the door and windows to make sure we can't be heard.

"Everything okay?"

"Everything's fine," I confirm, hoping he doesn't hear the hint of uncertainty in my answer as I lower my voice. "It's just that the whole getting me breakfast and heart shaped strawberries thing is a little too much too fast for me. I don't mind my friends knowing right now, but I don't need everyone in my business. Plus, I don't want Josh to think we're still distracted. This is our job after all. I still haven't made up my mind, so... baby steps, you know?"

He doesn't say anything, and regret musters in my gut like an army. I shouldn't have said anything. I'm taken back to my room in my old apartment, AJ standing in front of me, disregarding me like I'm a child. Telling me how I always have to be right—making the smallest thing into something more so that I can complain. I felt so small at the time, and he seemed like a giant, crushing everything I tried to make until nothing was my own. I feel myself start to shrink again as Mateo's silence looms over me.

"I'm sorry. I'm messing it up," I say, retreating into myself.

"No," he says quickly. He places his hands on my arms, gently bringing me to his attention. "I was just surprised, that's all. I thought you'd be okay with it, but we can go at your speed. It's no problem."

"Really?"

"All we have is time, and we have the whole summer to get it right, *manemea*." His hands come to my shoulders, and I imagine them sweeping behind my neck and into my hair as he pulls me into a kiss. Why does he have to be so good? "Baby steps."

I relax as relief washes over me. "Thank you, Mateo."

The summer of a lifetime.

His words give me an idea, and I tell him to wait outside while I go into the cabin to grab something. I pull my duffel bag from under my bed and pull out the plastic bag tucked inside. Right where I left him, I hand him the bag as he eyes at me curiously. "Just open the bag," I scrutinize.

He pulls out a disposable camera and smiles. "If this is for nudes, I'm all for it. Very old school."

I roll my eyes, regretting my choice already. "Stop being gross. It's for *the summer of a lifetime*. I thought it'd be nice to have it on camera or whatever you want, really. I bought some extra for anyone who might want one."

"And you weren't going to give me one?" he asks with amusement.

I shrug. "I had a change of heart. Just let me know when you need more film."

"I'll take it," he says, starting to walk back to his cabin.

"Oh, one more thing," I say. He turns back to me. "How did you know I like buttermilk pancakes?"

He shakes his head, leveling his gaze. "Your pajama shirt—International Pancake Day. Figured it wasn't a coincidence."

Heat rushes to my cheeks, and a tinge of sweetness pools at the back of my throat. It washes over me as I find my way to my bed, noticing a small piece of paper tucked under my pillow. Turning my back away from the girls, I open and smooth the neatly folded paper. There are no words, but a drawing of a teddy bear holding a heart. I take my time looking at every detail. The fine fur and the gloss added to the bear's eyes. I didn't even know he could draw. And just like that, I'm back on air.

CHAPTER 18

For the rest of the morning and afternoon, I occasionally peek at the drawing. I must look like a fool grinning down at a piece of paper, but who wouldn't? It was a nice touch and an even better substitute for the real plush toy. Knowing that Mateo can draw somehow makes him more attractive. At every turn, there's a new facet of him I've yet to unlock, or maybe they simply went unnoticed because of my own narrative of who and what he is. It makes me ask myself what else I could have missed out on being so one track minded. I neglected to check up on Valarie, and I missed out on so many family game nights that I thought I might be disowned. Maybe it is time to shift gears.

For our Rec hour this week, Kennedy, Maeve, Sasha, and I settled on taking up ceramics. It's by far one of my favorite art forms and the only one all three of us could agree on, given that Kennedy wanted to try gymnastics—I'm still too afraid to attempt a cartwheel—and Sasha wanted to do tennis. Maeve, her usual gleeful self, was indifferent. Wanting to do something together, I suggested ceramics since it was something we've all done before, and it was guaranteed that no one would break a bone or leave with a knot on their head the size of a tennis ball.

As we pull on our aprons and take our seats to wait for the instructor, Mateo and Beck walk through the doors of Arts and Crafts. Beck takes a seat a few places over from Maeve, and I watch her face fall. My head shakes as her eyes wander over to him.

"What's that head shake for? Not happy to see me?"

"Did you know I would be here?" I ask Mateo as he sits on the stool next to me.

"Would it be terrible if I said I did?" he questions, a glint of humor in his eyes.

"Only if you don't mind getting embarrassed by my mad pottery skills," I challenge.

"All these years and you're still so cocky."

"Who are you telling?" We both split into laughter as the instructor takes her seat at the front of the room. After a brief introduction and going over some ground rules, she instructs us to weigh out some clay as we'll start with working on centering it, and getting used to the wheel alongside the positioning of our hands and bodies.

Mateo offers to grab a portion for me and Kennedy, and I thank him before grabbing Beck's attention. "Beck, don't you think it would be better to sit next to Maeve since you're both here?" I say low enough for only him and Kennedy to hear.

"Oh, no, I think it's fine where I'm at," he says nonchalantly.

I sigh, scratching my head impatiently. "Okay, but maybe you should. You're exploring new things, and it would be good to talk."

"In the middle of a ceramics class?"

I slap my hands on my thighs, letting Kennedy take the lead because, as much as I love Beck, he can be so clueless at times, and Kennedy has the patience of a goddess.

"Okay, Beck, you and Maeve are essentially dating. You may have known her for years, but not as a potential partner. It might make her feel wanted and special if you sit with her. Think of it as starting anew."

He looks over to Maeve, who's waiting her turn for clay. "I know," he breathes. "To be honest, I'm nervous. I don't want to fuck up and disappoint her."

"That may be true, but it might make her feel worse that you're not showing any interest. Trust me when I say I know how it feels to have your wants ignored. It's not a good feeling."

He nods his head as he ponders Kennedy's words. He straightens, rolling his shoulders back as he walks over to Maeve, offering to take her clay back to her station for her. Her demeanor shifts as a wide grin spreads across her face, tucking her hair behind her ear.

"When did you become the couple whisperer? I thought you said you've never dated anyone?" I ask, turning my attention to Kennedy as I twist my hair up and clip it in place.

"Oh, I haven't," she says as she averts her gaze. "I'm just an observationist, like you said."

Minutes feel like seconds as the class goes on. I know it's been a few years since I've done this, but by my skills, you'd think it's been decades. Muscle memory fails me, and now I wish I had taken up Ceramics for my arts elective in college instead of Introduction to Theatre.

Others around me appear to be doing fine, while I feel like I'm just wasting water. It's either I'm spinning too slow and adding too much pressure, or too fast and can't gain control. Meanwhile, some people have already begun to open up their clay to form a small bowl.

I groan in frustration the tenth time my clay spins off center. I had already asked the instructor for a few more minutes after the class was over, promising I'd clean up after myself. As everyone else fizzles out of the building, Mateo stays behind, lingering on the other side of the room. I'm too busy focusing on finding the right speed and right amount of pressure to notice him until a stool screeches across the floor and he plops down next to me.

Out of my peripheral vision, I see him lean his arms on his knees, watching my hands.

"Can you not do that?" I ask, irritated.

"It's just fascinating not seeing you be able to do something perfectly—"

"Mateo," I groan through my teeth.

"Alright, alright." He puts his hands up in defense. "Do you want my help?"

I keep quiet as annoyance creeps up on me. If I wanted help, I would ask. Clearly, I'm trying to focus, so why interrupt?

The wheel stops spinning as I shut my eyes in an attempt to calm my nerves so that I can concentrate. I hear Mateo get up and assume he finally took the hint and let me be. I stretch my neck, rolling back my shoulders as I loosen the tension in my limbs. A hard chest presses against my back, and my eyes shoot open. Mateo reaches around me, sprinkling water onto the clay.

"Start spinning the wheel, easy on the pedal, and lift off."

"I don't want your help, Mateo," I say dismissively.

"You may not want it, but you need it, and I'm going to give it to you. Now start spinning the wheel, please."

My first thought is to push him away, tell him to leave me alone, and that I can figure it out. That's always my response when people offer help when I'm frustrated and can't find the solution. It's not the nicest thing to do, but it's how I am. I'm so used to doing things on my own and getting things down pat on the first try that I often don't realize when it's okay to ask for help or accept it. I've always seen it as me being a burden and being utterly useless. Solving things on my own is a pressure I've felt since childhood. Seeing my parents be the best at what they do—in everything they do—being rewarded when I did something right, it became an exceptation for me. Above all else, I need to be the best, or there's no point in trying. I know I should take that weight off of my shoulders, but how can I when I'm the only person I can truly depend on to get it right?

"It's easier for you," I complain. "You work with your hands all the time; you're a mechanic, and you can draw? Art was never my strong suit."

"Since when do you consider the written word not to be art?" he asks, his voice knotted with concern.

"It's not the same. I'm not molding pretty things with my hands for people to gift or to put on their coffee tables."

"Yeah, but you're molding minds, molding hearts, and *that's* a beautiful thing." His words bounce off the walls, offering me reassurance and encouragement.

The impact writing can have on individuals and society is the reason why I feel so passionately about journalism. It's shining a light on truth and making that truth accessible to the public. But when it comes to my own truth, in some areas the light is dim and gray. I feel so close to turning that nozzle up, adding brightness to the shadows of my mind that refuse to let me see the whole picture outside of my career aspirations—outside of the polished and elaborate frame that I call my life map.

Baby steps.

Inevitably, the angel of reason and logic tricks me into submitting, and I halfheartedly ease my foot onto the pedal.

"Good, now try and center the clay like you were before." I wet my hands and add horizontal pressure to the sides of the clay. Mateo's hands come over mine, his arms wrapped around me, causing a flurry in my stomach. He molds his hands to mine, showing me where to adjust my pressure. "There. Try using your body instead of your hands so you don't add too much pressure... Lean into it, rest your arm on your knee for control."

I follow his instructions while ogling at the way his hands shape the clay. The way he easily guides me, indirectly demanding me to be right where he wants me. There's no denying the sensual nature of it, but I try to ignore it as a twinge of excitement pulls at the corner of my mouth as I work the clay. For once, it isn't flying off the wheel as my body finally syncs with my hands.

"Oh, it's working," I exclaim, giggling to myself.

"It is. You're doing so well, Aubree." Maybe it's my imagination, but his voice drips with seduction as his breath tickles my cheek, and heat surges through me. I almost lose my grip if not for Mateo's hands still covering mine.

I turn to face him, leaning my body into his, his mouth inches away from mine. The pout on his lips, and the way I can tell his gaze is tracing over the curve of my mine, draws me nearer to him. Our breaths mingling between us as his dark scent fills my lungs with pleasure. I nibble at my bottom lip thinking of the consequences if I allow his lips to touch mine. Before I can experiment with the thought further, a wet, slimy substance is streaked across my neck, and Mateo laughs at his proud work. I raise an eyebrow in shock before taking my clay covered fingers and spearing a much larger streak over his cheek. He gives me an "oh, it's on" look before dipping his hands into the water and flicking his wet fingers at me.

Our laughter fills every corner of the room, puddles of water covering the wooden floor as I join in his antics, but my mind freezes this moment in time. Marveling at the crinkles at the corner of his eyes as he smiles, the redness in his cheeks as he tosses his head back in laughter, the lines around his mouth that indicate a life of happiness, and the way he holds onto me firmly to keep me from tipping off the stool.

Life truly can be this easy.

Chapter 19

My back leans against a tree as I flip over pages of Valarie's poems and short stories. Some I can tell her pen was trying to keep up with her mind as words spilled onto the page. It made me happy seeing such similarities between me and her. Late at night, I'd sit in my bed writing down every idea, line, word, and phrase that came to me. I'd take each one and turn them into a poem or a story and read them aloud to my parents, but only when I felt my drafts were finished and sufficient. I sacrificed so much paper just to have the right word in the correct structure with the most perfect handwriting. Once my dad was fed up, he got me a laptop and printer, and I never looked back. I promised Valarie that I'd read every last one and provide my feedback by the end of the week, and I was already a little behind, being so wrapped up in spending time with Mateo.

The last few days have been nothing but memorable in all the best ways. He no longer gets me breakfast in the morning, but little things like carrying my laundry and offering to grab me a snack between breaks.

He's even given me more drawings; my favorite has to be the one of a bird nestled in a pile of leaves while it sleeps. I've tucked each one inside a book, and occasionally admire them as much as I can in the darkness until I can no longer keep my eyes open as I drift off to sleep. Just as I'm full to the brim with wonder, the devil walks in, blocking out the light in favor of its dark presence.

Penelope stands over me, her arms crossed over her chest like I'm the one bothering her.

"Shouldn't you be with you're new arm candy?" I ask, piling the papers onto my lap.

"He's getting me some ice water, not that it's any of your business," she replies coolly. For the show they put on about how coupled up they are, you'd think she might bother to correct me about calling him out of name to prove something. "What about you and Mateo? You two look especially cozy all of a sudden."

Penelope's barely said two words to me since camp started. But if there's one thing about her, she can never let anything go, especially when she feels it's something she deserves. We've never run in the same circles or had the same interests, but she always found a way to weasel her way into places where she doesn't belong. I should have known she'd start up again. Although it does feel good to know that the guy she really wants is spending most of his free time with me. But this time, I'm not letting her get one over on me.

"Why? I thought you and Gale were so happy together, or is that just the fake bullshit you want everyone to believe, like everything else about you?" Her eyes darken as I move toward the cabins.

"You know he's only acting this way because he feels sorry for you. I heard him say so to Beck."

A lump of uncertainty forms in my throat. I thought that I had gotten rid of that insecurity. Tucked it away at the bottom of a drawer to be forgotten. But her words slowly seep into my veins and tear into old wounds. Penelope trying to get under my skin isn't new, but I can't quiet the buzzing of my past that plays in the back of my mind. How the words leave a bitter taste in my mouth, how those same words were said to me in my last argument with AJ. Two years of my life were wasted because someone felt sorry for me, because I felt sorry for myself, and there's nothing I could have done to stop it. Mateo did come in with Beck yesterday, and I never thought to ask Mateo if that's the reason he's doing all of this. I was so wrapped up in it all, it felt good not to think about it. But I guess that's what he's good at.

Trying to suppress the doubt that threatens to take root inside me, I turn to face her. "Even if that were true, he still doesn't want you."

I enjoy the tightness in her jaw and the flare of her nostrils at my remark. "Whatever, I was just letting you know the truth. I only came over as a favor to Josh; he's looking for you."

Well, next time Josh needs to use the loudspeaker instead of sending the devil to find me. With that, his voice booms over the speaker, telling me to make my way to the office. I guess impatience got the best of him.

With a huff, I make my way inside. With every step, the more my body tenses with the weight of what's to come when I open my email. I'm not sure I can handle any bad news with the doubt that's already coiling around my bones.

I knock on the door and open it to Josh leaning far back in his chair, his leg crossed over his knee. "You rang?" I ask, closing the door behind me.

"Mm, apparently there's a new email awaiting you," he says, getting up from the desk and offering me his seat.

Anxiously, I take it and open up a new window to log in. From behind me, I can see Josh leaning over me, watching the screen.

"Do you mind?" I toss over my shoulder.

"Oh, yeah, yeah. Sorry." He backs out of the room, and once I see the door shut, I get to work, the email popping up immediately. My pulse drums as I read the words "The Intersect" in the subject line.

The Intersect is a smaller publication, but still a top choice. It was the first magazine I picked up that wasn't about celebrity gossip, and one of the reasons I studied journalism to begin with. It would also allow me to stay closer to home instead of moving to Columbus if that's what I choose.

As I drag my cursor over the email, I'm more excited than nervous compared to last time. The Intersect could be a place where I can easily fit in, maybe it can even feel like home since I'm clearly never hearing from the Franklin Gazette. Either option would be a dream come true, but before I can click the email open, there's a knock on the door that prolongs the excruciating wait.

"Yeah?" I yell out, hoping that it's just someone for Josh to make the interaction quick. To my surprise, it's Mateo whose head peeks around the door.

I put on a reserved smile as if a dark cloud was looming over him. The closer he gets, the more my smile starts to falter and feels more forced.

My mind barks at me to say something and share this with him, but my nerves keep me in place, and I'm sure my smile looks more psychotic by the second.

"I heard your name over the speakers and decided to come." He stands in front of me now, excitement sparkling in his eyes. "I trust that's okay. Sasha and Kennedy are downstairs too, but they insisted I come up," he adds quickly.

"No, yeah, it's cool. You were here the last time, so…" I wave for him to take a seat, and he pulls one up next to mine. I shift away slightly, breathing out a laugh that I hope sounds natural, but I can't ignore the beads of mistrust that fill me at what Penelope said. Every attempt I make to shy away from it only makes it greater—makes me more aware of it.

"Mateo?" I let out. "I need to know something first before I open this email and can't properly react to it because of how I'm feeling right now."

"Yeah, sure," he says, leaning in to capture my every word.

"I know that Penelope is the last person I should be listening to, but I'm feeling super insecure now, and I need you to be honest with me." Pausing with regret that it's too late to go back now, I fold my hands in my lap. "Did you tell Beck you felt sorry for me and that that's why you're spending time with me?"

The words sound worse out loud than they did in my head. I bite down on my lip as his hand comes to the back of his neck and his expression becomes stern, and my heart begins to slowly sink.

"I did say that to him yesterday," he says softly.

"Right," I conclude, slapping my hands on my knees. I move to turn my chair around, but he stops me, grabbing onto the armrest.

"But it's not like what Penelope is making it sound like. Jesus, I... he was talking to me about Maeve and asking for my advice. It led up to us talking about me and you, and I did say that I felt bad for you after what you said in the shed, and that I wanted to spend this summer with you because of how shitty it made you feel. I've just never seen you look so defeated—but that's not the sole reason."

"Then what is it, Mateo? Because I'm starting to feel really shitty and stupid right about now." There's no hiding the quiver in my voice that becomes more ridged with each word. I can't believe I allowed myself to get sucked into his stratosphere. All of the things I opened up about—things I'd never confessed to anyone else. Embarrassment boils within me, spreading rapidly, and a big, fat 'I TOLD YOU SO' imprints itself at the forefront of my mind.

We sit in complete silence as his eyes dart back and forth in contemplation, and the more time that passes, anger replaces my embarrassment. I watch as his mouth opens and closes like a fish gasping for air.

"What? No excuses this time?" I ask.

"It's not that, it's—"

"You know what?" I ponder with the click of my tongue. "I'm not sure why it matters to me anyway. I never said yes to whatever this is. Besides, at the end of the summer, I'm leaving Coventry and we won't have to worry about who said what or why."

A small voice tells me to reel it in, that it's not too late to take it back, but what's said is done. My plans were never changing for anyone or any reason.

He nods his head slowly as I watch realization fall over him. He doesn't say a word as he stands up and leaves the room, leaving behind the weight of dread in the air. My eyes stay glued on the door, a part of me feeling like I'm suffocating the more it dawns on me what just happened. But it's for the best. The last thing I need is sympathy or pity.

Then why do I feel so guilty?

My lungs fill with air as I turn toward the computer screen. My curse still hovers over the email, and I reorient myself to remember my purpose for being up here. Although it feels less like I'm holding my future in my hands and more like a dumbbell with the word 'obligation' on it.

I don't waste another second on clicking the email open and scanning over the paragraph quickly until my eyes land on the words I'm searching for. Relief washes over me, and I should scream, jump up and down in revelation, but my mind keeps going back to Mateo. My nails dig into the flesh of my palm to distract myself from it, and I focus instead on outlining the requirements and deadlines flushed out in the email for the position before printing out the attached documents along with the email itself. It's about time that I get back to what I do best and focus on what will get me the results I want. It was a good distraction while it lasted.

CHAPTER 20

T he next few days are what I imagine a cold day in hell feels like. Mateo and I haven't said a word to each other since I confronted him about what Penelope said. We work around each other and pretend the other doesn't exist, like normal adults. On one hand, I couldn't care less, but on the other, I wish I hadn't let Penelope get to me like that. Still, it turns out she was right, and I was right to question Mateo. I have to continuously remind myself that I'm only mourning who I wanted Mateo to be, not who he is. It's my own fault for being so naive. It's one of the first things he said to me, and I can't fault him for it. My discernment has gone down the drain in the past year, and I need to get back to remembering who I am and the woman I worked to become, no matter how callous she may be.

In better news, I've started to get the hang of ceramics. The somewhat lopsided bowl I made might disagree, but I only had a week, and I'm proud of it—it's unique. Throwing is surprisingly more fun and relaxing when you stop worrying about the piece being perfect. Our final glaze firing will be done today, and I can't wait to see the final project. My fingers are crossed that it comes out in the pretty pastel green color I was going for.

I flinch at the crack of Josh's hands coming together, signaling that our staff meeting has been adjourned. My mind had wandered off thinking about if I was going to take the job with The Intersect. Although they stated I wouldn't start until the beginning of August, giving me plenty of time to come to a sound decision, it's still hard to move on from what could have been with the Franklin.

"I need a shower," Kennedy whines. "Why do the kids have so much energy after lunch? I spent 20 minutes chasing around a camper to get them to stop using the mini catapult to throw cherry tomatoes at a family of ducks." She shoots daggers at Beck, and his hands fly up in defense.

"Don't look at me. I told them to use them responsibly," he clarifies as if that makes it any better. "It'll be good practice for when you start teaching in the fall."

Kennedy sits down at a picnic table, massaging her calves. "Yeah, except I won't be chasing around a bunch of 15 and 16 year old sophomores around the school. Instead, I'll likely be hounding them to turn in their homework on time."

"When do you hear back from them about the position? Do you know?" I ask.

"They said it might be a few weeks before I hear back about an offer if I get one at all."

"You're getting it," says Sasha. "Put only positive thoughts into the universe."

"Thanks, but I don't want to get my hopes up."

"I should've been a teacher," Beck chimes in wonderment. "Mr. Santos, science teacher." He casts his hands out in front of him like he's envisioning the writing on a big billboard in neon lights.

"You'd be miserable," says Maeve, breaking the illusion in his eyes. "You hate discipline, and science was never your strongest subject." Beck shrugs with an agreeable frown.

"When you finally get the job offer, we should celebrate," I declare. "Maybe dig up an old tradition and take a dip in the lake at night after lights out?"

"Aubree threatening to break the rules? Where's my best friend, and what did you do to her?" Sasha begs as she covers her mouth with her hand in horror.

"Mateo really has changed you for the better." Our heads swivel to look at Beck, who looks as clueless as ever. That suffocating feeling comes back as his words sink in. Maeve pulls Beck—who mumbles about what he said wrong—away, making up some excuse about needing to do something before third block. I try to remain as carefree as possible, snuffing that flame out before it turns into a case of emotional arson. I rest my arms back on the table, staring off into the woods. Closing my eyes, I focus on the wind as it blows through my hair.

"So," Kennedy whistles. "When are you going to tell us exactly what happened between you two?"

"Nothing happened. We called it quits before either of us could get ahead of ourselves."

I hear Kennedy shift, and I know she's getting into therapist mode. "Was it a mutual decision, or did you get scared and cut things off?"

"I don't need you to psychoanalyze this, okay?" I snap, sitting up to face her, making sure she can read the seriousness in my expression.

She lifts her hands up before slamming them back down on the table. "Well, excuse me for wanting to help you process it."

"I don't need that right now, Kenny. One second it's 'let's give her her space and privacy,' now it's 'let's pick this apart and leave her bare.'"

"Whoa, Bree, let's chill for a second," Sasha interjects. "It's not us you're mad at. Remember that before you start coming at us."

My head falls into my hands as I massage my temples. "I know, I'm sorry. I don't want to think about it is all."

"I forgive you *this* time, but next time I can't be too sure," Kennedy says, puckering her lips.

"You love me, even at my worst," I giggle.

Her arms come around my shoulders, pulling me in for a warm hug. "I do. I just thought that maybe if you let it out instead of bottling it up, you might feel better. Maybe a little less fierce."

My head rests on her shoulder, and I continue to stare into the distance as I visualize my options. I can keep pretending that everything is fine and dandy while my pride slowly eats away at me, or I can fess up and deal with the scrutiny I'll face from my friends. I'll take the former for now, and I'm saved by the bell to escort our campers to third block.

The rest of the day goes by without incident, and I'm mostly feeling better about the Mateo situation. More importantly, I'm ready to see my final ceramics project. After dropping the campers off for Rec hour, I practically skip over to the Arts and Crafts building to retrieve my bowl. How something so small and fragile could spark so much joy was beyond me, but I was more than happy to see how it turned out.

My friends are already there when I step into the busy space as everyone stops around the front table to marvel at their projects. Sasha, as talented as she is, settled on making a jewelry dish for her rings. It's shallow and carved to look like a lily pad, adding a sculpted white flower for a finishing touch. My bowl sits at the end of the table, a bluish glaze mixed into the pastel green, giving it a subtle ombre effect. It came out more beautiful than I thought it would. I was never good at art—I still struggle to draw an even heart that doesn't look like a botched letter *B*—but this lopsided and somewhat lumpy piece of art is mine. Now I know what Sasha means when she says creating visual art is so much more exciting than only consuming it.

After admiring some of the other pieces, I waste no time picking mine up to take back to my seat. Turning around to find a spot near my friends, I feel a hard object knock into my arms. In slow motion, I can do nothing but stare in shock as my bowl hits the floor below, shattering into large pieces. The room goes silent, and I stand there frozen as I take in the mess. A tattooed arm steps into view as I suddenly grow hot with irritation. Of all people and of all things, it has to be Mateo and my bowl.

"Shit. Aubree, I'm so sorry—I didn't see you—"

"Please, I wouldn't want you feeling any more sorry for me than you already do," I spit out like throwing knives.

Ignoring him and the eyes I feel piercing into us, I squat down to pick up the pieces.

"Let me help you," he whispers as he comes to the other side of me.

"Please, don't," I ground out in a voice low enough only he can hear. I refuse to look up at him as he hovers near me, contemplating my words before backing away and leaving me to pick up the remaining chunks.

The instructor advises everyone to stand back from the broken shards, but Beck comes over with a broom and dust pad to sweep up the fragments I can't see or pick up without potentially cutting myself. I thank him before tossing the chunks into a nearby plastic bag and discarding it into a trash can. As sweet as she is, the instructor offers to help me mend what we can, but I can only politely shake my head before seeing myself out. The energy in that room, the way people were looking at me, is too much to bear, and it's exactly what I wanted to avoid. Except this is worse because now I look like a bitch, and everyone knows something is going on between Mateo and I.

The further I walk away from the building and into the night, the more my chest shrinks in upset. The entire time I was cleaning up the glass, it felt like picking up broken pieces of the short yet memorable time I spent with Mateo. Seeing it like that, I want to scream into the sky or run until my legs fold beneath me from exhaustion. Anything to stop myself from admitting that it's more than just the bowl, but that I was hurt by Mateo. That without his constant presence, everything feels empty.

Chapter 21

"Guys, there's only 346 s'mores kits here," I say as I sift through the pile again to make sure I counted correctly. I hear a crunch behind me and catch Beck trying to wipe away the evidence of graham cracker crumbs from around his mouth. "Beck!"

"What?" he pleads. "I got hungry."

"I swear, if I see you take one during the bonfire, it'll be up your ass."

"Geez, okay. Message received."

"Don't mind her, she's just on edge because she's in charge of the bonfire tonight," Kennedy says as she readies the hot chocolate and apple cider.

"Yes, I am, and I don't need another reason for Josh to be on my ass."

After last night, Josh pulled Mateo and I into his office for yet another talking to about teamwork and remaining a sense of professionalism, even when we're on break. Thankfully, he didn't ask what was going on between us. Technically, fraternizing with other staff isn't against the rules as long as everyone is being safe and appropriate, but it wasn't a conversation I wanted to have. I'm still angry at Mateo, and with myself for being angry at him. Feelings aren't supposed to be involved, and I fear I'm too deep in to dig myself out. I've been contemplating all morning about where they came from and when, and why I didn't stop myself before it got to this point. Mateo has me all out of balance, the realization ramming into me and turning in my stomach. I don't get it, and I don't want to. What I *need* is for him to get out of my head.

"Okay, Kennedy, make some extra kits just in case. Remember, it's three per kit. I'll have to remind Josh we're running low on marshmallows." Tapping my thigh, I try to remember what else I could be forgetting. "Oh, the speaker."

"Got it," Maeve says, setting it in the box with the kits.

"Not on top," I wince.

"I know, relax," she giggles. "Don't get so worked up. It's just a bonfire."

"You're right," I breathe, closing my eyes briefly and opening them to the sight of Beck drinking the cider. "Beck!"

He shrugs. "I got thirsty."

I look to Maeve who only ogles at him until she notices my glare. "Okay, babe. How about we go look for extra blankets?" She drags him away to the storage closet while I sit down before my blood pressure is through the roof.

"You good?" Kennedy asks, sitting next to me.

"Mhm, I need a nap, I think."

"Me too," Sasha adds as she sits on the bench across from us. "But, I feel like something else is bothering you. You're extra cranky today."

"I'm not cranky, I need—"

"Things to be done right." Sasha and Kennedy say in unison. "Yeah, we know," Sasha finishes.

I roll my eyes. "Whatever."

"You know what we're talking about, Bree. We don't want to push you, but your bad mood is coming down on all of us."

"Yeah, like yesterday when you almost took my head off for borrowing your sunscreen." Kennedy raises an eyebrow.

"You didn't ask, and that stuff is expensive," I say in defense.

"You brought three with you and told us we could borrow it."

"Oh yeah."

"Yeah," Kennedy sings, bobbing her head slowly. "So, spill."

Taking a deep breath, I accept my fate and let it all out. Everything with Penelope and Beck, and how it made me question Mateo, and how he didn't deny it when I confronted him. I leave out the part where I'm conflicted because I suddenly care about Mateo and may actually like him to spare myself the added lecture. A lightness floats over me, but the looks Kennedy and Sasha give each other only make me nervous.

"Well?" I say, anxious for their opinion.

"Uh, well." Kennedy rocks back on the heel of her hands, shrugging her shoulders.

"Yeah?"

Sasha leans forward, resting her hands on her knees. "It feels like you kind of jumped to conclusions."

"Me?" I gasp in shock. "He didn't deny anything Penelope said."

"No, but it's Penelope. She doesn't exactly tell the whole truth. Did you give him a chance to explain?" Kennedy asks.

"Yes," I confirm with confidence, but when Kennedy's eyes meet mine, I know that's not true. "He just sat there with his mouth hanging open."

"Maybe he needed a chance to gather his thoughts."

"Whose side are you on?"

"Aubree, we're always on your side, but that also means being honest with you. I think you got scared of being rejected and cut him off before he could potentially hurt you." Kennedy's mouth ticks up apologetically. I look over as Sasha, whose expression only cosigns what Kennedy is saying.

So what if it's true? I'm wrong for that? He had every opportunity from then until now to say something, but he's choosing not to. That's all the confirmation I need. I don't want to have to pull teeth to get the truth.

"So, what? I'm just supposed to talk it out with him?" I question.

Kennedy pats my shoulder. "That's up to you, but you have to decide what's more important to you, knowing the truth or knowing that you let a good thing go to save your ego."

I shrug her off. "It's not about my ego being bruised, Kennedy."

"Then what is it? Because right now, all I see is a stubborn girl who thinks she's too good to admit when her feelings are hurt."

Being open and honest about my emotions is something I've always struggled to do. I've always masked it well by keeping myself busy, taking it out on things that can handle the pressure so that I don't break. Lately, it's all been too much. I'm at the end of my rope with excuses, and I have no choice but to face the music. There's no class I can blame it on or stress from work. Out here, it's just me with nowhere to hide. And it wouldn't be a good look to blame it on a bunch of kids who have been more or less sweet to me the past two weeks. Being stubborn about it is second nature—a defense mechanism.

"Look, we're not trying to be rude, but we don't want you to do something you might regret later because of fear," Sasha says.

I stand up when I hear Beck and Maeve returning from the supply room. "Nothing to be regretful over. There's about a month left, and we agreed to go our separate ways anyway."

I begin folding freshly washed blankets to keep myself busy, but my attention is where it's secretly been all morning. Through the window, you get a clear view of the basketball court where Mateo spends some of his free time before dinner. Between eyeing his sleek frame and the way he seems to easily fit in with any crowd, recollections of how sweet and gentle he's been with me spin on a carousel in my mind. With each reminder, the invisible string pulling me toward him becomes more noticeable as it tightens in my chest, nuzzling its way in and nesting. The rough tugs have begun to ache the longer I've ignored it and the more stubborn I am. I've convinced myself it's only because I got too relaxed, but that lie doesn't even work in my sleep.

CHAPTER 22

The warmth from the bonfire coats my skin as I work on assembling a s'more for myself. The speaker blasts an upbeat song I don't recognize, but it keeps the energy between campers and staff lively. I successfully convinced Josh to let us use my phone and the wi-fi for the night to listen to music and take requests rather than relying on someone to play guitar or tell a story to keep the energy flowing throughout the night. Some campers stand above the Quad dancing and singing, while others talk or play games. Kennedy, Sasha, and I are playing our fourth round of Uno because someone—that someone being Kennedy—can't help being a sore loser. I place down a draw four intended for Sasha, but she doubles it, making Kennedy draw eight.

"Nah, you guys are cheating," Kennedy exclaims as she reluctantly draws a handful of cards from the stack. Sasha and I can't stop laughing as the 10 cards in her hands become 18. "You're using some sort of secret code or something."

Ironically, when Sasha and I were younger, we did use secret codes when playing against others two on two. Scrunch your nose if you're changing the color; move your hand around once for red, twice for blue. We won a lot of bets those days, but this was just too funny to consider using our cheat sheet.

"You're smart enough to catch when we're cheating. This is too good," I say between short breaths of laughter.

"Yeah, right. Next time, I'm coming prepared."

The blanket wrapped around my back slides off the same way it's been doing all night. Annoyed, I shrug it off and set it down in front of me.

"Ugh, I forgot my jacket," I say as I slip my cards into my pocket before dusting off my shorts. "I'll be right back."

"But it's your turn," Sasha reminds me before I can track up the stairs. I take out my hand and toss down a skip to which she sticks her tongue out and mutters something about me being a meanie as I make my way up and out of the Quad.

All of the lamps outside of each cabin are on, illuminating the smooth dirt path. I take to kicking a small rock to keep me distracted until I make it down to my cabin. Posters, photos, and artwork litter the walls, giving the cabin a more homey feeling. I zero in on my jacket folded over the headboard of my bed and sidestep the pile of clothes I told Valarie to pick up before the bonfire started. Clearly, the daily reminders do nothing, and I need to turn up the ante. A groan escapes me as I grab the jacket and turn to leave when my breath draws taut at the sight of a long, orange vase filled with wildflowers sitting on top of my dresser. Carefully, I marvel at the delicately carved petals and leaves at the mouth of the vase before my eyes catch sight of something that peers around the body of the vase, my hand immediately reaching for my once shattered bowl. Gold lines run up and down the bowl, revealing where it had once been broken and adhered back together. The string tightens as I admire the work and give notice to a white card placed on the opposite side of the vase. Reaching for it, I let out a small breath as the words "For No Occasion" imprint themselves in my chest. A heaviness consumes me as I read the words over and over again, and my legs suddenly carry me out of the door back toward the Quad. The swelling in my chest throbs in tandem with the light thuds of my steps, only slowing when the source of the trouble comes into view.

Mateo leans against a tree a short distance away from the Quad. The light from the bonfire dances over his face, highlighting the sharp angle of his jaw and defining his toned arms as they rest crossed over his chest. His eyes flicker in my direction as if he could feel it too. He wastes no time as our strides widen to meet each other.

"What is this?" I challenge, holding up the bowl, its golden adhesive shimmering in the light. "You know I don't need fixing, right?"

"I do know that," Mateo says. The sincerity in his tone bringing me closer. "That's not what I meant by it, and it's not what I mean when I spoke with Beck."

"Then tell me what it is that you meant. Is this just some way to redeem yourself? Because—"

"No," he interrupts. "You were concerned, and you had every right to be. I'm sorry for not being more honest with you sooner. I wanted to say this the other day, but I didn't want it to seem like I was saying it to save face or for it to scare you."

I hold my breath as I anxiously wait for his confession as he rocks back on his heels.

"Aubree, I've wondered about you ever since I moved back to Coventry a few months ago, but if I can be honest, you haven't left my thoughts since high school. I wondered what you'd be like now, what you'd look like, and the look on your face when we saw each other again. If you still had that fire behind your eyes, the crinkle of your nose when you laugh too hard, and that small pout to your lips..." His gaze drops before allowing me to plunge back into the depths of his brown eyes. "What I'm trying to say is I like you, Aubree. I always have, and I've never stopped. It was hard enough coming back here and pretending like I still didn't have these feelings, but I can't keep pretending. I've wasted too much time already, and I don't want to waste the rest of the time I have arguing with you. I haven't been a perfect person, but I want more than anything to be that for you."

"Mateo," I whisper as shock and esteem dip in the cavity of my chest. Did I really miss all the signs that he felt this way all those years ago? I always assumed I was just an easy target, the girl who nobody really cared for unless they needed something from me. Looking back, he was the only guy who never asked anything of me. Looking at him now, I can't figure out what to say, where to start, or how to put into words that these past few days have shown me how much I crave him. His presence, his compassion, his kindness—I want it all. The realization had unwound in me, blooming with every thought of him. Even if I can't have him forever, I want him now.

Stepping toward him, I bring my hands up to Mateo's chest as his hands come to my waist, closing the gap between us as he tugs me against his frame. The brush of his hand as it comes to my neck, his thumb slowly caressing my jaw, sends a bolt of electricity down my spine. I suck in air as my lips part, and my breast press against him. The look in his eyes is unmistakable, and I nod, giving him what he needs to send his lips crashing into mine. The world softens around us as my arms move around his neck, and my knees go weak, but my mouth moves with greed. His arm moves around my waist, and I dread the moment he'll have to let go.

We break apart briefly, his breath tangling with mine. "Just in case it wasn't clear, I like you too, and I'm saying yes," I confess. He simply smiles before pulling me back into a gentle kiss that melts away any question in my mind that this is where I want to be.

CHAPTER 23

A grape flies into the air, springing off of Beck's spork catapult as I attempt to aim it into his mouth. It hits the corner of his mouth, bouncing onto the table before rolling off onto the floor.

"Dammit, I was so close. One more try," I say, loading on another grape.

"You said 'one more try' fifteen tries ago, Aubree," Mateo says as he chews on a grape of his own.

"It's harder than it looks," I complain. "It's not like you can do any better."

He makes a 'give me' motion with his hand, and I scoff as I shove the catapult his way. Beck throws his head back slightly, opening his mouth wide for the grape to be cast into the abbess. Mateo lowers his head as he pulls the spork back, and with a swift motion, he launches the grape, and it lands like a bullseye in its target. Beck pumps his arms up in victory and high fives Mateo as he raises his eyebrows at me.

"You got lucky, so what?" I cross my arms in mock humiliation.

"I can always teach you." He leans closer to me, deliberately as he drops his voice an octave. "If I remember correctly, you're an excellent student."

"Ah!" Sasha jabs her spork in our direction. "I'm glad you two have made up and all, but some of us are still eating."

I giggle. "He meant no harm; it's just his nature."

"Hey, I've got self control," Mateo says defensively.

"Could have fooled me," I say as a sly grin spreads across my face. The clashing of trays on the ground brings me back to reality, and I remember we're in a room full of kids who don't need to see this, at least not on my account. I don't recall ever being so caught up with a guy before, especially not with one who made me feel so comfortable being myself.

Mateo winks at me before returning to his breakfast, and I struggle to wipe away the silly smile that seems like it's permanently implanted itself since last night. Kennedy slides onto the bench next to Beck without regard for any of us. The lack of steam coming from her half eaten breakfast sandwich serves as proof of her long absence while the rest of us waited for her to come back. Yet, she says nothing.

"Seriously, Kennedy? Come on," I whine. She knows we're waiting for her to tell us what they said, but if there's one thing she loves, it's a dramatic pause. But when she bites down on the inside of her cheek to keep from smiling, a shriek of glee bubbles up from inside me. My excitement can't be contained as I make my way around the table, practically pouncing onto Kennedy's back as my arms wrap around her.

"I told you you'd get the job. I'm so happy you get to stay," I exclaim, making sure I don't squeeze her too tight as she pats my arm while others offer her their congratulations.

"Thank you. I'm glad I get to stay," she says.

I imagined this moment being more celebratory for Kennedy. That she'd be smiling from ear to ear and gushing about finally having her own classroom, and what her students would be like as she made them fall in love with science. Rather, her demeanor yields with precaution, something like alarm or relief flashing in her eyes. I don't get a chance to decipher when Beck declares that I follow through on my promise that we sneak out to the lake tonight and celebrate.

Breaking rules with the high risk of getting caught was something I left behind long ago after Camp Whisper Lake closed. It was like watching the door close on my childhood as I began solely focusing on academics and meeting the impossible standards I set for myself. But a quick post-midnight swim to relax and celebrate a friend's success is never off the table. Given that Kennedy was the one being honored, we let her decide. Being the voice of reason, she chose to do it right before dusk so that we could celebrate her within our free time and still meet curfew, but the timidness in her response doesn't bypass me.

The ring of the bell for cabin cleanup breaks the moment as everyone scatters toward their designated stations, some of us being assigned to stay after to clean up the Grub Station and the common areas on camp.

"Walk me back?" I ask Mateo, but it really comes out as more of a question of reassurance.

His hand slips into mine like it's natural, fitting like a glove. "Always."

I feel less exposed and more liberated by the idea of being so open with Mateo. The fear of judgment or resentment that would be waiting around the corner at the slightest hint of disapproval fades into the background the closer I get to accepting that I can't control my feelings or desires. It's still a scary realization to live with, but maybe this is what Sasha means when she says desire knows no borders.

Mateo's thumb encircles the palm of my hand as he smiles down at me sweetly. "What's on your mind?"

"Nothing," I lie, wanting to keep the conversation light.

"I can always tell when the gears are turning, *manamea*." Mateo's arm comes around my waist as he pulls me against his side.

"It's you," I mutter with reluctance.

"I did tell myself that by the end of the summer I'd consume your every thought," he jokes.

"What makes you think I still don't hate you?"

"Unlike your perfect mouth, your body betrays you." His hand moves to the small of my back, a finger sliding into the belt loop of my shorts. That's all it takes for a rush of pleasure to pool between my thighs.

Quickly, I move on as I attempt to control the stupid grin on my face. "I just have so many questions. Like when did you start reading Shakespeare? I thought you always hated it."

"I never hated it," he corrects me as we come to a stop in front of my cabin. "It's probably my one guilty pleasure I started really getting into once I moved back to Samoa with my family."

"Hmm," I sigh, cocking my head to the side. "Now you really have me curious. Who is Mateo Opetaia?"

"Maybe we can have some alone time tonight?" He raises an eyebrow, leaning into me until my back is pressed against the wooden wall of the cabin.

A blushing laugh escapes me. "You'd be lucky."

"I'll take my chances." The intensity of his gaze heats my core, and it takes all of me not to pull him in to a satisfied kiss. I settle for the ginger kiss he leaves on my cheek and hear quiet giggles coming from the open window above me, breaking the spell I'm under as I watch the swank in Mateo's walk as we part ways.

"You guys better be cleaning up in there," I exclaim. Climbing up the stairs, the girls scatter to their designated areas to resume cleaning. The sternness in my stance lights a fire under them, but doesn't stop the occasional giggles and whispers.

CHAPTER 24

The orange, pinkish hues of the sunset add a sense of serenity as the colors reflect onto the surface of the lake. The campers being away at Rec allows us to have this time to enjoy ourselves without interruption. Watching my friends be so carefree reminds me of how much I missed summer days like this. How frequently and abruptly I'd drop everything for a sliver of time to forget everything and enjoy myself. Looking out over my friends, I wondered how much of this I missed being obsessed and preoccupied by things I made into mountains. How many hours did I spend meticulously planning out a future I was never guaranteed?

The shifting of the boards on the dock interrupts my thoughts as Kennedy sits down next to me, handing me a can of pop.

"Are you enjoying yourself?" she asks through sips. "I haven't seen you get in the water."

My eyes drift to Sasha, Maeve, and Beck who've been at each other with water guns since we came down here. "I could ask you the same thing."

She shrugs as she taps the rim of her can. "Watching you guys be happy for me is more than enough."

"I know the stuff with your mom has been hard. Do you think you'll tell her?"

Kennedy shakes her head. "It's not worth it. I need to move on and let the past be the past."

"I hear you on that," I say as I lift my can in solidarity. "But Sasha and I are always here if you want to talk about it."

"Thanks, but..." She nods down the dock where Mateo is approaching us, a slow smile creeping onto his face. "It looks like you've got *bigger* plans."

Kennedy leaves me to it as she goes to join the others on the other side of the lake. Mateo takes her place, his legs dangling in the water below. I rest my head on his shoulder as I watch Maeve tread through the water, trying to get away from the windmill of splashes Beck is sending her way. Sasha lies out on a flamingo floatie nearby, a dolefulness in the way her body seems to hang over itself like she's made of stuffing.

"I missed you," Mateo says low in my ear before kissing my cheek.

"Can't stay away, huh?" I tease as my foot sways in the water, admiring the ripples the movement creates.

"Never." His hand comes around my stomach, pulling me to his chest as he lays a kiss on the back of my neck. "Come on."

Mateo pushes me forward slightly to ease himself up before taking a few steps back, taking a running jump into the lake. My arms come up to my head too late as the water from the impact splashes me. Mischief dances at the corners of his mouth as he tries to keep from laughing.

"That was so unnecessary," I exclaim through broken giggles.

"Oh, it was very necessary," he smolders. "Jump in."

"It's cold—"

He flicks water up at me, causing me to flinch and freeze in shock. "In the water. Now."

All I want to do is knock that cocky smirk off of his face as he wades in front of me, his overconfidence casting a shadow over me and giving me the perfect idea.

I lift myself up slowly as I drag the tips of my fingers just beyond my inner thighs. He tracks my every movement, and it sends a rush of an unfamiliar desire over me. The way that his expression grows hungry fills me with a taste for power I didn't know I had, and I'm suddenly in the mood to satisfy my cravings.

I pop open each button of my shirt starting from the bottom, leaving the reveal of my breasts for last, remembering how his eyes dipped between them that night at the Belfry. The shirt flies open to reveal the navy blue two piece underneath that stretches over my curves, hugging in all the right places.

"Whoa, take it off!" Kennedy yells from the background, but my gaze is trained on Mateo. Watching the way his Adam's apple bobs up and down, and the way his forearms flex with an eagerness that tells me he can't wait to get his hands on me.

Mateo's tongue runs over his bottom lip slowly, sending warmth to my cheeks as hunger strikes like lightning in his eyes. The fact that I can draw this reaction out of him just standing here makes me believe that all the wild fantasies I've dreamed up about being wanted—craved for—aren't so far out of reach. That I'm not too much or too imaginative when it comes to intimacy. The look on Mateo's face makes me realize that what I really want is to be desired for anything more than just an obligation.

I lower myself into the water with a small splash and make my way over to Mateo, whose arms are outstretched, waiting to take my hands under the water. Taking hold of his, he pulls me out toward a deeper part of the lake and a short way away from everyone, spinning us gently as he does. As my feet leave the floor of the lake, I instinctively wrap my legs around his waist, and he doesn't hesitate to press me closer as one of his hands comes to the small of my back.

"I can't believe I haven't been in the lake all summer," I say as I wrap my arms around Mateo's neck. "It's so relaxing."

"If I had known you'd feel that way, I would have gotten you out here sooner." He kisses the annoyed wrinkle formed between my brows before continuing to pepper kisses down the side of my face, lingering when he gets to my mouth. "Especially if I'd known how sexy you'd look."

"You didn't know that already?" I tease.

"The real thing is better than anything I could dream up." The words brush across my lips. I revel in it, teasing the tension in the space between us as my lips barely graze his.

"Is that so?"

Mateo's hands slide down to my thighs as he begins massaging the skin there. My pulse skips and jumps as if dancing under a forgotten sun that only grows brighter with every second I spend in Mateo's atmosphere.

Everything that he does—everything that he says—brings me closer and closer to the edge. The closer I get, the quieter my nerves, and the more ready I am to take the leap.

"You don't believe me?" he questions, his hands coming up to my hips.

I wind one of his curls around my finger, taking in the feel of my body against his. "I'm someone who believes in what they can see."

"What about what you can feel?" Mateo's voice is low and husky as he brings his mouth to my neck. If not for his strong arms holding me up, I would have slid down into the depths of the lake at the feeling. His kisses are like silk, and I allow myself a soft moan.

The string of kisses grows as they trickle over my collarbone and land on the other side of my throat. Each one is deliberate and savory, but grows more desperate the more I lean into him. Opening myself to him to make room for all I can bare. The last of it lingers on my shoulder before Mateo looks up at me innocently.

"Why'd you stop?" I ask in what's almost a panic. But when I shift to adjust my weight, the hard length of him drags against my ass. "Oh."

I can't help but laugh, especially as he begins to flush red like he's been caught in the act itself. He walks back towards the shallow end of the lake near the dock, and my laughter dies out as I realize that he seems more worried than embarrassed.

"Mateo, it's okay," I soothe.

His plush lips purse as he still avoids my gaze. "I don't want to do anything that might make you uncomfortable."

I push against his chest and force myself down to stop him from moving any further. "But I wasn't uncomfortable. It's fine."

"It's easy to get caught up when desire is stronger and moves quicker than what we actually intend," he sighs. "I don't want things to get confusing between us because we didn't stop when we should have."

This man. If I could make ten thousand carbon copies of him, I would.

Sex isn't something I've been able to offer whenever and with whoever, and the fact that Mateo understands and accepts that only makes me want him more. But, he's right. When I make that choice, *if* we ever get there, I should make it when my legs aren't wrapped around his waist, and it only takes two tugs at our swimsuits to get the job done. Maybe it's my fear of seeming too easy or being easily manipulated and discarded, but is that not what AJ did to me? We were together for two years, and he used and discarded me as easily as a grocery list. Just the thing you need when you occasionally realize you have other responsibilities. I hate that the little monster in the back of my mind burns a permanent reminder of how easily I fell into a pattern of allowing him to use me when he pleased, just so that I could say—or so that I could convince myself—that we were doing okay. And then all of the months leading up to our breakup without him even so much as brushing up against my arm. Like I was some contagion. But Mateo isn't AJ, and it's not fair to me or to him to put him in that box. While Mateo's spent the majority of my life being the bane of my existence, what he never was is cruel.

My hands reach up to cup Mateo's face. Reassurance forces him to lean into my touch. "You're right. I'm not there yet, and it wouldn't be fair to either of us to force it. Even if a large part of me wants to, I'm not 100 percent." I press myself against him, leaving no room for doubt or fear as the words escape me with ease. "But I'm horny, and my magic wand is at home."

Looking over at the others a distance away from us, Beck and Maeve are wrapped up in their water gun fight while Sasha seems to be dipping in and out of sleep. Kennedy is nowhere to be found. I raise an eyebrow in challenge at Mateo who doesn't miss a beat as he tips my chin up and meets my lips with his. All of our other kisses had been sweet and desperate, but this was submission tied in a neat bow. His mouth moves over mine with a slow depth that leaves me feeling bare and exposed. For a second, I thought he was going to have his way with me right here until he pulls back, and I moan at the disconnect.

His kisses trail down the sides of my face, lingering sweetly as he makes his way to my ear. "Let's get out of here, *manamea*."

You don't have to tell me twice.

CHAPTER 25

We manage to gather our things and make our way to the cabins reserved for instructors beside the Grub Station in record time. I hadn't known there was an empty cabin until Mateo slid his hand behind the door frame, popping out a hidden key. He pushes the door open, illuminating the untouched furniture as I venture inside and prop my clothes on top of the dresser.

"You've been holding out on me."

He grabs my arm, turning me around to face him. "Being the camp's handyman has its perks. Plus, if I had shown you the place from the start, would you have stayed?"

I shrug. "Previous Aubree likely would have called you out of your name and ended with 'you disgusting prick.'"

His head falls back slightly as he chuckles deeply. "Yeah, that sounds like her." His hands come to my hips as he pulls me into him. "But what would New Aubree say?"

"I'm not sure she'd be up for much more talking."

My gaze lowers to his soft, pink lips, swaying my body towards him as his hand wraps around the back of my neck. I always imagined when he was like this that he'd be more rushed—starved. But when our lips finally meet, he takes his sweet time, and all of our surroundings dissipate into this one savory kiss. I match his pace as it grows deeper and more refined. Mateo gently tugs and nibbles at my lower lip, and I groan with the need for him to be closer—to have more of him. I shift up on my tiptoes to deepen the kiss further, and the length of him brushes against my stomach. I step back slightly.

"Sorry," he murmurs, his breathing heavy. "Is it too much? We can stop."

"No, that's not it. It's more than enough," I say with a giggle. "I just wasn't sure if it was okay that I... can I touch you?"

A slow grin creeps across his face. "Aubree, baby, you can have me however you please, especially considering what I'm about to do to you. But I really want to take care of you for now if that's okay."

The huskiness in his voice heats my core, and I waste no time locking my lips with his. His hands come to my ass, cupping and squeezing, and suddenly my back is against the dresser as I let out a soft, pleading sigh. I lick at the curve of his bottom lip, commanding him to open more to me, and allowing my tongue to tangle with his.

Mateo's arm comes around my waist, pulling me to him as my hands run up his chest. He rocks into me, his cock thrusting against me. The feel of him sends me into overdrive as all logic and reason take a backseat, and an untamable greed takes over me.

"Fuck, Mateo," I breathe. My fingers dance at the lining of his shorts as he lays kisses down my neck and across my chest.

Mateo's hands travel up my sides, grazing the sides of my breasts before filling them into the palms of his hands. His tongue glides between my tits, and I press into him, longing for his tongue to reach every inch of my body. When he finally frees my breasts from the confines of my top, I gasp as he blows cool air over my nipple, and it perks up instantly before his tongue swirls around it, sucking the bud into his mouth. I whimper under the heat of his wet mouth. The way his tongue flicks repeatedly at my nipple, combined with the sensation of his thumb and forefinger rolling the other between them, leaves neither without the feel and pleasure he has to offer. When he releases my tit to drag his mouth to the other, my hand finds the back of his head, fisting his hair to press him closer.

He releases me only for a moment to sit back and admire them. "Fuck, I can't get enough of these tits. You're so beautiful, Aubree."

His words rush to my pussy, and I need to see more of him. My fingers hook around the elastic of his shorts, but before I can pull them down, he grabs my hand and leads me to the bed, laying me on my back. Hot kisses trail over my face and my chest, and I draw in a sharp breath as Mateo's fingers slightly graze over the sides of my bikini bottoms.

"Is this okay?" he asks, stopping himself before he goes any further. When I nod in agreement—too focused on the need to feel his touch to speak—he slowly lays a wet, lingering kiss on my lips as he forces my legs further apart before drawing the fabric to the side to expose my dripping pussy to the hot air in the cabin.

"Shit," he breathes. He leans over to get a better view of its sleekness, and I feel his hand flex on my thigh as he tries to resist the urge to explore more.

I pull Mateo back down to me, sending his lips crashing back into mine. He only obliges for a moment before pulling away, breathless.

"Open your mouth for me, sweet girl." On command, I do as he says and let out a moan as his middle and ring fingers slide over my tongue. My eyes lock with his as I let the need to please fully take over me, and I wrap my tongue around them before slowly sucking them between my lips—not that he needed the lubrication anyway. He basks in the way my lips form around his fingers, and the way his mouth parts when I flick my tongue over the tips of them, sending his erection jerking against me.

Mateo slips his fingers from my mouth, replacing them with his tongue as his fingers finally slide over my plump clit and through my lips, spreading them until he finds my entrance and thrusts a finger inside, causing me to arch with desperation as I groan into his mouth. Before I can reach for my clit, his palm rests against it, grinding as he pumps in and out. Releasing from him, I cry out as a second finger slides in, and he moves faster against me.

"Oh, fuck. Mateo," I whine. "Don't stop, please."

"Fuck, I love the way you say my name like that." He slides a third finger inside me, and I can't help but fall into another fit of moans. "Mmm, your pussy is so wet. I love that shit."

Mateo keeps a steady pace, but the pressure in me keeps building as I move against his hand as he presses further. His tongue flicks at my nipple, nipping and tugging between his sucks and swallows. Each quick pass of his tongue and the way he rocks his palm against my sensitive clit pushes me closer to climax, my chest rising and falling as I try to catch up before it takes over me. I just need a little longer.

"Please, I'm gonna come." I grab onto his forearm as it threatens to wash over me.

"Come, *manamea*. Let me see how pretty you look when you do," he says, moving my hair out of my face.

"Oh, fuck!"

I arch off the bed, Mateo still pumping against me as I come, spilling over his fingers as I cry out in pleasure. I hold his arm there as I catch my breath and allow myself to come down while he trails soft kisses over my shoulder.

"Does your magic wand do that?" Mateo questions mockingly before sliding his fingers out.

I giggle as I sit up on my elbows. "Shut up. Fuck, I really needed that."

He reaches down to grab a towel and starts to clean me up just as the bell rings for the next block. Mateo takes his time, and I let him as I enjoy watching him care for me.

"What about you?" I ask, realizing that he didn't get off.

"Don't worry about me. Pleasing you is more than enough."

He kisses me sweetly before dropping his head down. "Had we more time, I would have shown you what else I can do," he whispers in my ear before getting up and stealing my breath away with him.

Chapter 26

The storm pounds at the windows as it rages over the camp. I wanted to use this time to relax and take a well deserved nap, but that's nearly impossible with 10 screaming girls and the smell of nail polish filling the humid space. So, I decided to spend my time reading the revised versions of Valarie's poems and short stories while she sits on the bed next to me, eagerly awaiting my feedback. I shake my head as her leg bounces up and down on the mattress.

"Well?" she asks, and I have to stifle a laugh at the vibrato in her voice from how hard she's shaking her leg.

"Do you think you were a chihuahua in a past life?" I remark.

She does that teenage eye roll that says 'nobody asked you for all that', and now I understand why my mom hated it whenever I did it. But at least it got her to stop bouncing her leg.

"Sorry," I chuckle. "But you're anxious for nothing. Like I said before and for the umpteenth time, your writing is impeccable and there's nothing to change. Don't sweat it."

She picks up one of the sheets of paper scattered on the bed. "But what about this?" She points to a stanza on the page, and I shrug, clueless as to what she's referring to. It looks the same as the last ten times I read it.

Valarie huffs in frustration as she shoves the paper closer. "I moved the 'I' to the second line instead of ending it on the first? Couldn't you tell the difference in fluidity? It's literally in your face."

My chin cocks back at the shift in attitude in her voice. "Okay, I think we need a breather. I'm down to help you, but there's no need to take your frustration out on me. I may be your friend, but I'm also your counselor. Either way, it's not cool."

Her head hits the wall behind her as her eyes close. "I know. I just want it to be—"

"Perfect." The word slips from our mouths in tandem. "Yeah, I know the feeling. Trust me when I say you *will* smash this contest because your writing is special."

She peeks at me. "Amanda Gorman special?"

"Eh." Valarie leans over with a groan, cracking me up. "No, but seriously, stop comparing yourself. It's okay to study your influences, but you don't need to be them. Your world, your experiences, are unique to you. When you compare, you lose yourself. And when you lose yourself, you risk losing the thing you love."

The words hang heavy in the air, but offer solace I didn't know I needed. The thought comes so easily to me, but it's been difficult to put into practice over the last few months. Just when I'd think I'm at the cusp of freedom, I'm sucked back into the chamber I call my mind. I've compared myself in vain since I was old enough to realize—against my will—that I was bigger than other kids. As I got older, I outgrew the habit, but made friends with the haunt of perfection. It took the shape of AJ at some point, and it was like being stuck in the eye of a hurricane. I came out of it with my self image intact, but I questioned more than ever if I can trust again and trust myself to know when to let go of my ego rather than trying to save face. I know that I'm not a perfect person, but for so long, I blinded myself with the belief that I am. A small part of me still hangs on to the idea, but the more time I spend at camp, and the closer I get to Mateo, the looser the cord that ties me to it.

Out of the corner of my eye, I catch movement outside the window. I slowly lift my head to see what it is, but when I peer over, there's nothing but the pounding of the rain. Just as I'm looking away, there's more movement, and this time I catch a glimpse of the top of an umbrella. Discreetly, I move over to the window, making sure not to fully face it, only to be greeted with Mateo's smiling face as he holds the umbrella up like a trophy. He gestures for me to come outside, and I shake my head as I try to suppress the giddiness brewing within me—begging for trouble. Mateo clasps his hands together, raising to his toes in a plea. I quickly scan the room behind me; the girls are occupied either napping on top of their freshly made beds or chatting about whatever gossip they didn't finish at breakfast. When I swing my body more to the left, I jump slightly as I notice Valarie behind me watching the entire altercation.

"What the hell, V," I exclaim, my voice breathy as my hand clasps over my heart. "You scared me."

"Did I scare you, or is your heart racing full of love?" Valarie sings.

"You scared me," I say firmly. Mateo throws up his hands as I turn around to undo the knotted curtain so that it falls straight, covering the window. I hope that he could see the apology in my expression as his face disappears as the curtain flows shut.

"That goofy smile on your face when you saw him says otherwise." Her braids brush my face as she flips her hair with confidence before walking back to the bed to collect her pages.

"Love is out of the question. We hardly know each other, and we're simply spending quality time together," I say, dropping my voice just above a whisper as I follow behind her.

"But why? You do know each other. You went to school together."

"We were kids then. We're adults now, and we didn't really get along then."

"But you kissed?" Valarie raises her voice a little too loud for comfort.

"Will you be quiet?" I hiss as I look around the room, as if everyone didn't already know Mateo and I have been closer than two coworkers should be lately. "And why do you even know that? Have you been talking to Sasha?"

"Don't look at me like that." She shuffles the papers, gathering them at her stomach. "I didn't commit a crime."

Valarie scurries off before I can reprimand her and squeeze more information out of her about what they've been discussing about me. I accept that she at least was honest, but I can't let go of the thought of loving Mateo. Of course, I've thought of it—and if this were a different place or time, maybe it would go that route. I thought I had completely left the idea alone, but now I'm questioning if anything that I've told myself about him and our inevitable end is true. What would it look like if I—no. It's too late to go down that road and reconsider what's already been decided. This is a one time thing, nothing more. Enjoy it while it lasts.

Speaking of, my curiosity pulls at me to look and see if Mateo still happens to be standing outside the window. He is, as to be expected, and his smile seems to grow even wider at my reappearance. I click my tongue against my teeth as I pull my rain boots from underneath the bed, stepping into them as I grab my jacket and umbrella.

The rain has lightened up since the few moments it took me to get dressed and outside. As I round the corner of the cabin, trying my best not to slip on the now muddy path, Mateo stands soaked from the waist up. I can't keep myself from laughing at the sad image while he continues to grip the umbrella that does absolutely nothing to protect him. The laugh turns diabolical when he walks forward, his socks squishing in his shoes.

"This is funny to you?" he asks, failing at hiding his own laugh.

"You look like you just came out of the lake," I say as I try to catch my breath.

"Well, it's your fault." He points. "You left me out here like some beggar."

"I mean, you were begging, were you not?"

"That might be true," he says, flashing a smile before reaching out to cup my cheek. His thumb tracing over my bottom lip. "But it's nowhere near as hot as the way you begged last night."

Mateo closes his mouth over mine, pulling me in deeper as my insides turn to slush.

"You're amazing, you know that?" He says more like a statement than a question.

"It might be my greatest superpower." I look up at the pathetic excuse of an umbrella Mateo is holding and pluck it from his hand, handing him mine, which is big enough for three. "Sorry, but I can't look at this thing anymore. You really need a new one," I say, realizing a few of the metal rods are broken as I close it.

Mateo moves in to keep us both dry. "That's okay. It still works for the most part, so it'll do for now."

"Mateo, this thing is falling apart, and it doesn't even keep you dry." I gesture to his sopping wet tennis shoes as we start walking away from the cabins aimlessly. Looking at them, I'm worried that he doesn't have another pair.

"Hmm, I'll think about it."

My fingers intertwine with his, stealing some of his warmth. "You do know it's okay to have new things, right?"

"Yeah, I just don't think I need a new umbrella, especially since I'm usually not out much."

"Then take mine," I declare. "I have another one at home, and I brought a raincoat anyway."

"I can't—"

"Stop saying you can't," I say, taking a page out of his book. "Some things may seem small, but that doesn't mean they aren't a priority, especially if that small task means helping yourself. You always take such good care of everyone. I'm not taking no for an answer."

He sighs as we stop in front of the greenhouse. "I know. It's not easy for me. I'm so used to putting things off because I figure there are bigger problems that need solving, and they usually aren't mine. I'm trying to do better, though—at being more honest—and that's actually why I was coming to see you."

He pulls out a thin, blue book from the inside of his jacket and hands it to me. *Hamlet.*

"It was my grandfather's," he adds, nodding down towards it. "He gave it to me when I first got to Samoa. It's what started my collection of his plays and some other awesome playwrights I found."

The corners of my mouth cork up. "Let me guess, it was because you kept complaining that you were bored and there was nothing to do?"

"Ouch, and no." He places his hand over mine, claiming my attention. "It was because of you."

"Me?" I question, pointing to myself.

"Will you always look so shocked when I bring you up in my past?" he teases.

"I mean, can you blame me? I went years thinking you were obnoxious by nature—and you are—but I didn't think past that."

"Are you glad you did?"

I run my tongue along my bottom lip before sucking it between my teeth. "Finish your story first."

"Since you asked so nicely," he says as he rolls his eyes. "I think my grandfather could sense I missed Coventry Falls a little more than for the town itself. Long story short, I told him about you and he gave me the book, and—anyway, what I'm trying to say is that I wasted so much of my time not following through when it came to you. Back then, I didn't know how to approach you, so I did the next best thing—which I know now wasn't the greatest—and it wasn't fair to you. Still, I blame myself for holding back, and even now I still feel myself falling back into that pattern because it's easier to pretend and joke around than say how I feel."

"Like Hamlet," I whisper, running my hand over the cover. My chest grows heavy as I bring myself to look up at Mateo, who beams with admiration that warms every inch of my body. He takes my hand in his, running his thumb over my knuckles, but my pulse only quickens.

"Aubree, you said before you want to know who I am; this is it. Obviously, you can tell it's my favorite read, but it's my favorite because of you. It made me realize how much time I'd wasted not being upfront about my feelings and how I spent most of it second guessing myself. I don't want to do that anymore, not with you, and even if it's just for now."

I thumb the pages at the corner of the book as I let out a slow, steady breath through my mouth, but all of the breathing in the world can't stop the tears that well in my eyes. Dammit. When did I become such a crybaby?

"I didn't mean to make you cry," he says softly as my vision begins to blur. "I know it's a lot, but after last night, I didn't want to hold anything else back from you."

I force my eyes off the ground to look at him. "It's not that. I just don't understand why you never told me any of this sooner," I exclaim in frustration.

"'Conscience doth make cowards of us all.'" Mateo smiles, a glossiness in his eyes. "I never thought I was good enough then. But I knew I could never move on until I tried."

I shake my head. "Okay, now you're just trying to make me cry."

Mateo's arm wraps around me like a blanket as he lets out a laugh. My eyes flutter shut as I press my ear against his chest, relying on the steady rhythm of his heart to bring me a similar strength, for it reassures me that I'm safe.

"Mateo." I exhale as the tears dry up. "This is beautiful, thank you. Thank you for trusting me, and thank you for everything, really."

"No, thank you, *manamea*. You make me feel like I can be whole with you."

"Your jacket," I say, swiping at where the fabric absorbed some of the tears.

"It's okay. I'm one step closer to matching my bottom half." He smiles sweetly.

I offer one of a similar kind, capturing his hand in mind. "Since you were so honest, I want you to know that I enjoy every moment with you. You've been so understanding, which makes me feel a little bad."

"I don't want to pressure you, I just needed to get that off my chest."

"Good. I'm glad you did." I lift myself onto my toes, grabbing onto his shoulders for support as I give him the softest kiss.

CHAPTER 27

In the background, I hear my dad yell at the television. From the sounds of it, I know he's watching one of his stories again. While other dads are big on sports, mine found guilty pleasure in soap operas and reality TV—an obsession he gained after meeting my mother. I love that about him. It made it so easy for us to bond together when I was growing up. Being an only child has its perks, but it can be super lonely, especially when you have to rely on your parents to be your first set of friends when you have none, or they're busy.

"What did you say, Ma? I couldn't hear you."

"Hold on." There's shuffling followed by a door closing before her voice comes over the phone again. "Sorry, baby, your dad is loud as usual." I can hear the irritation in her voice. "I told him to go in the basement with all that shouting, but no. He has to have an equal distance from the kitchen to the bathroom."

"Ma."

"Oh, right. Sorry. I was saying that I haven't gotten anything, honey. No emails, nothing."

I sigh, anxious for some answers. "What about their website? Did they publish anything about new staff joining or anything like that?"

"No. I'm sorry, Aubree. I know you're anxious for answers."

"No, it's fine," I say, although I'm really trying to convince myself. "It's been almost three months, and no one from the Franklin has contacted me. I just don't understand why they wouldn't say anything to me. I've had a good relationship with the editor since freshman year. We're on a first name basis!"

"I know, but maybe this is a blessing. You did get that position at The Intersect. Are you still thinking of taking it?"

"I don't know," I say quickly, changing the subject. "How's everything at home?"

"It's been fine. We aren't doing much of anything these days besides work. Is camp everything you thought it'd be?"

My hand twirls around the phone cord, and I can't help the obvious smile in my voice when I reply. "It's great. Better than I thought."

The click and flash of a camera goes off beside me. Mateo stands there holding the camera up to his eye, angling it in my direction. I wave at him to go away, but he keeps on, taking another photo.

"What? You look so beautiful today," he says in admiration. "I had to."

"Go away," I whisper.

"Who was that?" My mother asks, nosy as she is.

"Nobody, Mama. Just some campers talking to each other. You know how kids get in close quarters sharing the same air and all." I muster up a fake laugh as I stumble out the excuse.

"Is that your mom?" Mateo asks, coming closer to the phone.

"Oh, it looks like we're getting ready to leave. Gotta go, love you!" I slam the phone on the hook before Mateo can step any closer.

"That wasn't dramatic at all," he remarks playfully as he drops the disposable camera into his backpack.

"You say dramatic, I say saving myself from a long winded conversation about my love life."

"Why not? Parents love me."

I eye him, admiring his strong, lean frame as he stands against the wall. "That's besides the point. I was calling to see if my mom had heard anything about the Franklin Gazette."

His cocky expression slowly shifts to one of concern. "Nothing yet?"

I shake my head, and he pulls me into his side, kissing the top of my head as I move past him to leave the phone box. "I need to just give it up. It's just so hard to let it go. I put so much of my life into the Franklin Gazette, and they just cut all contact? It's shady, or maybe that's business."

"What about that other publication? The Intersect?"

"It's my only real option. What other choice do I have? I should have applied to more places." I brush my hands over my temples.

I can plan out anything—predict the outcome of pretty much everything—but this I didn't bother to consider. Now I'm stressed and stiff, and I need a week long nap. On top of that, I'm extra cranky because I've been spending the past few nights on the steps of the cabin reading

Mateo's notes on *Hamlet*. But it's more like a diary, and there's so much I want to ask him since we haven't had much alone time lately, starting with his concept that love changes a person's destiny. If I'm being completely honest with myself, I've never seen love that way, and I can't stop thinking about why I haven't until now. I'd have to find another time as the sight of the buses pulling up to the camp entrance reminds me that I need to get the campers together for our field trip to the Science Center.

After making sure my cabin had cleaned up their bedding areas and taking them for a last minute bathroom break, we make our way to the front where the buses are lined up and campers are filing in. I haven't been to the Science Center since I was about 12, so I'm mostly relying on Kennedy to be my unofficial guide since she worked there part time. I'm excited to see what's new, especially now that I have my own money to spend on unnecessary things from the gift shop that I'll never use or see again.

As my campers climb onto their bus, Mateo appears beside me, strands of hair from the bun piled on his head coming loose.

"Do you want to ride with me?" Mateo points to his red Mustang, shining just the same as it did the first day we got here, and I wonder if he comes out here sometimes to wipe the dust off.

"How did you swing that with Josh?" I question as I escort the last of my campers on the bus.

"Faith, trust…" I narrow my gaze at him. "He trusts me."

"He'll regret that later," I laugh.

"Fine, I told him he could drive it back—with me in the car, obviously."

I smirk. "I don't know. Are you sure it's a good idea to leave Axel on his own?"

Looking up through the bus window, Axel pretends he's a duck with two Pringles wedged between his lips to look like a beak. The other campers around him snicker and egg him on to what is now transforming into a walrus bit as he takes out two pretzel sticks from his backpack and sticks them in his mouth. Really, he's harmless when he's not getting into trouble or the cause of someone's stress, but he can also be a handful.

"I think he'll be okay on his own for 30 minutes," Mateo suggests.

"Really? Because you left him with me for 5 minutes and he vanished."

"Oh, so you've got jokes now?" He crosses his arms as amusement spreads across his face, widening his soft features.

"No jokes, just facts," I tease through a shared laugh that coasts between us.

"Fair, but I really do want you to come with me."

"I know, but I can't. I promised Kennedy and Sasha I'd sit with them. I have to balance my relationships efficiently or I'll never hear the end of it."

"Are you saying we're in a relationship?" His signature smirk makes its reappearance as he looks down at me, shameless.

He really can't help himself.

"You're always getting ahead of yourself," I say, as I climb the stairs to the bus.

"Or maybe I'm just miles ahead of you."

There's nothing to stop the taut grin that breaks free on my face and the bliss that trickles down my spine.

The Science Center is more fun than I remember as a kid. I'd honest-ly forgotten about the dome and how cool the projections are. When you're looking up like that in a dark room, you forget that you're inside and that it's all a picture. They even show movies on the dome some nights. It would be nice to come back here with Mateo once camp's finally over as a last, and more official, date. It's nice to sneak away and have small 'dates' when we can, but something more formal would be nice too.

While the campers are eating lunch, Kennedy and I decide to head to the gift shop for a little browsing before we eat something ourselves. It was much bigger than I recall. Full of fun trinkets and toys, and some things I think Mateo might like. But what I was really looking for was the thing I always wanted to try as a kid.

"Oh my god, they still have it!" I pick up the shiny silver bag and hold it up to Kennedy. "Look!"

She narrows her eyes. "That's what you dragged me down here for?" I nod my head enthusiastically. "It's just a freeze dried ice cream sand-wich."

"Exactly! I always wanted to try it when I was younger, but I could never get it, and now I can." I look over the rest of the section. "They even have mint! Do you think I should get them all? I'm gonna get them all, Mateo might want to try some too." I squeal a little as I pull one of each flavor off the rack. Two of each for both the cookies and cream and the mint chocolate chip.

"Okay, let's go before lunch is over. I'm starving."

"Did someone say starving?"

Kennedy and I whip our heads around to the sight of Mateo strutting over, holding two brown paper bags.

"Are you always lurking around every corner?" Kennedy asks with mock irritation.

"No, but I come bearing food for your kinship." The paper bags crinkle as he holds them out to us.

"In that case," Kennedy snatches one of the bags and heads off.

"You're not staying?" I question.

"Nope. You two love birds have fun without me."

I watch her walk off a distance before turning my attention to Mateo as I plant a soft kiss on his lips that quickly grows urgent. His hands come to my ass, squeezing and lifting before I lean back slightly out of his grasp.

I grab at his hands that still dig into my hips. "There are kids here."

"You're right," he says. "Let's go to the car."

He pulls my hand toward the direction of the exit. "Hold on. Lunch is over in like 30 minutes, and I haven't eaten."

"We'll just loop around the block, I promise." He crosses his heart as he continues to lead me out to the parking garage.

"So, you expect me to tag along and sneak away with you?"

"That was the plan," he says sheepishly.

I eye him, puckering my lips as if it's really that hard of a decision. "Fine, but we're not leaving this block."

He pumps his fist in a silent victory before grabbing my hand again.

"You're ridiculous," I say. "How did you find me anyway?"

"Your laugh."

"Is that supposed to be a compliment?" I challenge.

Mateo glances down at me as if I should know better. "I could pick out your laugh in a crowd, *manamea*. It's sweet with sultry undertones. Smooth when it's casual, but round and vast when you're really comfortable. Light and airy when you're enjoying yourself and think no one's watching."

CHAPTER 28

After finishing my lunch and circling the area for the fifth time, Mateo pulls over on a side street that just overlooks the lake. I don't mind the opportunity to stretch my legs as he opens my door and offers me his hand. The breeze coming off the lake is a cool contrast against the beating sun. The only thing that would make this better is a real ice cream sandwich, especially when it can distract me from the way my heart is beating out of my chest. The way Mateo described such a small part of me, like it was the easiest thing in the world, sent a swarm of butterflies into my stomach. No one's ever paid so much attention to me that they could describe my laughter the way a painter would describe the stroke of their brush.

Mateo pulls me to his side and kisses the top of my head as it comes to rest against him. "This is such a beautiful day," he says, taking in a deep breath as we lean against a nearby railing.

"I know. I wish I had come out here more often if I wasn't so afraid of driving downtown. The streets are so confusing, but there's this restau-

rant that everyone's been raving about that I want to go to before I leave...
Are you listening to me?"

Mateo's eyes shift from where they were on my lips to my eyes. "Of
course. I'm just admiring that pretty mouth of yours."

Shoving him gently, he chuckles. "What's the point of talking if you're
just going to get distracted?"

"I could listen to you through every sunrise." His hands rest on either
side of me before lowering his lips to mine. I meet him for another before
relaxing back against the railing.

"Kissing you is great, but I want to know something more about you,"
I say as he continues to loom over me.

"I'm listening." His voice is teasing.

Ignoring him, I ponder on what I've been asking myself for the past
few days. "I've been reading through your notes—several times, actually—and you say a lot of interesting things, but you commented on love
a lot. Isn't *Hamlet* a tragedy?"

"I couldn't disagree with that." He shrugs.

"Are you going to elaborate, or are you going to make me work for it?"
He raises an eyebrow, and I can tell he's thinking up all the ways in which
he could make that happen. "Please? I'm trying to get in your head."

He faces me, looking into my eyes as if they hold the answers. "'Where
love is great, the littlest doubts are fear; Where little fears grow great,
great love grows there.'" Mateo pauses for a moment like he's letting
the words sink in—become a part of him. "If to love is to fear and to
fear is to love, then love and fear are intertwined—almost inseparable.
We see how Hamlet struggles to make up his mind. He also struggles
with the idea that the love he has is often overpowered by fear. He tries

to separate the two with logical and overwhelming complexities, but really, the validation he's looking for to avenge his father doesn't exist. It stops him from getting revenge, and it not only kills him, but it also kills Ophelia in the process. I think it's because he allowed his fears to overshadow love; for greatness, for his father, Ophelia... Love can change the course of our destiny, and it allows paths to align, but so can fear."

I pick at the paint on the railing, somewhat jealous and impressed at his analysis. "But what if Hamlet didn't love at all? Maybe he was enraptured by the allusion to it through the great poets and writers he looked up to. Then would he really be operating out of fear and love, or fear and the chase for perfection?"

"A good point, but isn't perfectionism just the fear of failure?"

"Touché," I remark as my arms fold over my chest.

"Too close to home?"

"Moving on," I sigh as he lets out a slow chuckle. "Let's say fear and love do go together. Eventually, one snuffs out the other like you said."

"In the case of Hamlet, yes, it can lead to insanity at its extreme. Still, one can't exist without the other, and I know because the fear of completely losing out on my chances with you brought me back here."

A lump forms in my throat. Anxious and dazed, my eyes lock with his. "Don't say that."

"Why? It's the truth." He reaches for my hand, pressing his palm into mine. "I came back for a lot of reasons, but no matter what I did, I never forgot you. I can't. Coventry is my first home, but it's not the cause of the beating in my heart when I'm there. The fear of losing what I never had but always wanted brought me to you, and it will time after time. If we're moving forward, we can't keep running back."

Every thought that jets through me feels wasted compared to what he gave me. For so long, I let fear in like a thief in the night. Cutting away at my ability to live freely, chaining me to the routine of shaming what I believed to be superficial wants, writing them off as selfish in favor of the skewed perception of what I was meant for. There is no running, and there's no denying what I now know to have been there all along, waiting to be sparked to life. Assurance, humility, and the space I needed to learn how to follow my heart without the chains.

I think I'm falling in love with him.

"What did you say?"

"What?" I question, furrowing my brows.

Mateo's smile widens. "You just said you're in love with me."

My heart drops as desire dances across his expression. "No, I didn't," I say quickly, pushing off the railing and out of his reach.

"I heard you, and as you know, my hearing is impeccable."

Oh, I wish I could wipe that stupidly handsome and cocky grin off of his face, and I would if I wasn't too busy spiraling over the fact that I indeed said that out loud. Fuck, my stomach hurts.

"We should get going." I hurry to the car, biting down on a nail. Is it really a bad thing that he knows, though? It's not like I said I love him, just that I was falling. Two completely different things. I knew I should have listened to my mom when she told me to stop talking to myself.

Dolefully, my weight transfers from one foot to the other as I wait beside the car door and try to ignore the fact that we might actually be late if he doesn't hurry up. As usual, Mateo is in no rush as he takes long strides towards me, wrapping his arms around my waist and lowering his mouth to mine in the warmest kiss before cupping my face in his hands.

His forehead rests against mine, disrupting the magnitude of the desire that rouses in me. "You know it's okay, right?"

"Yeah, I'm still getting used to that..." I bite down on my lip. "Things being okay."

Mateo pulls me into a hug before kissing the top of my head. "I know."

"We should go," I say, pulling away from him.

Mateo obliges me by opening the car door for me to slip inside, and we're back onto the road with ease. Although my head is still reeling with embarrassment that my own mouth would betray me with such a heavy confession, it's hard to sit still in my seat as childlike glee skips through my veins. I never imagined I could feel so light and energized after openly admitting that what I feel growing more fierce by the second is love. It's different than before, and it's scary, but I drink it down anyway like it's the promise of immortality.

Glancing over at him, I bite down on the inside of my cheek to ease some of the pain from smiling so hard. When he notices, his hand slides onto my thigh.

"Why are you so happy?" he questions.

"A girl can't be happy without a reason?"

He chuckles low. That, alongside the angle I'm looking at him from and the way his pinkie caresses my inner thigh, sends my arousal through the roof. You always see moments like this in films and TV shows, but nobody ever mentions just how hot it is in person. The way his hand grips the wheel, the long veins coming up his forearm from the pressure, the tiny smolder he has because he's so focused on the road. Fuck, I'm needy.

Reaching over, I slide my hand into his lap, moving slowly enough that it grazes his cock. Mateo glances over at me as I suck in my bottom lip with innocence.

"Aubree?"

"Hmm?" I say. My focus is still on teasing him with gentle caresses.

He sighs as I feel him hardening with each passive graze. "Don't start what you can't finish."

I smirk at how he underestimates me, which only grows more sinister by the gasp that escapes him when I finally palm him through his pants. "Baby, I'm just getting started."

Unbuttoning his pants, I find my way into his boxers, springing his cock free from their constraint, and giving him no time to prepare as sighs and moans file out of him with every long stroke of my fist around his cock, and all I care about is making him come.

"Fuck, that's good." Mateo grasps at my thigh, and seeing the pleasure on his face as he tries his hardest to stay focused on the road only excites me. The cum already dripping from his cock allows me to speed up my movements, twisting and pumping at a steady pace.

"I need to see you come for me, Mateo." His eyes close briefly at my notion, and I lick my lips with the need to see him lose control for me the way I do for him.

When we come to a stoplight, he pulls me to him, our lips meeting roughly as his moans fall into my mouth. I only part from him briefly to pull my shirt up and unclasp my bra in the process. The moment my breasts drop, Mateo's cock jerks in my hand, and the way he throws his head back makes my core ache. He pulls himself together long enough to notice the light turn green again.

"Don't hold back for me, baby. Come for me," I moan into his ear.

"Fuck, Aubree!"

I slightly cover the tip of him with my fist, allowing his cum to drip down my hand and between my fingers. Beautiful.

I dust kisses down his throat as his breathing comes down in time enough to make the next stoplight. Mateo squeezes my thigh once again before taking my hand to his mouth and licking his cum from my fingers. The gesture alone has my panties soaked through.

My tongue runs over my bottom lip as my gaze falls to his cock, still hard and glistening; my mouth waters at the thought of what he tastes like. I don't give it a second thought before my mouth is around him, sucking at the tip.

"Ah, shit." His hips thrust upward, forcing more of him into my mouth, and I try not to choke on his depth.

My tongue swipes over his shaft, licking up as much of him as I can as my head bobs up and down his length. He groans when his cock meets the back of my throat, causing him to thrust his hips, sparking the corners of my eyes to water as I will myself to take more of him.

"Holy—"

I twist around him as his hand runs through my hair, his cock jerking with pleasure and the need to come again. I thrust him into the back of my throat again, swallowing as I do and sending him over the edge. His warm cum seeps down the back of my throat as I pull up and release his cock with a *pop*.

"Mm, I've been wanting to do that for a while." I wipe at the corners of my mouth when I notice Mateo turning onto a side street.

"And you think I'm going to let you without my fix?" Mateo throws the car into park and reaches over to bring my lips to his before reaching down to slide my seat back.

"We're going to be late. We have like eight minutes." My breath catches in my throat at the feel of Mateo's mouth closing around my nipple. He pops one out of his mouth in exchange for the other, making me lose my train of thought completely.

"I only need three," he says. "But if you want me to stop, I will."

"Don't," I moan, barely above a whisper. "Please."

His eyes darken as a grin snakes across his face. "Anything you want."

He lays me back against the door with rough kisses, his fingers working to undo the button of my shorts before sliding the fabric down to my ankles. I rest my legs over the center console when Mateo's hands come to my knees, spreading them open for all of him to see. His hungry eyes land right where I need him as he lets out a low hum of approval.

"God, you're already soaked. You really do love me." Mateo's voice dances with a hint of amusement.

"Shut up," I snicker as the heel of my foot jabs into his side.

"What? You teased me, and now I can't get my turn?"

"I—Oh!" My words are lost as Mateo's fingers press against my clit through the fabric of my panties, moving in a slow, torturous circle.

"Oh."

The kiss that comes after washes over me with thoughtlessness as the pressure of his fingers only builds a pressure of its own within me. Despite the uncomfortable position, my body pleads for more of him in a way that I hadn't felt in too long. There was no panic, no guilt, only pure yearning. A wish that I had long forgotten.

"I need to taste you, babe." The words leave his lips just as fast as my panties are off, and his mouth spreads kisses of fire along my inner thigh. My hands run through his thick hair as I watch him hone in on my pussy once again. "Fuck, it's so much prettier up close."

Mateo spreads me open, his mouth falling open as I feel the slickness of my pussy fall to the curve of my ass. He looks back up at me, his eyes never leaving mine as he lays a single kiss at my core, sucking gently as he pulls away.

A shiver travels down my body, and my grip on his hair tightens. "Please, Mateo."

I don't care how needy I sound, I'm not below begging at this point. I need to come, and I want him to have every last drop.

Exhaling sharply, my back arches against the door as his tongue dips into me, a playfulness at my entrance. The way his mouth works to suck and pull at my lips—his tongue only teasing with brisk passes over my clit—has me rethinking if I've ever even had a real orgasm before with anything other than a toy. But when he presses further into me, his tongue exploring deeper, I know it for a fact that nothing would top the feel of his mouth on me.

Mateo moans over my clit before latching on, spending my hips up into him. "Uh, yes! That's it."

His hands knead at my flesh as he continues to suck and lap at my entrance. I truly think I've reached a place a bliss until his fingers plunge inside me, caressing me where only I've ever been able to find.

"Shit, shit, shit." My moans turn into pleading as I rock against him, the groans escaping him sending me further into my climax when a third finger enters me and—*fuck*. "I have to come."

That phrase alone seems to work magic as his fingers begin to curl inside me, and his tongue flicks over my clit with fervor. My chest rises and falls in short breaths as the pressure climbs to new heights. He pins my hips to gain full control over my orgasm.

"Mateo, I'm gonna—" The cry that leaves my throat fills my ears as his fingers slide out of me, his tongue quickly moves over my entrance, lapping up my cum as my orgasm jerks through me.

When I start to come down, Mateo doesn't part from me without leaving gentle and satisfied kisses down my pussy and up my thighs before finally finding my mouth once again. I suck on his bottom lip, tasting the saltiness of my cum on it.

"You're amazing," he whispers between a few more peaks.

"Me? I don't think I've ever come that hard."

"It helps when the participant is as sexy as you." A smile spreads across my face as I give him one more long and deep kiss. We are definitely going to be late, and we'll definitely deal with the consequences later, but the only thing I can think of is when I can find the time to have him again.

Fuck my stupid rules and a five year plan, but thank fuck for tinted windows.

CHAPTER 29

"Care if I save the rest of the fudge filled marshmallows for myself?" Sasha asks. Although I'm not sure why she bothers asking, since she's already shoving the bag into her backpack.

"Be my guest," I laugh. "There are only two more weeks left anyway, and the last week is the trip to the county fair. I don't think Josh will miss them."

"He's been running around like he lost his head all day. I doubt he'd notice," Kennedy says as she snags an unopened bag for herself. I give her a funny look, to which she shrugs. "What? You said it yourself, they won't be missed."

"I didn't take you as a thief," I rebuttal.

"Considering what they're paying us to work here, these marshmallows are compensation to make up for it. Do you know how hard these are to find in stores?"

"Whatever, but no more. I don't need a guilty conscious," I say.

"*She says while she fucks the camp counselor next door,*" Kennedy narrates, causing Sasha to snicker as I shoot daggers in their direction.

"I'm taking this box outside," I mumble, leaving their laughter at my back.

I march the surprisingly heavy bags of popcorn and candy outside to the Quad. A team of men are still setting up the inflatable screen for the movie projector, and there's a small thud of sadness as I remember we're watching *Chicken Little*. It wasn't my first choice, obviously, but unfortunately, the decision was Josh's.

As I'm walking, I step on something squishy and hear a sharp yelp and growl from behind me. Sweetly, a smile creeps across my face when I turn and find Penelope grabbing at her foot.

"Oh, it's just you," I breathe with satisfaction.

"Yeah, it's me. Watch were the fuck you're going next time," she spits, rubbing the top of her foot.

I readjust the box that's starting to cause a burning strain in my arms. "Or you could learn to stay out of my way."

"You just think you can get whatever you want, don't you?" Penelope steps closer.

"It's obvious you think I do, so why not?"

"Well, the world doesn't revolve around you and what you want. You're not as in demand as you want everyone to believe, so back off."

"Excuse you?" The box makes a thud as it hits the ground beside me. "It was clearly an accident. I didn't see you. I get it, you hate seeing me have the one thing you can't; you've been pissy about it for weeks. Get over it."

As she moves in, I notice the mascara smudged at the corners of her eyes. "At least I know better than to mistake being a cum rag for affection."

My hands form into fists at my side as I step closer to her. The sweet glory I taste from being so close to doing what I should have done a long fucking time ago falls from the tip of my tongue as a hand wraps around my wrist. I attempt to pull away, fully ready to face whatever the consequences may be for one easy high I can ride for a lifetime, but Mateo's hold is firm enough to keep me in place.

"Don't," he whispers close to my ear.

I stare at him in disbelief, my anger still bubbling over and expanding by the second. "Are you seriously sticking up for her?" I gesture.

Mateo lets go of my wrist and steps in front of me. "No, but I don't want to see you go home because of her shit, and I don't think you'd want that either."

Quickly, I glance over his shoulder at Penelope, whose expression dances with smug amusement. Mateo must sense the intensity of my chagrin because he steps closer to block my view of her and tilts my chin up to meet his gaze, his finger tips sliding down the side of my neck.

"I know it's hard, and I know you don't think I know, but I do. Now, if you want to kick off any other time, be my guest, but not tonight. I have a surprise."

I raise an eyebrow as a speck of keenness enters my bloodstream. No, I don't want to go home, but a part of me feels like I'm letting Penelope get away with her shit, again. Allowing her to do it now, especially after what she said, feels like I'm *letting* her walk all over me. Confirming that

I'm just as weak and inferior as she believes me to be. But Mateo's right, and I can't afford to be wrong right now.

My eyes drop to Mateo's mouth where I lay a soft kiss. "When did you become more reasonable than me?"

"Someone has to do it, but I can't lie—you're hot when you're pissed off." His solid frame presses against me as he pulls me in for another quick kiss.

I roll my eyes, letting out a laugh. "Forget to use a coaster and you'll see a lot more of that."

"Looks like we both know a good lap dog when we see one," Penelope says as she steps around us, because of course she can't go without another sly remark or the last word.

I step away from Mateo as I watch her go. "What the fuck is her problem lately anyway?" I question as I reach down for the box that Mateo slides toward himself to carry instead.

"Besides her usual issues? She and Gale have been fighting a lot. You didn't hear that yelling earlier?"

"No." I shrug. "I was inside and couldn't really hear much aside from the air pump."

"Well, it was pretty heated." Mateo walks in front of me to set the box down near the rest of the snacks on a foldout table where some other counselors are helping lay out blankets and set up mosquito repellents. "She ran past me crying. She looked really hurt."

"Don't tell me you care?" I ask as I start unpacking. "I'm sure whatever it is, she'll find a way to flip it to play the victim as always."

"I don't," Mateo says quickly in reassurance. "Still, I like gossip just as much as the next person."

"Mmm, or are you just trying to distract me from this so called 'surprise' you have for us?"

"For *you*," he corrects, his voice low in my ear, sending my nervous system into high gear as I shiver in delight. His arms come around my waist as he pulls me back against him.

More curious than ever now, I look up at him with a newfound eagerness. "Well, I'm not opposed to that. Tell me more."

"Uh uh, I don't want to ruin the surprise." He smirks.

"Surprise? Okay, now you have to tell me, or I'll get anxious."

"No can do. I want to see the look on your face when you realize falling in love is of no regret."

"You're too cocky, you know that?"

"Ambitious is a better word." He gives me a quick kiss before walking off in the other direction, ensuring I don't get the last word this time. Fortunately for him, I have a surprise of my own for him tonight.

Setting up takes a little longer than it's supposed to, but by the time we're done, there's a makeshift concessions stand including nachos and pizza. The blankets laid out over the grass are all occupied with campers piled on top of them with their friends. My friends and I sit closer to the back of the arrangement, where Beck and Maeve are already cuddled up and whispering to each other. I give them to the end of the opening scene before they sneak off and ask us to cover for them. Mateo, on the other hand, might just miss it as he's nowhere to be found.

"I don't remember the last time I saw *Chicken Little*. I had to have been like 13." Kennedy tosses a piece of popcorn in the air before catching it perfectly in her mouth.

"I think Bree and I were 10?" Sasha looks to me to confirm.

"Don't ask me, you were the one obsessed with it," I say, groaning at the memory of how many times I had to hear her sing *Wannabe* by the Spice Girls.

"You're one to talk, Miss I Own A Custom Painted Goofy Movie Denim Jacket," Sasha says pointedly.

Kennedy laughs. "What? How come I've never seen this jacket?"

"She refuses to wear it," Sasha replies.

"It's not meant for daily wear. It's for special occasions," I correct.

"And what special occasion do you need that kind of jacket for?" Kennedy challenges.

"Try Homecoming 2016," Beck says, taking a break from the bubble he and Maeve have created around themselves.

Kennedy gasps. "She did not."

"Oh, she did," Sasha says before she and Kennedy once again start cackling at my expense while I give Beck the hardest side eye I can muster. He mouths an apology after Maeve elbows him with a dirty look. While I hate being exposed like that, I can't help but join in too. The distraction is enough that I don't notice Mateo when he walks over until he's plopped down next to me, stealing my nachos in the process.

"What did I miss?" Mateo asks, licking cheese from his lips before smacking a kiss on my cheek.

"Nothing important," I say quickly, adding the distraction of a firm kiss to drown out the cackling from beside us. "Where were you? Can I know what the surprise is now? There was a surprise, right?"

I don't catch that my fists are balled in his shirt until he untangles them and takes my hands in his, soothing me. "You think I would lie about that? Especially after you confessed how in love you are with me?"

Mateo's teasing smile wraps my skin in a warmth that tingles all over, and I can't help but gush at how evilly precious he thinks all this is. "You're cute when you're annoying."

"Is 'cute' a code word for 'love'?"

I shoulder him and let out a giggle. "Stop. Now, tell me what the surprise is."

"Just watch," he answers in suspense.

"Watch what?" A blue screen appears on the projector screen, and my heart leaps as my favorite opening fanfare plays before the famous laugh. I squeeze Mateo's hand. "Shut up! You didn't?"

"I had to. I remembered it was your favorite growing up, and you used to hum the song to yourself sometimes." He squeezes my hand back, using the other to brush a few of my twists out of my face. "I love seeing you happy."

"Oh my gosh, you remember that?" My lip turns into a pout before pulling him in for a kiss.

"Aw, you guys are so gross... I love that." Sasha coos. "I'm happy to sacrifice *Chicken Little* for you."

"Oh, how thoughtful," I mock. "Maybe we can do a comfort movie marathon after this."

"Oooh, that'll be so fun," Maeve says. "I'm pitching for *Doctor Dolittle*."

"And add *Fat Albert* and *Princess Diaries*," Kennedy adds to the growing list.

I allow my friends to shoot movies back and forth as the list goes on and on, but my eyes are on Mateo, who has his eyes on me, reflecting the love and radiance I swore would never grow in the space between us that shortens day by day.

CHAPTER 30

I'm tentative to pull Mateo away from the movie as Max is 15 minutes away from getting his big moment with Powerline—my favorite part. But I've been planning this all week, and I wanted to do something special for Mateo before camp is officially over, especially after I realized just how much he's been doing for me. He didn't need to be kind to me after how I've treated him, but the fact that he never cared is what got us here, and I couldn't be more thankful.

"I can't believe you're dragging me away from the movie," he says, sounding more confused than excited.

"It's my *favorite* movie, and my *favorite* part is coming up, but I'm willing to skip it for this. Unless you wanna finish it?" Tugging him toward the empty cabin, I slide my hand behind the door frame for the key.

He shakes his head. "Maybe one of the other a thousand times you'll make me watch it."

I refrain from groaning at his comment as I unlock the cabin. "Okay, so I know I wasn't the fairest person to you at the start of camp—really, since the Belfry—but despite that, you never stopped trying with me. You've been there for me when I needed you, even when I swore you were the last person I wanted to see." Mateo chuckles to himself, his smile softening as he listens to me.

"You've taken care of me for the past four weeks, so I wanted to do something special for you this time." Pushing the cabin door open, the once empty cabin glows as it's now filled with candlelight. A pile of blankets and pillows rests neatly in the middle of the floor. Similar to the picnic he made before, but this time there's no food and a deck of cards.

Mateo gleams down at me. "Is this our 'chill' portion of the evening?" he asks, a slow seduction in his tone.

"Not necessarily what I was thinking." Mateo's hand grazes the small of my back as he makes his way inside. "But mostly, I thought I'd be nice to talk, spend some alone time together. I know it's not much, and I know you used to like board games, but I couldn't find any that didn't have pieces missing. I hope cards are okay—it's my personal deck."

His grin softens as he turns to face me, planting a kiss on my lips. "This is amazing," he says, wrapping his arms around me. "It's perfect, and more than enough."

"Good. I thought it would be nice since camp's almost over." The smile on my face doesn't help to suppress the disappointment that suddenly aches in my chest. Less than two weeks until camp is officially over. Until we're over. I spent so much of my time adamant that I didn't and couldn't want this to go further than it has. But with me accepting this new job and everything that's happened between Mateo and I—what he's made me realize about myself—I'm not sure I'm ready to let it all go. There's no denying how I feel, the way my entire body sings for him when he's near, like I can't get close enough to him. Mateo is the best thing I never saw coming, and I wouldn't have wanted my summer to happen any other way. Still, I haven't figured out how this will work for me, my plans, my future. Not to mention what it means for Mateo. I know he says he wants us, but what if it's too much?

Mateo kisses me again before releasing me as we move to cuddle up on the floor, and I begin to shuffle the cards.

"You have to let me do some things for you from now on. I feel so spoiled with you, not that I'm complaining." I rest against him and find comfort with the way the tips of his fingers lightly stretch my upper arm.

"You don't have to. I like doing things for you."

"I know," I agree. "But you like doing things for everyone. What happened to relaxing and coming back to Coventry to find the part of you that was missing?"

"You were that part," Mateo hums as he kisses my shoulder.

"You know what I mean."

He sighs. "I know, but it's hard. I'm so used to being the glue and putting everyone above myself. Sometimes, I'm afraid I act too fast or not fast enough, like I did when I separated our team on the first day. I still don't know what I was thinking."

"You thought you were doing what was in the best interest of the team. And to be fair, other teams did it too. But, yeah, I get it. I think I worry too much about what others will think or say. I was so sick of being overlooked, I guess I just snapped at some point and solely focused on being good enough." Sitting up, I hand Mateo the cards. "I put myself before others because I'm scared that if I don't, I'll lose out on the things I want. Now, I'm not so sure what that is."

"We're not so different. I'd say we both love the same." Our eyes meet briefly. It's not hard to tell that there's more to be said, and I've been the only one getting in the way of it.

"So, I'm sending the paperwork off tomorrow for that position with The Intersect." Taking a deep breath, I press my palms to my knees and let it go. "Mateo? I know that we agreed to end things when camp is over, and to stay friends, but I feel like there's more to it than that. Maybe we need to be more transparent about what we really want?"

The silence between us makes the pulsing in my temples more noticeable as it begins to ache in my neck. And the way Mateo's gaze stays trained on the wall behind me doesn't help the fact until he finally breathes the words I'm anxious to hear.

"I don't want it to end." I didn't imagine that what I'd already known would bring such relief. "But I don't want you to move to Columbus either."

Deafened, everything inside me tenses and falls away as his confession sticks to me, hot and hard. "Oh." I push myself back, keeping my distance.

Mateo does the same, sliding his hand down my arm to bring my hand into his lap. "And I would never ask you not to go. I knew what I was getting myself into when we agreed to this, and I'm okay with the outcome."

I shake my head. "No, Mateo, it's not okay." Trying to control my breathing, the air in the room is suddenly heavier than I recall as fear makes its dominating presence.

"It is, and I was prepared for things not to work out in my favor when I came to Coventry." Mateo tries to sound as reassuring as possible, but my stomach won't still. "Bree, I'm not trying to change your mind—"

"What am I supposed to say to that?" My voice quivers as I sharpen my gaze on Mateo. Mateo moves closer to me, but I turn out of his view from the fear that that quiver in my voice might become a hiccuping cry. I fiddle with a fringe on one of the blankets to distract myself from the growing ache in my chest.

"You don't have to look at me, but I'm not saying this to your back because I want you to know that I mean it." He moves to face me, grabbing my hand again. "I would never ask you to put your life on hold for me. Coming back here in hopes of sparking something familiar with you was a decision I made on my own, but it wasn't one I made lightly. My life will go on with or without you, but I'd never say no to you being in it—I don't care in what way. I love your ambition, your passion, your need to be who you are unapologetically, and I wouldn't take that away from you because then you wouldn't be the woman I love."

The fringe falls from my hands, unraveling from my fingers. "What?"

Mateo swallows as a glint of panic shines in his eye, then goes glossy. "I want you to live your life, and I know that that means I might come second sometimes—"

"Mateo," I say over him.

"But it's alright because I'd follow you anywhere if it makes you happy—"

"Mateo!" He inhales sharply, and I squeeze his hand, hoping to ease the worry stamped between his brows. But when I finally have his attention, I realize that I'm the one who's shaking.

My grasp on his hands stiffens, replacing fear with an eagerness that leaps at the back of my tongue. "You're not second. I care about my future, but I also care about you. There's no second place for you in my life because I know what that feels like, and I would never want to hurt you in that way. I am moving to Columbus, but that doesn't mean I'm leaving you behind or that I'm putting you last. I don't know where this will go after camp is over, but I want to try. I want this to work, and I'm not going to let a silly five year plan get in the way of it anymore, especially not when I love you too."

Mateo's hand comes to my chin, tilting it up so that my gaze is steady and sure. "Say that again."

"I know I can be a lot at times and demanding, and I need to work on that."

"Aubree—"

"Please, just let me finish," I plead, my heart beating rapidly. "I'm scared. I'm afraid of what I can't see, especially when it comes to love. But I love you. I'm in love with you, and I think deep down I've always known. I love you."

A weight lifts off my shoulders like a breath of fresh air, and the panic that contracted in my chest now beats with credence. The further I'm removed from my own uncertainty, the more incapable I am of withholding myself from the happiness weeding in the truth of my words. I'm in love with Mateo.

Mateo doesn't take his eyes off of me as I search for any semblance in his expression to tell me what he's thinking—what he's feeling. He doesn't say a word. Instead, the crescent of his beautiful smile crosses his face, and tears drop from his eyes.

"Mateo." I take his face in my hands, using my thumbs to wipe at his tears as they stream from his eyes.

"Sorry." He sniffs as he attempts to pull away from me, but I stop him before he can.

"Why are you apologizing?" I ask as I continue to caress his cheek. "It's nice to know you have more emotions than just that cocky grin of yours."

"Oh yeah?" he chuckles.

"Yeah."

Mateo's hand comes to my waist, electric and warm as he squeezes and pulls me toward him so that I'm sitting in his lap. He rounds to the small of my back and lays a soft kiss on my neck. "I love you," he whispers into my skin. A sigh escapes me as he lightly drags his tongue across my collarbone.

"I love you too." I shift so my legs are on either side of him, giving me enough height to dominate him as I pull him to me, sending his lips crashing into mine. I savor every breathless pass of our lips and release myself to him—something I should have done a long time ago.

Mateo squeezes at the handles of my stomach before his fingers curl under my shirt, gliding over my stretch marks. Sitting back, my eyes lock with the hunger in his as I peel my shirt off and toss it to the side. His eyes fall to my breasts, a small sigh escaping him.

"You're beautiful," Mateo whispers as his mouth falls over the curve of my neck, peppering kisses up my shoulder and behind my ear.

"Mateo, I need you," I sigh before bringing his face to mine, stealing another kiss as I rock back into him. "Say you need me."

Greedily, his cock jerks against my ass, and I oblige, continuing to grind my ass into him at the low groan that seeps in his throat. "I need all of you, Aubree."

My gaze meets his in challenge. "Then show me."

The warm air hits my nipples as Mateo single-handedly unclasps my bra, discarding it so that my breasts are in perfect alignment with his vision. Instead of his usual slow teasing, his mouth is quick to meet the peak of my nipple, sucking hard over the hurried swirl of his tongue. My head falls back as his grip on my breasts works to shove more of me into his mouth, but the ache for more only grows as the bulge in his pants brushes over my center. The moan that escapes him tells me that he's just as needy for it as I am.

Quickly, I rip his shirt from his body while he works at pulling off his pants. I pay extra close attention when he takes off his boxers, his cock springing free before its heaviness slaps back onto his stomach. Seeing him like this—the soft lines of his abs, the veins in his arms, the curve in his cock—almost makes me regret waiting so long.

"What?" Mateo's voice snaps me out of my thoughts. "Did you change your mind?"

"Fuck, no. I'm more than ready," I say, leaning down to cast a lingering kiss on his lips for reassurance. "Do you have a condom?"

Mateo's face pales as his hands run up my thighs. "Would you be upset if I said I'd been carrying one around for a week?"

I smile, shaking my head. "I'd say you're stupid and weird, but smart for being prepared."

Fishing the condom out of Mateo's pants pocket, I take my time rolling it over his tip and down his length; his sharp gasp at my touch sparks a sense of possession in me.

My hands slide over his chest, and I push myself up to pull off my shorts. Mateo's eyes track my every movement, leaving strokes of fire that move through to my core and down between my legs at the effect I have on him. Thankfully, I wore my good panties tonight, but soon those are lost too, and a trill of rapacity sounds from him. When I move to sit back on top of him, my pussy slick and ready for him, he stops me.

"No. I need to taste you first." His fingers direct me to move over him until he grabs me, tossing my leg up and over his shoulder. His tongue is on my clit before I can fully regain my balance.

"Ah—fuck, yes." My hand finds the back of his head as he continues to move and lap against me.

Mateo's hands find my ass, squeezing as he pushes me forward as if he can't get enough. The more his mouth tugs and pulls at me, his tongue dipping in and out lousily at my entrance, the harder it is for me not to collapse into him. He holds firm, diving deeper.

"Mmm, if you keep doing that, I'll come."

"Not yet. I need to feel you come around my cock this time, *man-amea*." He breathes out after getting one more long and antagonizing lick before he lowers my leg.

Without protest, I let him bring me to the floor, resting my knees on a pillow while my upper body falls onto the bed. When Mateo finally gets behind me, I push back when the tip of his cock brushes my ass.

"You're so fucking needy," he says through his teeth as he pulls my hips back toward him. "I love it."

He works the tip of his cock down the entrance of my ass and between the folds of my pussy, a wild moan escaping me. "Mateo, please just fuck me already—"

The tip of his cock breaks the barrier between want and pure hunger as satisfaction tears through us the further he buries himself in me. He doesn't allow me the pleasure of sitting my ass back on him, but insists on savoring the tight and wet sensation of his cock forcing itself into me.

"Holy shit." His groan turns manic as I clench myself around him, sending him thrusting into me.

My ass sounds in the small space as his hips clap against me. He plays with the speed and strength, moving quickly at first, and then with hard, slow strokes that make me scream for more. I find myself moving against him, swimming in the feel of his cock grinding inside me.

"Shit, you're going to make me come." Mateo's hips rock into me, the words rolling from his throat gruffly. His hand comes to my shoulder as he pounds into my pussy, our moans reaching a new height of ecstasy that turns into breathless whimpers when his thrust turn long and hard, and I enjoy the sleekness of his cock. But the urge to watch him, the way my pussy makes his jaw go slack, and the shift in his eyes when he finally releases, fills me with a different thirst. I rest my back against his chest, his mouth waiting and ready to take mine. He groans softly as I slide off of him and turn to face him.

"Lie back," I say, nibbling at his bottom lip and crawling on top of him as he lowers himself down.

Mateo's hands run up my waist until my breasts are in his grasp, his thumb and forefinger rolling my nipples between them. A smooth grin forms on his lips that quickly fades into a soft *O* as I slide over his shaft.

I lean forward to grab his cock from behind and line it with my center, easing back into him and sucking air in through my teeth as the force widens me.

"Bree." The way Mateo says my name like it's a plea sends a thrill through me, and I give him exactly what he wants.

My hands slide over his chest as I work my ass up and down his shaft, picking up speed with every pass, moans filling the space once again. Fuck, I never imagined it would feel this good, this intense, this safe. With the feel of his hands on my body—molding and grasping like it's something he can't lose—I remember what it feels like to have someone want all of me for me.

My hips rock into Mateo again, and a shiver rolls down my spine when he meets me with a thrust. Everything from the past four weeks builds in me, and I gasp for air as he tugs me to his chest to send his cock plummeting into me until I can't take it anymore. My heaving breaths come to a halt as I release myself, my cum flowing down the length of his cock and over my already creamy thighs. He follows shortly after, continuing to pound in me in spurts until we both groan and collapse beside each other.

Mateo folds his arms around me, allowing me to rest my head on his chest under the flow of kisses that followed. I breathe him in, wanting to stay here just a while longer as I hear the ending of the movie coming up and threatening to put an end to the cloud of bliss we're floating on. His dark eyes meet mine, and I feel the soft graze of wings inside my stomach; twirling, spinning, and gliding in agreement with my heart. I don't want to be anywhere else.

Chapter 31

My feet tap at the base of the office chair as I swing back and forth, running over the document I filled out previously to finalize my position as a staff writer at The Intersect. It's not the job I wanted, but the benefits are great, and I can still move to Columbus if I want to or do hybrid work after a period, so I can stay in Coventry and work at their smaller office a few towns over. This is far from what I wanted—far from what I expected—and I thought it would be easier to deal with, but I'm still wrapping my head around why I was essentially rejected from the one newspaper that I spent years networking and building a portfolio for. Representing everything they want and more. So, what more could I have done? Of all the things I anticipated from the Franklin Gazette, this was not it. I worked my ass off, and nothing? I deserve some sort of answer at the least.

The dial tone rings in my ear, followed by the beeping of each number as I dial the front desk at the Franklin before I lose my nerve. My nails dig into the firm, cushioned fabric of the chair beneath me as the phone rings once, twice...

"Thank you for calling the Franklin Gazette. This is Wren speaking. How can I assist you today?"

"Hi, Wren. It's Aubree Harper," I reply sweetly, but I'm not sure it hides my apprehensiveness.

"Oh, hi!" Wren exclaims, and her enthusiasm makes me feel slightly better about all of this. "I haven't heard from you in a while. Is everything okay?"

"Yeah, of course. It's been a busy past few weeks for me." I pull on one of my twists, twirling the ends around my finger. "Is Scott Peterson there? It's important."

"Uh... let me check, one second." The line goes silent, and I look over toward the window to make sure that Josh is still occupied outside with the canoes, assuming he's getting ready for the "surprise" inflatable water park that everyone's been mumbling about since the start of camp.

"Okay, hun. Let me transfer you."

"Thanks, Wren." My pulse quickens as the line rings again. The beating turns into a stream of acid in my throat as I realize I have no idea what I'm going to say or how to say it. I don't know if this is professional or if I'm making a complete fool of myself, but there's no time to decipher as the ringing comes to a halt.

"Harper," Scott answers indifferently. "How's it going? How's life been treating you?"

"Fine, Scott. And yourself?" I reply, trying to keep things brief so as not to lose any more momentum than I already have in the past 30 seconds.

"Oh, everything's the same. Wren said it was important?"

"It is," I declare. As I take a deep breath, I wipe my hands down the fabric of my shorts. Essentially, they already rejected me once. Nothing I say can make it worse. "Mr. Peterson, I... A few months ago, I interviewed with you for a position as a junior editor at your newspaper. I didn't hear anything back afterward. I was wondering if I might have missed a call or an email? I'm always up to date with my emails, so I thought to call and make sure I didn't miss anything."

At first, I don't hear anything besides a faint rustling sound in the background, hoping my confronting him makes him as uncomfortable as I feel.

"Right, well..." My suspicion is confirmed by the quiet disillusionment in his voice. "We had many candidates, and you know we've always valued your dedication to supporting the Franklin."

"But not enough to hire me without explanation." The words slip, and for once, I didn't want to catch them.

Scott sighs, and a ball of rage blooms in my chest. "Aubree, we've always appreciated your hard work—and we'd love to work with you in the future. However, our team felt the need to go in a different direction this time. I apologize that we never reached out."

The floorboard rattles as my leg begins to shake, trying to maintain my composure. "I understand it was competitive, Mr. Peterson, but what I'm failing to understand is why? I'm glad to hear that you appreciate my work, but could you please elaborate on what I can improve on next time?"

"Look, you've got great stamina and immense passion. Your interview—you did well as expected—but we wanted someone more experienced and... personable for this role."

"I see." Shutting my eyes, I attempt to take deep, steady breaths. Despite my best efforts, tears begin to cling to my cheeks, rolling off my chin. First, I'm too much and then not enough; there's always something I'm not doing right. My career has always been at the forefront of my mind for as long as I could express what I wanted. Did I really forget to develop a sense of identity along the way?

"It wasn't necessarily anything you did. You were a perfect candidate in the sense that you knew the company and the field well. But perfect isn't a default setting for success, and I've seen you at your most authentic, but you covered that up during your interview. Aubree, you're young, you have so much to learn and even more to experience. I'm sorry it didn't work out this time." Scott's attempt at encouragement turns in my stomach.

Covering my mouth with my fist to keep my cries under control, I gather up the strength to thank him for his time before placing the phone back on the receiver. In hindsight, it's just a job that I was never guaranteed, but it still hurts nonetheless. Inexperienced and *regular*. The universe has a funny way of reminding me of my place—of how small I actually am—and maybe that's what I need after everything this past year to finally get back on the right track.

Once I feel I've had my fill of tears, both mournful and angered, I clean myself up in the reflection of the window before sending off my paperwork and calling to let the hiring manager at the Intersect know that I've accepted the position as staff writer.

Putting on my best smile, I make my way over to my friends who sit at our usual table. I'm convinced that if Mateo had a tail that he'd knock himself over from how excited he gets when he sees me approaching. But as I move closer, the wide grin that warms his face shrinks with concern. I attempt to make my smile brighter when I sit down, but by the look on Mateo's face, I know he can see the faults in my facade.

"Did it go okay?" He asks, giving me a quick kiss on the cheek.

I move a little closer to the table and roll a grape between my fingers. "Yeah. I turned in everything, and I start in a few weeks."

"You sure? You look like you've been crying," Mateo says, keeping his voice.

"I'm just tired and hungry, okay? I'm fine." Refusing to look at him, or more like the frosty glare whenever I shut him down, I continue to pick at my lunch more than I eat it as my head whorls with hopelessness. Contemplating that if passion were truly enough, would I feel this way?

CHAPTER 32

S houts and splashes of water send campers into fits of laughter as
they slip and slide their way around the inflatable water park that
holds steady on the lake. Sasha, Kennedy, Maeve, and I sit in the designated No Splash Zone near the oak tree under its cool shade while
we watch the fun from a distance. I had my go around, but after belly
flopping for the 5th time, the sting of each one finally started to get
to me. On a brighter note, the popsicles, watermelon, and grilled hot
dogs the kitchen staff prepared proved to be an effective medicine to put
myself—and my mind—at ease.

It's been two days, and I haven't been able to stomach much of anything without the sickening feeling of guilt twisting in my gut, especially
when it came to spending time with Mateo. A part of me feels wrong
for being stand-offish and not saying anything, but another part of me
feels worse when I think about how much time I'm wasting not doing
something about my self conscious as it eats away at what feels like a
daydream, defining the rough edges of the cloud of softness I'd been

floating on. I love Mateo; there's nothing that could make me doubt that, but I do doubt where my attention has truly been since AJ. It's like I've been floating from one thing to the next with no real direction. Floating is nice until gravity decides to show you what it's all worth.

A tall figure blocks out the sunlight, commanding my attention as it stalks closer, holding a sizable water gun. Mateo smiles down at me, his curls dripping water onto his shoulders and down his chest, my gaze following each one.

"You better be careful with that thing." Sasha nods to the water gun that rests in his hands like he's ready for action at any moment. It's understandable given how Axel and his friends have been warned countless times to stop attacking people already in the No Splash Zone. Thankfully, Kennedy has already mastered that stern mother face, and he hasn't bothered any of us since we came to sit down.

"Oh, I'm sure he's used to handling big things." The sly remark from Maeve sets the other girls into a fit of laughter, but the only thing I can do is hold back the embarrassment snaking its way through me. Careful not to make eye contact with Mateo, or the perfect lines that point down to what has also been plaguing my thoughts, it doesn't stop me from feeling the heat of his gaze on my face.

"Maybe another time," he quips, and a round of "oh's" from my friends has me burying the smile that collects on my face into my hand. Damn them, but fuck my hormones because I didn't realize staying away from him would be so hard, and that's just the problem.

Once I feel I'm okay enough to speak without managing to laugh, I straighten. "Did you need something?" I ask politely.

"Uh, just wanted to know if you wanted to team up with me against some of the other counselors for a relay race. Winner can skip out on their section of clean up for tomorrow, and I know how much you hate picking up after lunch." I make the mistake of looking at him, and it's as if his eyes are pleading with me.

Dammit.

I tug at some grass, ignoring the brutal way my conscious chomps away at the lining of my desire. "I think I'll pass."

Mateo slouches over slightly, and I recoil at the fact that I'm the one who caused it, but I just can't be around him right now—at least not until I figure out exactly how I need to move forward from now on. I can't afford a distraction, no matter how good looking.

"That's okay," he says quickly, in that way I know he's trying to protect me from my own feelings. "I'll check in later?"

I can only muster a faint smile and nod before turning back toward my hot dog, plunging it into my mouth to fill the silence as he walks off.

"Really, Bree?" Maeve doesn't even try to hide her irritation and disbelief. "That was so sweet. Why would you turn him down?"

I shrug. "I didn't feel like it."

"My ass," Kennedy butts in. "You're always trying to get one of us to trade sections with you for clean up. "Don't think we can't tell you've been avoiding him. What happened?"

"Nothing happened. I'm not allowed to be tired?"

"Nope, we're not playing that game." Kennedy sits up, making herself clear this time. "You were on my ass, and now I'm on yours. What happened?"

"You're going to think it's stupid."

"Probably."

I roll my eyes. If there's one thing Kennedy isn't afraid of, it's honesty. It's the one way I know I can trust her. Still, I don't think I can talk about it out loud yet, especially when I'm not even sure I know for certain.

My career and school have been the one thing I've been able to afford the keep within my grasp. Despite what everyone else believes about me, I'm not so naive to think I can control every aspect of my life, but I can propel it in the right direction, and that's what I've always done. The last few weeks have been nothing short of amazing, but I can't help but to feel like I let myself get distracted again. It's not Mateo's fault, but it reminds me of what got me here in the first place.

"The other day, when I was supposed to be turning in my paperwork for the position at the Intersect, I called the editor at the Franklin."

Sasha moves in closer alongside everyone else, her expression scrunched. "Okay? And what did they say?"

"Basically, that I was impersonal and that I let myself get so distracted by everything else going on that I was a fucking robot in my interview." The words are bitter as they leave my mouth. "I did it to myself."

"Don't say that, Bree." Kennedy grabs my hand, and I have half a mind to pull away out of irritation.

Sasha takes the other. "What happened with you and AJ wasn't your fault; it can never be your fault."

"But it was!" I exclaim. "I knew I was throwing away my time and letting myself waste away in some pathetic attempt to fix things with him, all because I didn't want to mess up my plans and wanted a fairy tale ending. I fucked up. He didn't make me stay; I did that to myself. What if it happens again with Mateo? Then what?"

I feel my heart pound in my ears, sucking in a breath as I remember how numb yet broken I felt as months went by knowing there was nothing I could do to save my relationship. I wanted to be hopeful, I wanted to try, I want what my parents have, but at what cost? My career, my sanity?

What's wrong with me?

"Aw, Aubree." Maeve's arm circles around me, her head resting on my shoulder gently as she squeezes me close. "Even if you were distracted, and even if that were all true, do you really think that's worth giving up what you've found with Mateo? Why can't you have both?"

"It doesn't work that way. Clearly, I can't have it all. People like me don't get to have it all. What if I lose sight of what's really important?"

"Love is important," Kennedy interjects. "Take it from me."

I squeeze her hand. "But you're different. You walk around like you know what you want and like everything is within your reach; you're not afraid of losing it all. What if something goes wrong?"

"It won't, but who knows if you don't try? You can still have a fairy tale ending, it just won't look quite like what you thought it would."

Sasha runs her thumbs over my knuckles, a hint of sadness at the corners of her mouth. "You should talk to Mateo."

His figure moves out of the corner of my eye as he stands in line for a grilled hotdog, the muscles in his back shifting and flexing as he laughs and helps some campers while he waits his turn. He's too good and so easy, but this still feels so hard. Most of all, I hate that I know I can't just keep pushing him away because it's the exact opposite of what I want.

I nod to the girls, giving their hands one last squeeze before getting up and making my way toward Mateo. With each step, that little voice inside my head screams at me to turn around, to just let it go, and focus on the bigger picture. But I don't want to be the same girl who refused everything and everyone who didn't fit perfectly into her future. Mateo isn't the guy I saw for myself five weeks ago, but he is the right one, and I don't want anyone else.

Mateo must feel my presence approaching because he turns around to face me, offering me a cup of lemonade with orange slices, his favorite, which ultimately became mine. I mutter a thanks as I bring the cold liquid to my lips, allowing it to soothe me for this next part.

"Do you wanna go somewhere and talk?" I ask quietly.

"Sure, yeah. Lead the way." His response is chipper, but there's a slight sense of eagerness he can't quite mask.

A picnic table clears up as we walk over, the campers leaving their half-eaten watermelon slices and rinds behind. After clearing it partially, we sit next to each other, his eyes lingering on me as if they're searching for something.

I let out a sigh. "So."

"So," he breathes in response. "Is everything okay?"

I nod, a cramped smile on my face. "I guess so." Mateo's eyes frost with the same rejected gleam that they've had for the past few days, and my chest looms with regret. Why does he have to look at me like that?

"No," I admit. Shutting my eyes tightly, I try to shake this silly feeling off, but it just sticks like the summer heat. "It's not okay. This isn't okay."

Mateo moves closer, confusion clouding his expression. "I know, and I'm sorry—"

"Why are you apologizing? It's not your fault." He looks at me, eyes wide as he waits for me to continue, forcing me to communicate what I hoped to avoid. "It's not you. It's this whole job thing, my life map, my life feeling like it's falling apart at every corner I turn... You're perfect, and I'm just pretending to be."

Mateo pulls me to his chest, his hand squeezing my shoulder. "I hate when you say shit like that about yourself. I'm not perfect, and it's not about perfection."

"That's easy to say when you're all healed or whatever." I wave my hand around at the invisible life-sized bandage Mateo seems to wear over his scars. "I called the Franklin Gazette the other day when I was turning in my paperwork for The Intersect. I asked to speak to the editor—who I thought I had built a great professional relationship with over the past three years, by the way—but clearly I was wrong because when I asked him why they never got back to me, he basically said I wasn't good enough. I was too busy running after my ex boyfriend to fix a relationship that was never going to work to show them who I really am and why I'm worth the investment when I had the chance. I mean, what the fuck? Three years of my life, and I ruined it because of some guy who wasn't the person I built up in my head."

Mateo doesn't say anything at first, and I think I might have said too much, but he kisses the top of my head, and I swear he looks a little relieved. "Is that why you've been so distant?"

I nod. "I didn't mean to—I mean, I did mean to—but I didn't mean to hurt you in the process. I just needed a minute, I got scared all over again and immediately jumped back into control freak mode." I cork up one side of my mouth as I grab his hand. "I didn't want to lose sight of 'the plan', but in doing that, I ignored how great it felt to deviate from it, and it's all because you showed me that I don't have to hide behind it anymore. I'm sorry."

He brings my hand to his lips, kissing my knuckles softly before grazing his thumb over that spot. "I'm sorry too. I'm sorry that they didn't see your worth because you're a brilliant writer, and they should have been fighting for a chance to get you." I chuckle, leaning into his arms as he continues. "But I'm also sorry that in the beginning I didn't understand you. I want you to know that you can trust me to be there for you, and I always promise to try my best to understand, even if it does seem silly and slightly obsessive."

I punch him playfully before holding onto his arms as they wrap around me. "I'm going to pretend you didn't say that last part, but thank you."

Making sure no one is watching, we both have the same idea as Mateo tips my chin up with his thumb as his hand rests on my neck and kisses me. First one peck, then two, and if we don't stop now, I'm going to have to find a room because I almost forgot just how good his mouth feels. I'm first to pull away, grinning as his greedy mouth tries to follow mine. Mateo bites down on his lip, and I shake my head as I start to clear off the table. When I turn back to him, he has that same look of confusion on his face. Before I can ask him what it is, the she-demon comes trotting towards us, her slim waist shifting in a snake like manner. It suits her.

"What now, Penelope?" Mateo says as he stands up to take the trash from me.

She shrugs and sighs like she has not a care in the world, and I'm positive she doesn't. "Oh, nothing. You two just look so adorable." Her eyes are pinned to Mateo before shifting to me with mockery.

"Where's Gale?" I question, shifting the energy back onto her. "Finding out he's better off, I hope?"

"I wouldn't be so sure about that. People always learn the hard way." Penelope flips her hair before stalking over to the dock where Gale sits with a few other counselors. She takes one last glance back at me before sliding next to Gale, demanding his attention as she drags him away from the water gun fight that broke out seconds before.

"What the fuck is up with her lately? I mean, she's always a bitch, but... maybe it's Gale?" I move to Mateo's side to clean under the table, looking up at him for a confirming response, but he only shrugs. "Okay. I guess that's that. I shouldn't bother with her anyway."

"Yeah." His reply is so soft I almost assume he didn't say anything.

I lay my hand on his forearm, stopping him from heading toward the trash. "Hey, we're okay, right?"

"Yeah, I'm just thinking, that's all." He nudges my side.

My gaze runs over his features again, making sure there's nothing I missed. "Good. Okay, yeah, just making sure. Anyway, I should get back."

"Right." He offers me a kiss on the cheek that I willingly accept before turning away toward the oak tree until he grabs at my wrist.

"Aubree, wait." He swallows, and for a moment, I think I see a flicker of panic cross his expression. "Do you want to meet up in the cabin tomorrow after dinner? It might be our only chance before the fair."

"You know I want to." I drop my voice down an octave. "But I promised the girls I'd we'd hang out just us tomorrow. Sorry."

"No, I understand." His voice jumps as he responds hurriedly. "As long as I get to talk to you at some point. It's important."

"But not so important that you can't tell me now?"

"I'd rather do it in private." Mateo pulls me to him, my breasts pressing against him as he sprinkles soft kisses behind my ear.

"Mmm, I'll see what I can do. I'm sure I can find some time to squeeze you in."

"Oh, you will."

Chapter 33

"You know, when you said you had something planned, I didn't expect that to include stabbing myself." Kennedy wraps another bandage around the pad of her finger, checking the durability of the others before picking her embroidery ring back up.

"Girl, please. It's just a little prick," Sasha says with carelessness.

Kennedy holds up her hand with animosity. "I'm bleeding!"

"Good. Now we're blood bound."

"Can you guys not fight right now? I'm trying to concentrate," I chime as I thread my needle through Maeve's denim shorts, right next to Sasha's flawlessly embroidered letter 'S'. While it was annoying, I did appreciate that Sasha took the time to trace out all of our initials on a pair of each of our shorts; a reminder of our time here together, similar to how Sasha, Maeve, and I carved are initials into the baseboard of the cabin we stayed in together one summer. This time, we can always take it with us. It's cute, besides the occasional whining from Kennedy.

"I love this guys." Maeve's voice cracks a little, and we all look up to see that the water works have already started. I thought it'd be at least another 20 minutes before then, but I should have known better with Maeve. Each of us carefully sets down our rings and needles, forgetting them as we wrap our arms around her.

"Maeve, what did we say about crying?" I remind her.

"I know, I know. It's not like we won't see each other again, but I missed you guys so much." She rests her head on my shoulder before her attention shifts to Kennedy with a smile. "And now I have a new friend. And Bree, I can't believe you found love with Mateo. I was kind of afraid you'd end up alone."

"Ouch?" I say, poking her in her side and earning a laugh out of everyone, but I can feel the tears threatening to well in my eyes at the thought because the truth is that I can't believe it either.

It's so strange. Had you asked me a few weeks ago if I would ever fall for Mateo, I'd think you needed to seek medical attention. But now, I can't imagine life if I hadn't gotten to know him for all that he is, and there's still so much I want to know. Long distance will be hard for the first month or so while I get settled, but maybe then I might consider staying back in Coventry or him moving out to Columbus with me. Things seem so different now—I feel so different. I wouldn't mind either.

"Yeah, but you and Beck, though? I never thought I'd see the day." Sasha chuckles as she reminds us of how awkward they were with each other and how clueless Beck was.

"I know! I'm glad he snapped out of it because it was even getting hard for me to watch," Maeve jokes.

Mumbling in agreement, we all jump back into a group hug. Nothing could have made this a better summer.

"Okay, enough or we'll be doing this all night, and I'm still on my first pair," Kennedy says as she separates from us. It was good while it lasted.

"You're right, but I need to use the bathroom real quick," I say as I dash out of the cabin.

Mosquitoes swarm around the exterior lights of the bathrooms, signaling that it is getting late. Honestly, I've been dreaming of throwing myself onto my bed and sleeping until camp was officially over all day. Our counseling duties have doubled this week since we're closing up on Saturday for the fair. I didn't realize how hard it was going to be to help 10 girls make sure all of their things were packed and ready to go beforehand. Some of them have managed to collect half as much as they brought with them. At least now I know how my friends felt when we were packing for our drive up to Whisper Lake.

Everything's so quiet and still at this time of night. The water ripples in whispers, and the crickets chirp to a song of their own. I could learn to love it if not for the nagging feeling in the back of my brain that warns me of the potential danger that may or may not be lurking in the trees. Maybe Mateo and I could sneak out for a midnight swim like old times. Making a mental note of that, the door to the boys' restroom swings open, making me jump a little. Mateo makes no effort to hold back his laughter at my expense.

"Sorry, didn't mean to scare you." I would believe he was if he wasn't laughing so hard. "I forget how skittish you are sometimes."

"I'm not skittish," I claim, forcing the biggest eye roll I can muster. "You caught me off guard."

Mateo grabs me by the waist, pulling me into his body before resting his hands on my lower back. "We'll have to work on that."

"I can think of a few other things that might better suit both of our needs." My hands slide up the hard muscles of his arms, gliding over his shoulders and into the nape of his hair. The firm squeeze of my ass as Mateo presses himself into me lets me know he's just as starved as I am.

Bringing my mouth to his, my tongue swipes at his bottom lip, allowing me entry for my tongue to dance over his. A soft moan escapes me at the feel of his bare hands finding their way into my shorts, his touch sensual and deliberate. I hate to have him stop, but the last thing either one of us needs is for a camper to catch us like this.

Pulling his hands away and lacing his fingers with mine, I step back after leaving him with one more quick kiss.

"Are you sure I can't steal you away for a few minutes?" Mateo groans.

"I'm sure. I'm almost done with my embroidery, and I also need to pee, like right now. Maybe later? I was thinking of a midnight swim when everyone else falls asleep."

"You're not suggesting that we...?"

"Gosh, no." I chuckle. "Kids swim in that lake, but I have thought about it."

Mateo pulls me back to him once again, a pleading look on his face as he tucks a strand of hair behind my ear. "I love your idea, and I'm more than willing to do it, but just give me a few minutes? Please?"

No would be the right thing to say right now; it's what I should be saying right now, but when his mouth dips to my ear, his lips grazing my earlobe before planting the softest of kisses behind it, I swear my legs turn to jelly on the spot. "I swear I'll make it quick."

Stifling a moan, I shut my eyes in response to the low vibration of his voice. "Fine," I breathe in a mix of annoyance and lust. "Wait here."

Finally able to pull myself away from him, I rush into the bathroom. I forgot just how bad I needed to go because I don't think I could have held it any longer. Nevertheless, I make it quick and rush out to the sinks and quickly wash my hands as all I can think about is the 6'2 hunk of a man that's waiting on the other side of the door. My heart leaps in my chest at the thought of sneaking away with Mateo, but as I pull the door open, a shrewd voice cracks in the air.

"—then tell her you're lying!" Penelope's gaze lands on me, her eyes and nose slightly red. "Well, isn't this just perfect?"

"Penelope, don't." Mateo's voice comes as a panic as he moves to rush ahead of her, but she's faster.

"So, you're boyfriend here forgot to mention his pact with Sasha. Isn't that right, Mateo?" She looks back at him, and my heart drops as he refuses to look at me.

"Mateo? What is she talking about?" I ask, my voice shaky. He stands motionless, his mouth opening and closing, fishing for the words that don't come up, but Penelope is all too ready as a grin forms on her lips.

"It was when you had that little incident with your ankle. I overheard him and Sasha talking about it. Tell her, Mateo," Penelope demands with amusement in her tone as she gestures for him to speak. "Let her know just how special she is that her best friend set her up to get fucked—"

"That's enough!" Mateo exclaims through his teeth.

Penelope shakes her head, a laugh bubbling up from inside her. "This is too good. You picked her over me, but you can't even be honest with the woman you 'love'?" She moves to walk away, but her attention turns to me once again. "Gale is worthless, but at least I'm not as naive and shitless as you. You're welcome."

Empty and hollow, my hand finds my mouth as my lip begins to quiver. There are no excuses, no explanations, as he continues to stand stuck to the spot, shame etched into his expression. Disgust stirs in me, and I can no longer look at him. Everything between us flashes in my mind as the illusion of who I thought Mateo was shatters. I think back to that day of the training, the look on Mateo's face when Sasha was talking to him, and how quickly he cut her off when he saw me approaching. It was all built on a lie.

"So, it's true then?" I say as rage slowly seeps into my veins. "This was just all a lie."

"No, it wasn't a lie." Mateo takes a step forward, and I take one back, my hand outstretched. "It's not like that, Aubree. I swear—"

"Bullshit!" I shout, the word echoing and breaking the stillness around us. "You hid it from me. You made me believe this was real. I let you in, and you knew the whole time you'd been lying to me. When were you going to tell me?"

"I swear I was going to tell you sooner, I just couldn't find the right time—"

"You wanted to make sure you actually got to fuck me first? Get your end of the deal?"

Mateo shakes his head, a pleading in his voice. "Aubree, no! That's not what happened."

"Was it to make yourself feel better about coming back here and leaving your family behind? You finally got to fuck the one woman you couldn't have?"

"Now you know that's not true." His tone bites through my argument, sending a coldness down my spine. "It was more than that to me, and you know that."

"Then why lie?" I ask as I throw my arms up, tears staining the front of my shirt. "If I'm really that important to you, why not tell me the truth?"

"It's not his fault." Sasha steps beside me, her head hung slightly as she approaches. Kennedy and Maeve linger nearby, watching as it all unfolds. "It was my idea, and I asked him to lie just until after camp, and then I would tell you myself."

My chest descends further into a pit of betrayal as Sasha refuses to look at me, and my anger ebbs into heartbreak. For as long as I've known Sasha, she's always been the type of person to insert herself into everyone's business but her own. It was always annoying, always childish, but I never once thought she'd think to hurt me like this. She's been my best friend, my forever person, since we were kids, but I'm so sick of her excuses and tireless instigating.

My stomach turns as I recount her words. "What the fuck were you thinking, Sasha? And for Penelope of all people to tell me... Why?"

Her lip curves up at the mention of Penelope. "I just thought it'd be good for you. You were so stressed—I was trying to help."

"By pimping me out? All I needed was some good dick to chill the fuck out and relax, and the rest would work itself out?"

Mateo steps forward and moves into my line of vision. "That's not what I thought—"

"I'm not talking to you right now," I bark at him, retreating as I direct the same tone to Sasha. "Talk."

Sasha picks at the sleeves of her sweatshirt, but stands firm as she lifts her face to mine. "I wanted to do something for you for once. You..." Her eyes dart over to Kennedy before shifting down at her feet. "You and Kennedy got so close, I felt left out. She knew stuff about you that I didn't—it felt like I was second place, and I know that that's wrong now. I wanted to feel like I was still important and that you could trust me."

"Sasha, oh my gosh," I groan as I press the balls of my hands to my eyes. "You're so fucking selfish. This is what you do, this is what you *always* do. Obviously, I'm close with Kennedy; we were roommates for three years, but that doesn't mean you go behind my back like this. This is the reason I don't tell you things. You ruin things, it's what you're good at."

Tears well in Sasha's eyes, gathering at her lower lashes. She scrunches her nose, trying to hold them back, but they fall the same as mine—hurt and estranged.

"I'm sorry," she whispers, her voice shaking.

"Sorry isn't good enough this time, Sasha."

I'd never thought those words would leave my lips when it came to her. There was never a future that Sasha wasn't in. I couldn't even imagine it, but I can't forgive her this time. Chance after chance, and she still won't stop to think about how her actions only benefit her and hurt everyone else involved. It's been that way since we were kids. I thought she'd grow out of it, get herself together, and learn that it's time to finally grow up and accept that not everyone is her personal charity case. Clearly, I was wrong.

Kennedy and Maeve try to stop me as I make my way to my cabin, but their efforts float past me as I run off. Footsteps track behind me as

I reach the steps, and I only turn around to stop Mateo from following me in.

"Can we just talk? I'm sorry that I didn't tell you, I should have. Please, just give me a chance to—"

"We're done." Like a knife, I feel the weight of my affirmation cut through me, twisting until the sting of it becomes a permanent reminder. "You used me just like the guy you said you weren't anymore, and I was right... I don't want to talk to you or see you again."

He catches his hand in mine, holding tight to what I'm so desperately trying to let go of. "Please, don't do this. Tell me what I can do. I'll do anything. I love you."

I don't expect the quiver in his voice. The tightness in his throat as a sob threatens to break free. Since we've been here, he's been the strong one, the light that I needed when all I felt was shame. Now all I see is darkness. An abyss full of memories, the spoken and unspoken confessions of the love that grew between us, that crumble to dust as his betrayal constricts around them. There's nothing I wanted more than to be with Mateo, for him to be by my side more than I was willing to say aloud. I wanted him close, to be the person that we run to when we can't see a way out—my safety—and he destroyed it with one lie.

"There's nothing to do. You can't fix it this time. This was only meant to be for the summer anyway, so you got what you wanted. Please, go away."

The screen door shuts behind me, and I half expect Mateo to follow me in, but he doesn't. The image of the man I love twists into an ugliness I don't recognize.

CHAPTER 34

M y head knocks against the car window as we drive over yet another pot hole, this one sending my hand flying up to cover where there was sure to be a small knot forming soon.

"Ah, Dad!"

"I'm sorry, baby girl. Sorry." He rubs the spot as well in condolence. "It's so bright, and I forgot my sunglasses at home. Let's just not lean up against the window for now."

I cross my arms over my stomach, closing my eyes as the radio plays softly, cool air blowing into my face. I only want to go home. To lie in my bed and forget this summer even happened. Admittedly, I had fun while it lasted, but knowing that some of the best parts were built on a selfish lie because my childhood best friend couldn't handle not being in the middle of everything hurts. This was supposed to be an escape—a break until I could figure out my next plan of action. Instead, I'm right back where I started. Naive and way in over my head. Scott was right, and I was too stubborn to admit it at the time, but I see it now. I should have trusted my intuition, but yet again I put my trust in something that turned around to bite me in the ass anyway. Except this time, it's not my pride that's broken.

My dad taps his fingers on the stirring wheel; the thing he does when he wants to talk but knows no one else wants to, so he tries to come up with an icebreaker. "Original Pancake House is at the next exit. You too old to split a stack with your old man?"

Hesitantly, I open my eye just enough to see his bright smile of hope and know I can't disappoint him. If I eat enough, I can put myself in a food coma until this passes. "Fine, but I want bacon pancakes this time *and* a spinach and feta omelet."

"Whatever you want."

When we pull up to the building—circling the parking lot twice to find a good spot to keep up the tradition—we're lucky enough to be seated right away. Normally, we share a booth, but a table seems more proper given the number of larger families here. Truthfully, I don't recall it ever being this busy. Granted, I haven't been to a Pancake House since before college. I missed the cozy yet chaotic atmosphere. The food was nothing fancy, something you could easily make at home, but that's what I loved about it. It's comfort food, and who doesn't like that?

We don't need menus since it's relatively the same thing every time. We each pick a stack of pancakes we want and split them to share. Ordering a side of bacon for crunch, fresh fruit, and orange juice to wash it all down. My dad, being the father that he is, allowed me to pick each stack—bacon and strawberry.

"Tic-tac-toe?" My dad holds up a box of crayons I assume he swiped from the empty table next to us that had yet to be bused. With a nod,

I let him start the game on a napkin that the waiter left for us while he ran our order and drinks. I always choose blue, and my dad always grabs green, claiming that it's the color of winners. That didn't stop him from letting me win most of the time, though.

"Well," he finally says after a few tacs, and I brace myself for the inevitable question and answer game we'd play because that's his thing. My dad never really makes too many statements or advises unless he feels the need to. He just asks questions, and I hate it. "How was seeing everyone again at camp?"

"Fine," I sigh.

"Just *fine*?" I glare up at him, and he shrugs as he makes his next move, forcing his win. "No big life changes or updates?"

"It's not my business to tell," is what I would say, but I know it won't suffice, so I simply settle on, "Maeve got into the veterinary school at Ohio State."

"No kidding, good for her. What about Kennedy? Did she hear back from Principal Ellis?"

"I'm sure you and half the town already know the answer to that," I tease, feeling a smile tug at the corners of my mouth.

"Haha, yeah, I guess you're right." He crosses over his win again, and now it's time to concentrate because I won't let him win a third time. "How about you?"

I move back into my chair, leaning my head into my hand. I could say, *"Oh, yeah, I hooked up with a guy who turned out to be scheming with my best friend to find out the best ways to trick me into liking him,"* but I don't want to give the man a heart attack.

"Well, you know I start that job with The Intersect soon."

"Are you excited?"

I shrug because now I'm not so sure. I was excited to have my own apartment, pack up my things, and start a new journey. But a lot of that excitement extended from the fact that I might have someone besides my parents who loves me back home in Coventry. Once again, falling into the trap of my own imagination. It's why I lost that job with the Franklin Gazette to begin with. Moving into the city has always been the end goal, so why does it feel like I'm running away instead of running to?

"Yeah. Super."

Thankfully, our food arrives just in time to interrupt his next question. My fork meets a glazed strawberry, and I pop it into my mouth. Every muscle in my body relaxes as the sweetness spreads over my tongue, taking me back to the last time we were here. My dad was convinced it would be the last time we ever split a stack since I was already a distant teenager who wanted to "hang with my friends more than the only father I'll ever have," as my dad put it. He wasn't mad at me, but I'd be a fool not to notice how sad it made him. So, I paid for breakfast that day, and we talked and laughed until our ears were filled with the sounds of memories never to be forgotten. I miss that kind of magic.

Working to split each stack onto separate plates, my dad continues his interrogation, taking me right out of the moment. "Is that why you came back early?"

"Dad, please," I groan, cutting into the buttery softness of my bacon pancake. He stares back at me as he chews on a strawberry like he knows I'll answer him either way or deal with my mother, whose questions feel more like a stupidity quiz than an innocent conversation.

"It's not a big deal," I say.

"If it's not a big deal, then why wake me up out of my sleep at eleven o'clock last night saying that I needed to come pick you up this morning?"

I shrug, the memories of last night ramming into me once more as I recall their lie, the smug look on Penelope's face, and the shame and embarrassment that still clings to me as it forms a ball in my throat and stings at the back of my eyes. I don't want to repeat it out loud—it's too fresh a wound—but I know that if I don't, I'll drown in it like before. My vision begins to blur, and I keep my head down to keep from anyone seeing the small puddles forming.

"Was it a boy?" My dad softens his voice, reaching out to wrap an arm around me. I nod. "Did he hurt you?" His voice is firmer now.

I purse my lips, holding back as much as I can. "It wasn't just a boy... Sasha."

"Sasha?"

My grip tightens around my fork. "She set me up. She knew that I didn't want to get involved with anyone, and she did it anyway like she always does, and he went along with it. Mateo used me to fulfill whatever sorry fantasy he had about me. He filled my head with all these lies, and I hate him for it, Dad. I feel so stupid for falling for that shit again."

Tears roll down my face as a soft sob hiccups in my throat. My dad moves quickly to my side, wrapping his arm around me while shielding me from the stares of others behind us. He rubs my shoulder, giving me all the room I need to let it out.

He kisses the top of my head. "I'm so sorry, sweetheart."

"Dad... I loved him."

"I know." He dries some of my tears with the hem of his shirt. "Let's get you home."

CHAPTER 35

A light knock on my door pulls me away from my phone, and I raise my head to see my mom at the door. She'd made my bed with freshly washed sheets when she found out I was coming home early just for them to be stained with the evidence of my tears. I cried myself into a nap and only woke up when my dad came up to check on me and accidentally knocked over a stack of my textbooks.

My mom eases the door open slightly. "Can I come in?"

"Are you coming to pry?" I question.

"A mother can't comfort her daughter and make sure she's okay?" Her hands rest on her hips, and I roll my eyes before moving over in the bed so she can sit beside me. "I'm going to pretend you didn't roll your eyes and assume you meant to greet me with a smile."

Putting on the fattest smile I can, she bumps my shoulder before falling into laughter. "Happy?"

"Very." She looks down at my phone where a video plays of some random girl showing off the best looks for summer. My mom points out a pink floral skirt and a white top. "That one would look great on you. You always look so pretty in pinks."

"Yeah... I already ordered the skirt. It'll be here next week."

"Smart thinking."

Besides the video on my phone, the silence between us waits to be broken by the mumbling question my mom has been brewing since last night. Naturally, my dad didn't ask any questions about why he needed to come get me, but simply asked at what time, giving my mother nothing to work with. On the outside, my mom is cool and level headed, but on the inside, she worries just as much as I do. Her mind races faster than her mouth, allowing for careful and considerate speech, whereas I often say the first thing that comes to mind when I need answers—an outcome. So, this silence was familiar and expected as she flushed out all of her questions until she landed on the one she felt would yield the most results. It was slightly annoying, but appreciated. It gives me time to calm down, think, and figure out how to talk without anger, frustration, and pain at the forefront.

She settles closer, leaning her head on top of mine as the next video plays. "So, Mateo Opetaia, huh?"

I shut my eyes, breathing through the mention of his name. "Not my proudest moment."

"You're young, we all make mistakes... including Mateo and Sasha."

"Yeah, right, because setting your friend up with a guy after repeatedly saying no is such a mistake. And I guess playing along so you can finally get the girl is too." I huff as I angle myself away from her.

"No, that's not what I'm saying, Aubree. They were wrong, and they should be ashamed of themselves, especially Mateo. But is it so bad that Sasha was just trying to be a friend?"

"Ma, you weren't there!" I exclaim. "You know Sasha, and you know this isn't her first time messing everything up for everyone involved; it's what she does, and then to blame it on my friendship with Kennedy?"

"No, I wasn't there, and no, she shouldn't have blamed Kennedy." My mom shifts towards me so that I'm forced to hear her loud and clear. "Sasha should have come to you as a friend—"

"Ex-friend," I correct. I tap on another video as I let the word seep in. "I can't forgive her this time."

"Then don't." My mom puts her hand over my phone and turns it off. "I'm not saying to forgive her, but I'm saying to try and understand her perspective. I know I'm on the outside, and from the outside, you have gotten closer to Kennedy. Movie nights with Sasha turned into study dates with Kennedy, and skipping out on a weekend at home to go out with Kennedy. I'm not saying she was justified, but I see her reasoning for it."

I'm so sick of everyone making excuses for Sasha. I know that her life is different than mine—completely different—but it's not a good enough reason to go so far. I won't keep letting her try to manufacture the life she wants for me. I have my own plans; my own dreams. I didn't ask for her help, so why am I meant to feel guilty?

"I don't care, Ma. I don't think we can come back from this."

She hesitates a moment, pursing her lips. "What about Mateo?"

Abruptly, I shake my head. I let two guys screw me over in less than 6 months. I'll be damned if I let him try it again. "I want a relationship with someone I can trust, not one built on lies."

"Of course not, sweetie." She gathers me into a hug, squeezing me before pulling away. "Can I give you something?"

"What is it?" I roll over to see her pulling something out of her back pocket. One is a piece of folded up craft paper with my name on it. The other is an old photograph that I immediately recognize.

"Is this from Spring Fling?" I ask, grabbing the picture from her. Eleventh grade. Sasha and I have our arms slung around each other, our laughter caught in frame. We shopped for an outfit together every year, heading into town to Gloria's Boutique and trying on as many options as we could before picking for each other. I ended up in an off-the-shoulder lily white dress, and she danced the night away in a red top and skater skirt that year. We had so much fun helping each other get ready, but what I remember most about that night happened after the dance; it's hard to forget. The last thing I expected was to break my leg trying to climb into the old hideout that we found in a tree on the far edge of town. It had been abandoned for years and was a playground for tetanus, but that never stopped us from going there for a palate cleanser and good gossip where only the trees could hear. It was our special place, and she thought the best way to celebrate was to hide away in our cozy little tree house and drink a few of my dad's beers. It was a dumb idea, especially given that the thing was bound to fall apart at some point, but Sasha stayed by my side the whole time. Even with two broken ribs and staples in her scalp, she never left my side. I didn't care about what happened in the end because I was with Sasha—and she would never hurt me on purpose.

I shove the photo back towards my mom, seeping down into my pillows. "That was years ago. A few broken bones together doesn't warrant forgiveness."

She takes the photo, moving it back into my view. "Yes, but that night wasn't the whole picture." She points out the silver butterfly necklace I was wearing. "Remember you thought I didn't buy the necklace you begged me for every day whenever we passed by Gloria's Boutique?"

Continuing to scroll through my phone looking for nothing in particular, I nod. I still have that necklace somewhere around here. I only wanted it to match the dress, but my mom was clear that I could either get new shoes or a necklace. Now those shoes are sitting in a thrift store somewhere after I only wore them once.

"I'm not the one who bought it for you." My mom smiles.

"What are you talking about? You said that you and Dad decided to surprise Sasha and me with them right as we were walking out the door."

"I know what I said. I lied." She shakes her head at me like I'm supposed to be any less confused. "When I went outside to get the car ready, I didn't make it down the steps when I noticed a certain someone about to walk away, leaving the bag with the necklaces on the stairs. I stopped him thinking I caught him trying to pull a prank, but it wasn't that. He left them for you and Sasha."

Hot and sudden, blood rushes to my cheeks as my heart leaps in my throat. She wouldn't say it, and neither would I, but I know who this certain someone is. His mother worked there, and she helped us pick out our outfits. Did everyone know about his crush but me? Was I that blind?

"He said he wanted you to have it," my mom continues. "When I asked why he wouldn't give it to you himself, he wouldn't give me an answer. I tried to convince him otherwise, that you would love it and would want to thank him, but he just said there was no need since he was leaving soon anyway."

That's right. I forgot he left after that weekend; nobody really knew he was leaving. Surprisingly, the school days felt emptier without his constant taunting and prying. At the time, I was glad he was gone, but looking back, I wasn't used to a day without him. It felt strange that he would just leave without a word, and so quietly. I'd spent the last 17 years with him as a constant, never resting thorn in my side. Every day it was the same; I'd come in just before the first bell for homeroom, and he'd miraculously appear out of thin air as I made my way to my locker while he talked my ear off about nothing and everything. I'd initially ignore him, instead looking for my friends in the crowd of students who flooded the halls, but he'd eventually say something so ridiculous that I had to respond out of annoyance, or maybe it was curiosity. We only shared two classes and a lunch period, and yet he was always around. He always noticed me when I paid so little attention to him.

I shake my head. "That doesn't matter now. He lied then just like he lied now. He manipulated and humiliated me the same way he always did. He—" I clutch at my sheets, fighting to keep my emotions at bay. "Please, Ma."

She nods as she pats my hair. Before she leaves the room, she turns off my overhead light, leaving my bedside lamp as the only light source in the room. I wait for the patter of her steps to fade away down the hall before turning over to see the folded red craft paper she propped onto my pillow. Staring at it doesn't make it go away, and it doesn't make my palms stop itching to read what's inside. My name is written in silver permanent marker, the looped letter *e's* giving it's writer away. I hold it up towards the light as I unfold it carefully.

Aubree,

I know that I fucked up, and I know that I upset you. I was jealous and stupid, and I should have known better. I was so focused on myself that I thought I was helping our friendship. I know there's no excuse for what I did, so I won't try. I risked my best friend over a stupid guy because I thought I knew what was best for you, and I don't. I should have come to you, talked to you about it, but I was so selfish and obsessed with my plan that I didn't stop to think how it would hurt you. You don't have to forgive me, but I hope you can give me a chance to apologize in person. I know it won't be soon... but if you change your mind, I'll be at the park near the camp at 4PM tomorrow. If you don't come, I know why.

— Sasha

The letter is in a ball and tossed into the trash can beside my nightstand before I can let it get the better of me.

CHAPTER 36

C losely inspecting the cartons of blueberries at Evelyn's stand, I just about think I found a perfect carton before noticing some of the berries were crushed, and I put it back in its place. I want to find the perfect carton for the perfect blueberry cobbler I'm making for the annual Back to School Barbecue because no job was going to have me miss out on it, and I've gotten so close to nailing my grandmother's recipe. It would be dishonorable not to make it like she used to every year. Everyone else seems to miss it just as much as I do, so the perfect carton counts for all or nothing—at least that's what I was telling myself before Julian started to hover over me, just as rude as I remember. Now I'm taking my sweet time just to annoy him because the perfect blueberries didn't matter *that* much.

I pick up another carton, and he lets out a heavy sigh. "How many more times are you going to do that? There are other customers."

I look around noticing that the stand was getting a bit crowded. The farmers market is always a hit, so I shouldn't be surprised.

"As many times as I need to," I lie as I pick up the carton I had already decided on ten cartons ago and hand it to Julian. "You should be nicer to your customers. You'll scare them away."

He grunts, shaking his balding head. "You kids are a pain in my—"

"Julian!" Evelyn glares at him, daring him to test her. He sucks his teeth before bagging my berries up and holding out his palm for the seven dollars I owe him. I slap the money down into his hand.

"Until next time, Julian," I say sweetly, and I swear I hear him claim his luck that that won't happen as I walk off to the next stand, giggling to myself.

Julian is the Grinch of Coventry Falls, but I think he's just playing it up so that he won't be forced to actually engage with any of us. Deep down, I believe he likes the attention because after all these years, he still hands out candy on Halloween and comes to all the town meetings.

I'm sampling honey when my phone starts to ring, immediately recognizing it to be the camp's landline. My face falls in opposition with my heart as the number flashes on the screen. It could be anyone; it could be no one I want to hear from. It could also be important. Maybe I left something behind when I was in a rush to leave the other day. In a split second decision, I click the green button as the feeling of regret looms.

"Hello?" My voice comes out in a whisper. I move away from the stands, looking for a quieter and less noticeable place to talk.

"Thank god. I thought you wouldn't answer." Valarie's voice comes over the other end, and I shut my eyes with a sigh.

"Hey, what's up. Is everything okay?" I bite down on the plastic spatula that had my honey on it, glad to hear her voice. "Did you finish your edits for the contest?"

"Uh, yeah, it's coming along." The line is silent for a beat before she speaks again, hesitantly. "Are you okay?"

Putting more tension on the spatula, I shrug. "I will be."

"Good. I hope so. Things here are kinda weird, and I miss you."

"I miss you too, Val. Things will be fine, okay? Enjoy the fair tonight for us both."

"You still can't come?" she whines. "I wanted to ride the Mouse Trap with you like we always do."

I sit down on the bench beside me, a new ache drilling a hole of despair. I never break tradition, it's the one constant that I can always look forward to, and Coventry is full of them. It's hard not to honor them in a place like this. Not doing so felt like yet another heartbreak. They seem silly in the grand scheme of things, but it's a comfort you don't just turn your back on. Valarie and I still managed to ride the Mouse Trap every year despite her moving away. I don't want to disappoint her after leaving so suddenly.

"I'm sorry, but I don't think I can. I'll try, though." She doesn't say another word, but I can almost imagine the sadness in the way her shoulders slump over when she feels disappointed. "I'll really, really try—I promise. And if not today, we can do it another day. I'll pay for whatever."

"Okay," Valarie sighs.

"How are Kenny and Maeve?" I question, trying to change the subject.

"They're good, I guess. Kennedy and Sasha are getting along."

"Oh, good." My hand comes to my throat. "That's really good."

"Maeve and Beck are lovey-dovey as usual. It's getting gross."

I chuckle. "Give them a break. They've waited years for their moment."

"Yeah, whatever. As long as I don't look like that when I get older."

"You can't help it when you're in love." Images of Mateo and me float in my mind, remembering the pain in my cheeks from how hard I'd smile with him, and the butterflies in my chest every time he recalled every shared and unshared detail of myself with him that let me know he listens. I never had that before.

"Maybe, but I have to go now. My time's up," Valarie says.

"Okay, yeah. I forgot we were timed. I should have asked you about you."

"It's okay. I needed to know you were okay."

"Thanks, Val." I smile.

The line goes dead, and my back rests against the bench. The long line that was formed at the stand in front of me for Early Bird Bakery dried out, leaving no one left. I take that as my queue to walk over as I've been dying to sample one of their miniature creme puffs that I already knew I was going to order a dozen of. Juniper has magic hands that I swear are passed down from generation to generation in her family. Anything I was craving, she and her family could make.

"Well, it's good to see you back!" Juniper's bakery themed earrings swing as she waves me over. It never ceased to amaze me what kind of earrings this girl can find. This time, she opted for two miniature chocolate covered croissants topped with the perfect swirl of whipped cream that matched the life size ones in front of her.

"It's good to know I was missed." Offering her my brightest smile, I pick up a toothpick to get sampling. "Don't tell me that's your famous orange and chocolate cake," I beam as I stick the end of my toothpick through its moist exterior. I've been hooked on this cake since Juniper asked me to taste test it for her a few years back. It sounds odd when you think about it—chocolate and oranges—but the flavors together just worked like magic dancing on your tongue.

"How do you come up with such heaven?" I ask Juniper as she guides me down to the other end of the table.

"That's a secret I can't tell," she smirks. "But lately, it seems like one of the few things I can get right. I've been trying some new recipes with honey, but I don't know. It just comes out all wacky."

"You know I'm always happy to help."

"I'll keep that in mind." She points over to a wheel at the end of the table with different prizes to win. "Wanna spin them wheel? People have been trying all day to win the free cupcakes."

I shrug. "Sure, why not. I could use some free cupcakes."

With one firm push, the wheel spins clockwise, the words blurring as it does. Free cupcakes did sound nice, but what I'm really aiming for is the half off any dozen prize because I'm not leaving Coventry without my fix of Early Bird creme puffs. The wheel begins to slow, and I roll the toothpick between my fingers as it *tick-tick-ticks* before finally stopping.

"Holy cannoli, you got the cake tasting for two!" Juniper exclaims, her family joining in on her excitement. "Every couple has been trying to win that all day. You're so lucky!"

I nod, looking at each of their smiling faces as I take the pink prize ticket, which feels heavier than it should. I quickly fold it into my pocket, ignoring the hearts and Cupid's bows that litter the paper. With effort, I force a look of shining happiness.

"*Sooo* lucky."

I toss the slip onto my dresser, figuring I can at least take Kennedy or one of my parents at some point in the next week before I leave. Maybe it looked loser-ish, but at least it's free cake, and Juniper swears her grandpa's lavender lemon cake can cure any heartache. I've never tried it, but Sasha always orders it every year for her birthday and a single orange and chocolate cupcake for me because she knows I hate lavender.

Pulling down a photo I have taped on the side of my vanity mirror, I soak in our faces as Sasha poses with a mustache and monocle, and I with a cheap flowy dress I thrifted along with sparkling silver heels. The idea for my sweet sixteen to be a costume party instead of a regular birthday party came up after I saw it in some movie where the girl's party was circus themed. Sasha and I spent so much time planning the party and our costumes. She insisted on being Mr. Herriman from *Foster's Home for Imaginary Friends*, and I decided on Dorothy from *The Wiz*. Everything about that night felt right. We felt right.

The same itch overcomes me as I turn around and spot the letter I tossed into the trash last night. To my right is the new vision board I'd been putting together for my new and improved life map. On the back was a bigger written version of the road map that I had already drawn in my journal on my way home from camp. I'm nearly finished—I could have finished it—but everything about it felt out of place. I taped and undid things so many times, and I still can't fit the pieces together.

The itching turns into a burning as I draw my attention back to the photo that reminds me of everything I want to forget, just like the one from yesterday.

My keys are still in my pocket, and my feet are already moving before my mind is made up.

CHAPTER 37

My legs pump back and forth lightly as I swing, my hands clenched around the hot metal chains. This swing set is probably older than me, as the metal parts move against each other with a high pitched shriek. The only new thing about this playground is the fact that they took out the monkey bars and replaced them with a rope bridge after the bars kept popping out of place, and because kids kept breaking them. Honestly, the rope bridge looks more dangerous than the monkey bars with how wide the holes are. At least they kept the old swirly slide.

It's five minutes until four o'clock, and knowing Sasha, she'll probably be late or she got caught trying to sneak out here in the first place. All the campers and counselors were meant to leave for the fair at half past four, and the distance from here to the camp is at least a ten minute walk. She should have been here before me; she's the one who asked me out here to begin with.

"This is stupid," I mumble, kicking off the swing with a huff. I'm just enabling her and giving her what she wants. "I need to grow up."

The headlights on my car flash just as I see Sasha's arms flailing about as she runs toward me, but my mind is made up as I speed walk to the car door. Moving on is the only right answer; I should have remembered that and stayed home. Besides, my dad wanted to have game night, and it's not too late.

"Aubree!" Sasha jogs over to be, but I'm already stepping into the driver's seat. "Wait, please. I'm not even late."

My eyes could have rolled out of my head the way she tried to throw that in my face like I should give her a bone for doing the one thing she should do after countless reminders of how irritating her lateness is. Ironically, she's almost never late to things that benefit her.

"Get away from my car," I say, dripping with avoidance.

"Are you going to run me down with it?" Sasha challenges between heavy breaths while holding the car door open and placing herself in between. Her eyes meet mine, and I know this isn't going anywhere.

"I will if I have to. Now move." I go for the door handle, pulling the door towards me, but Sasha blocks it further with her frame, arms crossed.

"Just give me five minutes."

"No."

"Please?"

"I said no, or do you simply not care about what I want?"

She pauses, and her arms fall to her sides. "I do. I'm sorry," she says softly before stepping aside. The grip on my keys tightens as I watch the old swing from my windshield lose momentum, the photos flashing in my mind like a dream. Leaving is easier than staying.

"Start talking." I slam the car door shut behind me before I lean back against it.

"I'm sorry," Sasha says as her hands fold together behind her back.

"You said that already."

"I know. I'm—" She looks over her shoulder as if the words would appear behind her. "I messed up—and I know I mess up a lot—but you're my best friend, Aubree, and I took that for granted."

Anxiously, I run my hands over my arms, hugging my chest. "You always took that for granted, Sasha. You never think twice about anything, and you constantly make me feel guilty about it, like I'm supposed to accept your shitty behavior as a part of the package. That's not a friendship, Sasha."

"You're right, and I should have listened to you sooner instead of constantly going around you. I just thought that if I pushed you that I was helping you, but I ended up getting in the way." She leans against the car next to me, keeping her eyes on her feet. "I was so blinded by jealousy that I didn't bother asking or thinking about what I was doing. I know the thing with Mateo isn't my first time fucking shit up. I didn't see how selfish I was being. It's my fault."

"It is," I spit out, breaking a hidden barrier of resistance. "But you didn't act alone. Mateo knew what he was doing and chose to keep lying to me knowing how I felt—" The words hiccup in my throat as the face I want to forget the most appears in my mind with jagged beauty. I can understand why Sasha did it, but Mateo? I thought I knew him better than that; I thought he understood me better than that. Now I can't stop his stupid face from haunting my thoughts, or forget the way his body felt pressed against mine, the feeling of walking on air just from hearing his name like music that floats on the edge of the wind.

I roll my shoulders back as I find a steady rhythm of breath. "I felt hopeful for the first time in months. He made me feel safe—like it was okay for me to breathe and let go." Each breath becomes heavier as I reel through every built up thought and emotion I've bottled up. "I went against everything I knew because of him, just like I did with AJ. And for what? So I can look like some pathetic loser that can't tell her head from her ass? I looked stupid, I was humiliated, and you were a part of that!"

My fist meets the metal frame of my car as I no longer fight back the tears that hung heavy on a thread. "I'm so tired," I wail. Sasha's arm wraps around me, holding me up as the cries become more vigorous. "I'm so tired of pretending everything's okay, that I have everything under control, like I'm not hurting. And I'm so tired of being angry all the time. I don't want to do it anymore. I'm so fucking tired."

Sasha cups me into her chest, softly rubbing my back as it all falls apart. The facade of happiness and picture perfect blurs into the ugly mess I avoid at all costs. I don't remember the last time I really paid attention to it, and now it's festered and grown into a shadow I don't recognize, but I always felt nip at my heels. It's only ever breathed down my neck, but now every regret, every worthless thought and mistake faces me with the certainty that they were more a part of me than the illusion I created.

I straighten as I wipe my face and regain a sense of ease, although I can feel the tears building up again behind my eyes.

"I want to forgive you, but I just can't understand why or forget everything that you've done in the past when I explicitly told you I didn't want to."

Sasha takes a deep breath as she steps out away from me, tugging at the sleeves of her hoodie. "I thought that I was losing my best friend," she croaks. "Seeing you and Kennedy be so close after you came back made me feel like I was being left behind and discarded. It's not an excuse, but I hadn't really seen or heard from you in a year. You kept missing my calls and skipping out on weekends we were supposed to spend together. And when you did answer the phone or I managed to make my way to campus, you were always with Kennedy. Everything became about you and her, and I love Kennedy, but I felt like I was being replaced and that I knew nothing about you anymore.

"I stayed back in Coventry and you went off to school, and so much changed that I wasn't ready for." Sasha's head falls, and a stream of tears soak the light blue fabric of her hoodie. "And when you came back, you were so heartbroken, and I wasn't there to help you; it was Kennedy. It just brought up all these feelings of being a disappointment and how I'm always getting in the way. That's not your fault, but I wanted to be useful and prove that I could be selfless, so I asked Mateo to help me do it. I thought that if I helped you realize how much he liked you, you'd forget about AJ and the Franklin. I thought I was doing the right thing—that this would turn out differently than everything else I've done—I was wrong. I set you up for me and tried to convince myself otherwise. I'm so sorry, Aubree."

Sasha's arms wrap around herself as her breath becomes heavy with a silent cry. A range of emotions from bitterness to remorse flows through my fingertips as I contemplate what to do—what to say. There was no denying that I had left Sasha out for the past year, ignoring her calls, missing texts, and forgetting our plans. But this is a pattern with Sasha, a bigger issue than a simple lapse in judgment. She forced Mateo onto me and hid it from me for weeks. She crossed a line, but I also can't pretend those last few weeks weren't some of the best I had in a long time, even if it wasn't real.

Slowly, my arms come around Sasha, a natural and true feeling as hers wrap around my frame. "I know you're sorry, and I know you'd never intend to hurt me. You're not a malicious person... just really thoughtless at times."

"I know you wanted to say stupid," she says, hearing the smile she wears.

"Yeah, but I'm trying to forgive you right now, and it wouldn't be nice given that I haven't been that great of a friend to you lately."

"That's not what I meant."

"But it's the truth." Stepping back to look at her, I fix Sasha's hair while she taps at her face with her sleeves. "I hate what you did, and jealousy is a shitty reason, but I don't hate you because I knew what I was doing at times. I didn't want anything to get in the way of the future I mapped out for myself, and I treated you like you would because I was afraid you wouldn't get it. You were always so pushy. I didn't want to hear how I was wasting my time or how I was stretching myself too thin. I should have trusted you, and I'm sorry I didn't."

She nods. "You're right, though. I understand why you'd keep some things from me, but it really hurts when you do."

"That makes two of us." I offer her a small smile, to which she responds with another hug.

"I'll do better, I swear," Sasha whispers.

"We both will," I confirm. "But I don't think I can forgive Mateo."

"That's understandable." Sasha purses her lips as she falls back onto the car, twisting a loc from her hair between her fingers and thumb.

"What?" I question, narrowing my eyes at her.

She shrugs, keeping her voice cool. "Nothing. I support your decision. Can I get a ride back to camp?" Sasha walks around to the passenger side of my car with a teasing avoidance that's both annoying and slightly intrusive.

I've thought long and hard about it, and there's no scenario where I can see myself forgiving Mateo. It isn't as simple as not wanting him in my life, but it's the thought of letting him in again—letting myself love him again—that scared me. The people you love are meant to see all of you, hold your heart in their hands like an unforeseen treasure that can slip at any moment. We're meant to trust that they would never do anything to harm you or to break the intimate bond tied together with an invisible string that pulls you closer. I still feel that string tugging and yanking, weighing me down, and I can't be brought down just to have to pick myself up again. I know how this ends, I know what it looks like. I'll lose myself in him, forget his lies, and numb the pain until he's all that I see, and I can't be that girl again.

"You think I should give him another chance." The truth breaks through my spiraling thoughts and lands face up for both Sasha and me to acknowledge.

Sasha raises her hands in defense. "Well, I mean, you gave me one."

"And that was hard enough." The words come out harsher than I mean, leaving a sting that imprints itself on the tension slowly shifting in our atmosphere. "You're my best friend. I know you. I hate that you did it, but I know you. Mateo is just some guy—"

"Some guy?" Sasha shakes her head, laughing to herself as she slides into the passenger seat. I duck in after her as her laughter fills the tiny space. "Don't bullshit, Bree."

"I'm not, actually. Everything we've built was based on lies, and you of all people know that."

"But—"

"But nothing," I say. "I'm not talking anymore about it, and I mean it. I've accepted that it's over, and if you really are my friend and want to keep it that way, you'll leave it alone."

"You have my word. I won't mention 'some guy' ever again." Sasha pretends to zip her lips shut, locks them, and throws away the key.

The car ride is short, but feels so much longer sitting in restless silence. I never realized how much I was used to relying on Sasha's opinions to form my own outside of anything that didn't have to do with school or my career. To be honest, I never really gave anything else any thought. I assumed everything else would eventually fall in place after I finally settled into my career, leaving little room for dating, as if my lack of experience wasn't already evident. AJ just happened. I mean, I definitely wasn't opposed to it, but there was no road map or color-coded chart that led to him or Mateo—especially Mateo. Mateo crashed into me—one beautiful disaster—and no matter how hard I pulled away, the harder it was to deny that my heart was already his. But knowing that he lied after I confessed so much to him makes me question that feeling.

I was vulnerable and heartbroken, and he took advantage of that. If I forgive him now, I would be saying that I was okay with it, and I can't let my feelings twist reality.

Dust kicks up around the car as I pull onto the road leading to the Camp Whisper Lake parking lot, parking a distance away so that Sasha can sneak back in unnoticed. Remaining counselors run around helping campers pack their belongings before final pickup.

"The buses will be here soon; you should get going." I squeeze her hand before pulling her into a quick hug.

"We'll be back around seven thirty if you want to come by and hang out." Sasha smiles.

"I can't, but have fun," I say, hoping I don't sound too callous.

"Okay. Well, thanks, Bree." Sasha sighs as she looks me over. "I know you don't want to hear anything else about it—"

"Ugh!"

"Listen!" she exclaims with a giggle. "I know you don't care, but I want you to hear this... I've never seen you happier and as vibrant as I did this summer. And I'm not saying it's because of what's-his-face, but it looked good on you, and I hope you'll find that again once you move and start living those big city dreams—even though you'd be leaving me behind and miss me way too much."

"Okay, Sasha," I giggle. "Thanks for that. Now go before someone sees me."

She interlocks her fingers with mine, giving our hands a final squeeze before dashing out toward the panicked rush of campers. In the midst of them, my gaze catches the one figure I'd recognized from any angle or light. Mateo sits in a squat, and I can hear the tenderness in his voice as he tries to soothe the young girl he's with as she frantically searches her backpack. The crescent on his lips is more than enough to know that he will take care of it, whatever the problem is, because that's who he is. The kindness that's melted in his eyes is always one of a promise unbroken. Those eyes, that smile, seemed to always find me when I needed their warmth the most. And looking at him now, maybe that's the one thing about him that never changed.

Chapter 38

"Do you not hear me talking to you?"

"Hmm?" I sound, snapping back into reality as I rinse off the dish that's in my hands.

"I asked when you were going to be done? You might just wash the color out of that plate." My mom gestures to my hands before taking it and drying it off.

"Sorry, I was thinking." Thinking as in completely out of my own mind and body. Every time I tried to focus on the conversation at dinner or on the dishes, I daydreamed to the places I wanted to be and the person I can't stop thinking about.

I was just at the county fair, a light breeze against my face as the ferris wheel rotated around. Above me, Maeve and Beck shared a cart as they pointed out the different attractions at the fair that they planned to try next. But next to me, an arm rested over my shoulders, and his warm cherry scent filled my lungs with longing pleasure. We never said a word to each other, but the squeeze of my arm and the way his fingers brushed my shoulder said a thousand I missed you's. I met him in kind as my finger traced out our initials on his knee. I kept reimagining the scene in different ways, trying to decide if it would be better for us to talk or if the words would get lost in the moment. The way his lips might brush against my ear to whisper into the heat of desire that would fill my soul and lead to a night full of other things.

"Why are you smiling like that?"

My face drops, and so does my sponge before turning to my mother in confusion. "Like what?"

"*Like what?*" she mocks as she flicks her wet fingers at me, causing me to flinch back. "Do we really need to go there?"

"There's nowhere to go because you're just seeing things. When's the last time you've seen Dr. Krause?"

"My eyes are just fine, thank you." She dips her hand into the dish water and flicks some at me.

"Ma!" Moving back, I don't forget to block my face this time. Her laughter is contagious as she threatens to follow me over the kitchen island, this time with a big glob of soap bubbles to wipe across my face.

"What happened to not treating me like a little girl anymore?" I plead.

"I'm not treating you like one. I'm treating you like my daughter."

A mischievous grin spreads across her face as she finally grabs at me, only to miss me by the thread of my shirt as I lunge out of the way, and she loses the bubbles to the floor.

"Fine, whatever," she groans bitterly as I fall over in laughter at her loss. "Out of my kitchen. Your googly eyes were slowing me down anyway."

"Rude, but fair. I didn't want to help anyway."

Bed was calling my name alongside a long, warm shower. My pajamas are already laid out on my bed, ready and waiting for me to slide into because there's nothing like the feeling of soft cotton fabric on clean skin.

I grab my robe and shower cap from behind my door before catching a glimpse of an old vision board resting in the corner, peaking out from under some newer ones I made. Before pulling it out, I'm already certain of which one it is. My mom started the tradition of vision boards when I was around eight or nine, and every two or three years, we'd make a new one before I started doing them yearly on my own. This one happened to be the summer before my senior year of high school. I remember wanting to do something different. Instead of just pictures and affirmations, I wanted it to be a keepsake. I stuck six small envelopes to the board and filled them each with a memento of the things I achieved that year. Two of them were just photos of the moment in question, another crunched under my touch as I opened it to find the remnants of dried rose petals. It wasn't exactly a part of my vision for the year, but it was the best unexpected desire to come to fruition. Every year for Valentine's Day, the cheerleading team would raise money by selling candy grams ranging from a simple flower and sucker to a small bouquet and chocolates; hand delivered by our school's mascot dressed as Cupid. This year, I got a candy gram of my own that wasn't a Galentine's gift from Maeve or Sasha. I can remember the feeling of my heart in my stomach when they said my name and handed me the rose and heart-shaped sucker with an attached card marked 'anonymous' on the front. I'd spent the rest of the semester dreaming up the mystery guy who sent it to me and never came forward. It hurt a little not knowing who he was and why they didn't seem to want me to. But I had to stop wondering and guessing for my own good, as I was getting obsessed with the idea of Happily Ever After.

The rose died pretty quickly, but I did my best to salvage what I could of its petals. The only clue I had of who my secret admirer could be was the drawing they left me inside the card.

Carefully, I pull the small card out of the large envelope to admire the drawing of two swans, just as beautiful as I remember it. Their heads touch together to make a heart as they float in a ring of water. At the time, I didn't appreciate the drawing as much as I adored the fantasy of someone unknown having a crush on me. But now, all I can think of are the hands that crafted the image. Hands I'd seen countless times as they held mine; wrapped around my back as they pulled me in for a kiss, a hug, a reassuring grasp.

Digging through my jewelry box, I quickly find what I'm looking for as the shiny wings of the butterfly pendant hits my fingers. Pressing it into my hand, a sense of relief washes over me as a stark realization has me on my feet and down the stairs, headed for the front door, when my dad stops me before I can reach the foyer.

"Whoa, hold it there, Speedy." My dad's hand comes to my shoulder, slowing me down.

"Dad, I gotta go."

"Go where? I thought you were staying in for tonight, and what about game night?"

"We can do game night another night, but I really need to go."

"Why? It's almost eight o'clock and you know I'm in bed by ten."

"Dad," I groan, but he only crosses his arms, blocking my path to the door, knowing I won't bum-rush him.

"Game night is an important family tradition for the Harper's. Your granddad did it, and so did his dad, and we will—"

"Ma!" I exclaim. "Please tell Dad to leave me alone so I can go? He's trying to guilt me."

My mom peeks her head around the corner. "Go? It's almost eight o'clock at night."

So much for not treating me like a little girl.

Rolling my eyes isn't an option, so I settle for counting to three on a deep inhale. "I'm going to the fair. It's important."

"More important than us?" My dad jabs his fingers into his chest dramatically.

"Dennis." My mom eyes him, which causes his immediate retreat. I don't know if it's how scattered I look or the desperation in my voice, but I know that my mom knows. "Go on, but text us when you get there."

"Thank you, thank you!"

I only take a second to grab my hoodie from the couch before my house is in the rear view mirror behind me.

CHAPTER 39

It feels like I've been riding with my heart ready to shoot out of my chest when I roll into the Camp Whisper Lake parking lot. A few cars are left in the lot, but the camp is quiet and dark aside from a few lights that were left on for the bathrooms and outside several of the cabins. I search for Mateo's car as I pull into a spot in the back, but I come up just as empty as the void expanding in my chest.

My grip tightens on the steering wheel as my head falls hard against it. I might take notice of the throbbing from the impact if not for the pounding in my ears as I flood myself with thoughts of everywhere I went wrong, and everything I can do to salvage it. His car not being here doesn't mean he went home; he could have gone back to the fair with some of the others. Then again, everyone's supposed to remain here until all campers have gone home, but was Mateo ever one to follow the rules? Having his number might do me some good if I had any fucking service.

"Ugh!" I exhale, banging my head against the wheel again before rubbing the spot to soothe the ache that was continuing to spread to my temples. "What am I doing?"

If Aubree from three months ago could see me now, she'd be standing over me, shaking her head like an overly disappointed micromanager. She would never go after a man who did her wrong, but she also never felt a love like the one I'm fortunate enough to know. He's wrong, and in my playbook, he doesn't deserve a second chance, but maybe it's time to rewrite the rules and tell a different story. One where I don't have to sacrifice love for a career or acceptance. I can at least hear him out… right?

"No," I mumble. My foot is on the brake, ready to turn on the car, when two shadows pass over my passenger and driver's side doors. The scream I let out could get me first place as Coventry's Scream Queen at the fall festival. But the death glare I give after is only enough to make my friends find this hilarious. Sasha and Kennedy cackle into the night sky as I step out of the car, slamming the door.

"I hate both of you," I say, shoving my way past Kennedy. "That was so evil. How did you even know it was me?"

"You pulled in with your bright ass headlights and bad brakes. It could only be you." Kennedy wraps her arms around me through laughs.

"Shady and accurate. I love it," Sasha sings as she slides in next to us.

"It's nice to see that you two are still good after everything." I check their expressions for any slight changes to prove me wrong, but they both smile at each other as if it made them closer.

"We're good as long as Sasha doesn't pull anything like that again." Kennedy eyes Sasha, who nods in agreement.

"Cross my heart," Sasha swears as she completes the gesture over her chest. "No more shenanigans. No more keeping secrets."

I look to Kennedy, who cosigns the sentiment. "No secrets... as soon as you tell us why you're here."

"I'm not here. I just came because I forgot something in my cabin." The excuse leaves my lips with ease.

"You? Forgetful?" Sasha challenges. "The Aubree we know wouldn't even walk past a penny, let alone *forget* her things in the middle of the woods and then come to get them after dark by herself."

That might be true, but I'm not so afraid of the dark that I can't function when necessary—some things are important enough to let fear subside. Although I'd be lying if I said it wasn't slowly creeping back in from how the camp would make a perfect stage for a slasher film, and because I'm slowly realizing the sacrifice I was willing to take just to have Mateo back in my life. My dignity cannot be that shallow.

"I'm human, Sash. And what if I wanted to come check on you?" I throw from over my shoulder as I march toward camp and toward a light source.

Sasha's eyes grow wide at me. "And now she's admitting she's human? What did you do to my best friend who yelled at me for buying ballpoint pens instead of rollerball?"

My eyes fly to the back of my head as I scoff. "There's a clear difference between the two, I told you that multiple times before you even left for the store. And you're an artist! You should know that."

"Gosh, I didn't know you were so passionate about pens." Kennedy's arm links with mine, pulling me in a different direction.

"The right pen makes a difference." Sasha mimics me in unison with a giggle.

"I thought you said you weren't coming to hang out with us," Sasha adds.

Does this girl have to remember everything I say? Sasha's always been quick to remind you of the things you've said, especially the things you promise. It doesn't matter if it was a month ago or five years ago; she has it stored in a little filing cabinet, ready to pull out at any moment. It's both annoying and useful, especially when I can't remember what I'm supposed to get at the grocery store.

"I can change my mind, thank you," I say.

Kennedy chuckles. "Yeah, okay."

"What?" I question, confused. "I don't have a default setting."

"It's not that," she says, although I'm still not convinced. "It's just that you rarely change your mind once it's made up, so it makes me wonder... why are you really here?"

"To see you guys and get the stuff in my cabin." I point to it as we move closer. Kennedy and Sasha both stare at me in blank frustration as we stop near the stairs.

Kennedy's hand comes to her hips, daring another lie to cross my lips. "There's nothing left in your cabin, Bree. Josh made us check after you left in case you did so that he wouldn't be responsible for making sure you got your things back." Kennedy's voice turns with irritation at the mention of it. As caring and responsible as Josh is, he is extremely lazy somehow.

"Oh," I say quietly.

"Yeah, oh. So, spill," Sasha demands. "Because I'm pretty sure we can all put two and two together here."

Their eyes narrow at me, and all I can feel is my heart hammering in my chest. He's not even here, so there's really no reason for me to lie, but that doesn't make the truth easier to say. I could run. I could hop in my car, speed off, and call this a lapse in judgment. I could forget that this ever happened with my dignity still intact. But that wouldn't slow the way my heart beats for him. How my body yearns for him in ways so familiar yet unnatural. And it wouldn't make how he truly did care for me all those years any less real, especially not with the necklace burning a hole in my pocket. What makes it worse is that I didn't see that until now. I always assumed Mateo was just being annoying, but there were times he was a comfort to me. Times when he went out of his way to make sure I was okay when all I ever did was dismiss him. It feels different now looking back, but I can't keep wavering on the truth of how I feel now. Everything does have its place, but Mateo isn't just someone I can shove in a box when he feels like the world.

My shoulders relax as I take a deep breath and straighten. "I came for Mateo."

"We were hoping you'd say that." A smile spreads across Sasha's face, filling the corners of her mouth. Kennedy tries to keep hers concealed, but the twitch in her lip betrays her.

"I'm sure," I sigh with anticipation of their ridicule, but it doesn't come. Kennedy takes my hand and pulls me toward the direction of the lake, Sasha trailing in front of us with a slight skip in her step.

"Where are we going?" I ask, trying to guess what's up ahead, but all I can see is darkness since the lamp was out near the supply shed.

"You'll see," Kennedy says.

"You can't just tell me?"

"Girl, just wait." Kennedy pulls me to the side and positions me to face her, a glint of excitement in her eyes. A chill rushes down my spine, and I suddenly can't find it in me to fight her to tell me. The expression on her face tells me everything I need to know.

"Kenny, is Mateo here?"

Kennedy's hands come to my shoulders before a soft light illuminates across her dark skin. "You tell me."

Her gentle hands turn me around, and my breath catches in my throat. Fairy lights wrap around the old oak tree, the wires reaching from branch to branch as the lights sparkle on the surface of the lake. A warmth spreads from my core as I move closer and notice small rectangles hanging throughout the tree. At first, they don't look like much of anything, but as one spins forward, it reveals a photo of me. They're all photos of me. Some with friends, many of myself candid, and others with Mateo. I reach up to grab one, keeping it from twirling on the string. I'm sitting on the dock, my foot splashing up water in retaliation of Beck, but the focus is on me. I would have never taken a photo like this knowingly, yet I've never seen myself look more beautiful—more at peace. Something in my chest swells, and my breathing turns shallow as tears form at the corners of my eyes.

"I love that photo of you." A deep voice comes in a calm whisper from behind me. I stay where I am, facing the photo, looking at others nearby that can barely be seen through the gloss of my tears.

"You took these?" I ask, already knowing the answer.

"Most of them," Mateo says. His voice is closer, almost swiping across the hairs on the back of my neck, but he keeps his distance. "Some I got from Sasha, Maeve, and Kennedy."

I almost laugh. Of course they helped him. It's almost ironic given why we're here in the first place. Still, I can't help but be filled with awe. Nearly every moment—every memory I made with and without intention this summer—is before my eyes, captured in a light I never thought I'd find myself in. A joy I thought was lost with the part of me I buried long ago.

My hands come to my chest, squeezing my fingers when I feel an overflow of excitement and fear rise to the surface. "Mateo..."

"You don't have to say anything," he says in a rush. "Really, I know I don't deserve anything from you."

"But you knew I'd come because you asked Sasha to invite me here." I turn to face him, wanting to see the truth as much as I want to feel it.

He stiffens when my gaze finds his, holding him to the words he says. "I was hoping you might, but I was prepared if you didn't."

"So, you used her to get to me?"

Silence falls upon us, only the rippling of the lake cutting through. Mateo's hand comes to the back of his neck, and my feet feel heavy as the illusion begins to crack. I didn't come here to be tricked again. What's the point of any of this if using others to get to me is our only form of communication?

"It sounds really bad, and I'm sorry about that." He pauses, waiting for a reaction that I don't give. "But it was the only way I could think of getting you here. I thought it might be better and less creepy than showing up at your window with a boom box every night."

I shake my head. "Creepy, yes, but who you really need to worry about are my parents. They take sleep very seriously in their house."

A grin breaks across his face, the same as mine, and I let him move in toward me as his hands find mine. My fingers interlock with his, melting in his tenderness.

"Aubree, you've been the woman on my mind for years. Something I've always kept secret out of fear you might reject me—fear that I could never measure up to you. So, when I found out you would be working at camp this summer, I jumped at every opportunity to prove differently and to show you that I wasn't the guy you knew me to be. In doing that, I betrayed your trust. It was stupid and inconsiderate, and if I could tell you a million sorry's I would. I wanted to tell you the truth, but I was so caught up in the fact that I was finally with the woman of my dreams, even if it was only for a few weeks.

"The truth is that I love you. I've loved you for a long time, and my heart never forgot how that felt. You're smart and beautiful, and you made me realize I'm more than enough. What I did was cowardly and selfish. I never want to be that man, and I can understand if you walk away from me now, but I can't live without you. My soul is filled with you, my heart yearns for you, and I can't let that feeling go without a fight. I'd lose you all over again if it means I get to keep choosing you because choosing you is the easiest decision I've ever made. Please, give me a chance to show you and make it right."

My mind's been a thousand places since the start of the summer, and a thousand more since leaving camp. I've thought of every dream, every scenario, every life where I would never entrust all of myself with a man again. Where I'd hold the things dearest to me close, keeping them locked away without fear of them being used against me. But no matter what I dreamed up or what I wanted to believe, nothing compared to the comfort and peace I feel with Mateo. My mind would eventually end up back here. To the times my stomach ached from laughing too hard at Mateo's jokes, to how weightless I felt when he'd offered himself to me without hesitation, and the wit sharp on our tongues when we'd disagree with pleasure. There's nothing I can imagine that comes close to the way Mateo makes me feel.

I run my fingers up his wrist, resting my thumb on his pulse. Always steady, and always sure. Pulling my necklace and drawing from my pocket, I place them in his hand. He looks at me, unsure as I shake my head. "You're good for keeping secrets."

"I know. I'm sorry."

He goes to pull away from me, but I pull him back into my grasp. "I can't lie to you. I'm still so mad at you, and I'm afraid."

Mateo's hand comes to my cheek, brushing away a tear, only for his to fall. "I know, and that's my fault. I hate that I did that to you, especially knowing what you've been through. But I promise you, I will never be the cause of your pain again."

"You can't promise me that. One of us will always end up hurting the other in some way."

"Then what can I do?" Mateo's hand comes to my waist, keeping me still against him, and I notice the pleading look for an answer woven between his brows.

I shrug. "There's no definitive answer or solution I can give you. You'll need to carn my trust and show me how true your love really is without the mask."

"Whatever it takes and however long. I just need you."

"I need you too."

Mateo's arms wrap around my waist, lifting me off the ground and into a spin. My laughter fills the air between demands for him to let me down. I glance over his expression, familiarizing myself with his smile lines and swimming in the heat behind his eyes as they longingly dance across my face. Out of the corner of my eye, I notice Kennedy and Sasha huddled together, wiping their own tears as they silently cheer us on from a distance.

"I think they're waiting for us to kiss," I say, my hands coming up to his shoulders.

"You think they deserve a show?" Mateo smirks from behind his teasing tone.

"Maybe, but I need an answer from you first." His eyebrow ticks up as he leans in. "Were you ever going to tell me you were my secret admirer for the candy gram and about the necklace?"

"If I did, it wouldn't have been much of a secret," he jokes.

"No, but I could have loved you sooner."

Our lips brush each others shyly before Mateo's mouth covers mine tenderly. My guard falls as I pull myself to my tiptoes and breathlessly give him my all as we start again.

EPILOGUE ONE

ETHAN

I hand the man behind the stand another five dollar bill, making that the fifth in one night as he hands another stick of cotton candy to Lillian, who promptly plucks a chunk of it off to hand to me.

"Oh, how thoughtful of you." I hold it up in thanks, which is met with an infamous eye roll.

"At least I'm sharing. That's more than I can say for you and your funnel cakes."

"You don't eat funnel cakes, Lill."

"No, I don't eat funnel cakes smothered in strawberries and chocolate sauces, but you never offer either," she combats.

I stuff the cotton candy into my mouth, the blue raspberry flavored sugar melting over my tongue. I know she's right, but I won't complain. She was the one who convinced me to come out to the county fair tonight, even though I know she really wanted to go with her friends. Still, she insisted that it be only us two since we haven't come as a family in a few years. I'll admit, it's nice to get out of the house, and it's a much needed break after spending all week working on building Mr. Giovanni's back porch. That guy loved to micromanage for someone who's never picked up a hammer.

Screams and laughter fill the air as the giant boat swing flies past us. It was one of the first rides we always went on together. Despite how tame it is, the funny feeling you get in your stomach when you hit the highest point always makes us laugh. It also gave us a nice breeze from the humidity that hung in the air. We stuck to our tradition of riding the swing, but what Lillian really couldn't wait for was the Mega Drop. I remember the first time she was tall enough to ride it; she'd been growing like a weed all year, and it quickly became her favorite. We'd waited to get on the ride, thinking the line might get shorter, but the crowd this year is thicker than I can last remember.

"Dad, hurry up!" Lillian waves me over as she jogs to the line for the Mega Drop. It isn't my top pick, given I hate waiting in long lines, but I liked seeing Lillian so happy, especially because her happiness reminded me so much of where I need to be.

"Comin'," I say as I lightly jog behind her. This ride is one of the only ones on the grounds that has gates extending past the makeshift walkways, the line moving in a back and forth pattern. I squeeze past a few people standing in line at the Big Squeeze to get to where Lillian's standing. Thankfully, the line seems to be moving fast.

Lillian plops the last piece of her cotton candy into her mouth before tossing the paper stick into a nearby trash bin. At least this time she didn't hand it to me and force me to carry it around until I could throw it away for her.

"I'm so excited," Lillian gleams, her hands clapping together. Seeing her so happy about little things like this. It made me realize just how much time I've spent on autopilot these last few years, trying to keep everything afloat for us—for her. This last year has been so much lighter, like how things used to be.

"I'm just as stoked as you are," I say as I try to match her excitement despite my slight fear of heights.

"Stoked, Dad?" Lillian raises an eyebrow.

"What? Oh, am I out of the loop again?" I grin as her face scrunches up. "Don't do that like I'm not the world's coolest Dad."

"You are the world's coolest Dad, just a little outdated."

"Are you calling me old?"

"If the shoe fits," she giggles with no attempt to hide her true feelings.

"Ah, I see how it is..." I lift my two fists, positioning myself into a lowered stance before breaking out my best Lion impression. "Put 'em up."

She jumps into position with a burst of laughter as we go into our routine of play boxing, jabbing right and left until I let her defeat me with an upper cut—like always. *The Wizard of Oz* was one of our favorite family night movies when she was growing up, so it came as no surprise when she started repeating the iconic phrase, rolling her fist in front of her face whenever something didn't sit right with her. Playing along only made it funnier, and it eventually just stuck. It was our thing, and now that she's 15, I didn't think we would still have one. But so much has changed, and it's brought us so much closer.

"I'm the champ!" She declares as she raises her fists in victory. "Crown me."

"Absolutely not."

"Yeah-huh! The battle is won and I'm the victor."

Crossing my arms, I lean over on the gate. "The battle may be won, but the war isn't over."

"Whatever, you're just a sore loser." She crosses her arms at me.

I straighten up to defend myself, but breaking through the rowdiness of the fair comes laughter that perks up my ears. It tugs at me, and then I see her out of the corner of my eye. Her head thrown back as her laughter grows—warm and inviting. My gaze falls to her smile, her full lips, and then traces every curve of her form. She walks in full strides like she knows where she's going—where she belongs—yet I don't think I've seen her before. Not that I know most people in town; raising a kid at 16 means your circle grows pretty small. So, the chances of me recognizing her are already slim. Still, it doesn't stop the fire that lights itself ablaze in me from needing to know who she is.

Lillian's gaze follows mine, and her brows scrunch with curiosity. "Do you know her? Because you're staring really hard, and I think you might scare her."

"Hmm?" My eyes never leave her, and as she stops to point up at the Mega Drop just as the ride is plummeting back down, her eyes drop to mine, and I swear I see the faintest smile on her lips before her friends pull her away in another direction. Dammit.

"Dad!" Lillian exclaims as she waves her hand in front of my face.

Clearing my throat, I snap out of my daze. "Yeah? What, Lill?"

"You were staring and the lines moving."

Lillian pulls me forward, but I can't help but get one last look at the mystery woman. The view from the back is much better.

"Do you know that woman?" Lillian has a far better social life than I do—people usually refer to me as "Lillian's dad," followed by a nod of approval after I confirm their suspicion. She's my main connection to the outside world that isn't work or a quick grocery trip to Stanton's General Store.

"You mean the one you were drooling over like a stalker?" She asks a little too loudly. "No. Never seen her."

"Are you sure?"

Lillian rolls her eyes for the 500th time tonight. "Yes, Dad. I recognized the girl next to her, Aubree, from when she used to volunteer for tutoring a few years ago, but it's the county fair. She could be anyone."

Heavy with disappointment, I nod as I repeat her words softly. "Right. She could be anyone." But she doesn't feel like just anyone.

Something pulls at me to go after her—find her, know her by name so I know who I'll be dreaming of at night—but an anchor weighs me to the spot I've been for the past four years. Something about her calls to me, a feeling I never knew I'd have again, but I miss my chance as she blends into the crowd, and my luck spills through my fingers. If luck will have it, I'll get my chance again.

Epilogue Two

Mateo

Five months later

"Dammit, this is taking forever." Slamming the oven shut, I wind the timer for another five minutes. Cooking comes naturally to me. I get in the kitchen, turn on some music, and the rest falls together. But baking is a science I could never get behind. Everything always comes out burnt, under baked, or chewy when it's meant to be soft. I thought cookies would be easy, but I either made them too big or the oven isn't working because it's been half an hour, and they're still not done. As I look over the recipe again, my phone rings, Aubree's face popping up on the screen next to mine, and my chest swells.

Answering it, I put her on speaker as I work to clean the kitchen of the mess I've made. "Hey, babe. Everything okay?"

"Hey," Aubree sings over the sounds of traffic and Christmas music. "I'm okay, I'm actually outside. Can you buzz me in? My hands are full."

"What?" I croak, turning back to the phone as I set the dishes in the sink. "But you said you would be gone until six?"

"That was the plan," she says with a groan. "But the article can wait, and it's kinda creepy being at the office alone on a Sunday—are you gonna buzz me in? These bags are heavy."

"Yeah, yeah. One sec." Frantically, I look around the kitchen at the very large mess. Powdered sugar and splattered milk litter the center island alongside what I'm sure is the entire paper towel roll. This was meant to be a surprise. I'd scoured the internet for the best strawberry frosted sugar cookie recipe, only for it to turn out to be a complete disaster and more difficult than I originally thought. Juniper makes it look so easy that I didn't think I'd take the entire afternoon and a second bag of flour after I'd dropped the first one.

I buzz Aubree in before quickly tossing everything into a trash bag and wiping down the island with a damp cloth. Just as I'm getting done, I step into something slimy, lifting my foot to find the egg whites I'd spilled earlier and completely forgot about.

"Nice going, Mateo," I mumble to myself as I hop on one foot to grab a clean paper towel. As I work to wipe off the sticky substance, my heart leaps into my throat as I hear the click of the lock on the door.

"Mateo?" Aubree's voice rings out from the hall, lighting a fire under me as I toss the trash bag into the pantry and cover the egg whites with a rag.

"Right here." I rush to meet her at the front door, taking the grocery bags from her arms before rushing them into the kitchen.

"Do you want me to help you put them away?"

"Nope, I got it," I grunt as I set the bags down. "Just sit on the couch and relax. Don't worry about it."

"Okay—wait." She pauses, and the pulsing in my temples intensifies. "Is something burning?"

"*Shit*," I whisper as I turn to see smoke coming out of the oven. Looking at the timer, I realize I set it to 15 minutes instead of five. "*Shit, shit, shit.*"

Aubree stumbles into the kitchen, her eyes wide as I pull the cookies out of the oven—slightly burnt. "Babe, what happened?"

"Surprise?" I say, shrugging my shoulders. The confusion on her face lessens as she begins to notice the dishes in the sink and the spots of flour I missed on the floor.

"We're you... baking?" She asks as she lifts the rag on the floor to find the egg whites.

"I wouldn't call this baking since the cookies are ruined."

A laugh slips from her beautiful lips as she comes to my side, eyes the cookies and then me. I can never get tired of hearing that laugh or the look in her eyes when she's full of happiness and admiration. It's like coming home after a long day and finding the same warmth and love in every corner of every room that's always there waiting for you. How I got so lucky is beyond me, but I savor every drop she has to offer.

"It's not too bad. Only the bottom is burnt," she says as she flips one up with a spatula.

"No, it was meant to be your favorite," I sigh as I open the bowl of pink frosting. The only thing I'd managed to get right.

"Aw, Mateo." Aubree leans in to lay a soft kiss on my lips as her hands fall to my chest. "Thank you, and it's not all ruined."

"How? The idea was for you to have freshly baked cookies, not burnt ones." My hands fall to her waist as she moves into me.

Dipping her finger into the icing, she brings her finger to her mouth, swirling her tongue around the tip before sucking it into her mouth. Her eyes never leave mine, and I feel my cock jerk in my pants as it hardens. And I'm sure she notices from the wicked smile that forms on her face.

"I can think of a few other uses for it." She dips her finger in the frosting again, this time bringing it to my lips as I suck it into my mouth. Her mouth hangs open as my tongue flicks the icing off, the sweetness spreading over my tongue.

"Tasty." I lift her onto the island, my hands full of her ass before dragging them down to her thighs. Her lips lock with mine as her legs wrap around my waist. My mouth finds the curve of her neck, and I grab more icing to spread across the path to her collarbone. Aubree bites down on her moan as I slowly lick up the sugary frosting, leaving not a trace behind. The frosting is good, but nothing could ever top her taste.

My cock jerks again as my mouth begins to water for a taste of her pussy. Reaching down to undo her pants, she places her hands on top of mine before pulling out of our kiss.

"What? What's wrong?" I ask, searching her expression as I try to ignore the ache in my cock.

Aubree smiles as she places her hands on my shoulders. "Nothing, but there's something else I want to do first before we get too comfortable."

I wait for her to tell me more, but knowing her, I should have expected the anticipation that follows as she leads me into the living room. We'd spent hours decorating the apartment to get in the holiday spirit, which Aubree insists started the day after Halloween. Since I moved to Columbus with her, I've let her take the lead on deciding what and where to put things when it comes to decorating. But for Christmas, she wanted the space to feel like home for both of us. We filled the space with homemade Christmas ornaments and trinkets, both old and new, decorating the tree with randomness that glistens with the spirit of Christmas past. It was a stark contrast to the usual organized and well patterned decor she usually goes for, but it rings true to her love for tradition.

A few presents are already under the tree as she dips down to pull out a small envelope with my name on it. A spark dances in her eye as she hands it to me.

"So, I know you said we weren't doing early presents because it ruins the fun, but I really hope you'll make an exception for this one." Aubree beams up at me, and I just want to kiss the glow on her face.

"What is it?" I ask, shaking the envelope.

She rolls her eyes, but her smile remains. "Just open it, please?"

Obliging her, I tear open the seal and pull out a piece of folded paper. I eye her, but she gestures for me to continue, almost dancing as she watches me. I chuckle as I unfold the paper, my gaze freezing on the words Pago Pago International Airport. My heart rate triples as I peer up at Aubree, who nods at me with a wide grin.

"Is this real?" I ask, a ball forming in my throat.

She nods. "Yeah, I bought the ticket a month ago. You always talk about how you miss your family, and how you wish they could be here for Christmas since this is your first one without them. So, I decided to bring you to them."

I try to swallow as the sting behind my eyes builds, but it's all too much to keep at bay. "Babe, I don't know what to say. I—" Tears roll from my eyes as I exhale sharply. No one's ever done something like this for me before.

"Say you'll go," she says as she takes my face in her hands, wiping at my tears. "We'll have plenty of Christmases together. Spend this one with your family."

"But what about you? You're not going?"

She shakes her head. "Not this time, but I'll be fine. Plus, I'm excited to spend Christmas in Coventry this year. I really miss the Winter Wonderland Festival. Family is important, and you're important to me. Please, go. They're expecting you."

There's a tick in my chest as I think back to my home in Samoa as a newfound excitement overtakes me. Swiftly, I pick Aubree up, spinning her around as our laughter fills the apartment. I've spent so much of my time and life observing others, I never realized how much I craved to be seen with the love Aubree has for me. This is what I want. This is love.

Acknowledgements

Thank you for reading my debut novel, *Flowers for No Occasion*! It means the world to me that you decided to give my novel a chance, and I hope you loved it just as much as I do. From start to finish, this novel as when a roller coaster of emotions for me, but it wouldn't have been possible without a few very special people.

I first want to thank Hannah Latham for the beautiful artwork for the cover of my novel. You truly brought my characters and vision to life.

I want to take the time to thank Ms. J. Miller. Without your undying support and dedication to your students, this novel wouldn't have been possible. You took the time to teach me how to be a writer when no one else would, and I'm forever grateful for it. Your love for what you do is what brought me here.

And thank you, Mrs. J. Patton. You have always been my biggest cheerleader. When I doubted myself, you never let me keep my head down. Because of you, I remember my worth and the talent I have to offer and continue to grow each day. I aspire to have your strength and passion.

I would also like to thank my sister, Jasmine, and my mother for the relentless reminders of how I've always preferred pen and paper over toys. Thank you for encouraging me and giving me the space to be the writer you knew I'd become.

And to my little sister, Jessalyn. Thank you for being a badass and constantly getting on my nerves whenever I get insecure. As you like to say, "You doin' too much." And to that I say, thank you for being the honest reminder that I need.

And to everyone who's made it this far, thank you again. I hope Aubree and Mateo stay with you and that their story inspired you.

ABOUT THE AUTHOR

Andre'a Delaney was born and raised in Ohio where she spends most of her days wishing she could live between the pages of a hopeless romance. When she's not writing romance novels of her own and figuring out how to live her modern day Victorian romance, she uses her passion to chase dreams too good to sit pretty on a bookshelf.

Find Her Here:

Instagram: authorandreadelaney

www.ingramcontent.com/pod-product-compliance
Lightning Source LLC
Chambersburg PA
CBHW050009120726
47903CB00006B/1697